Three Fifty-nine and a Wake Up

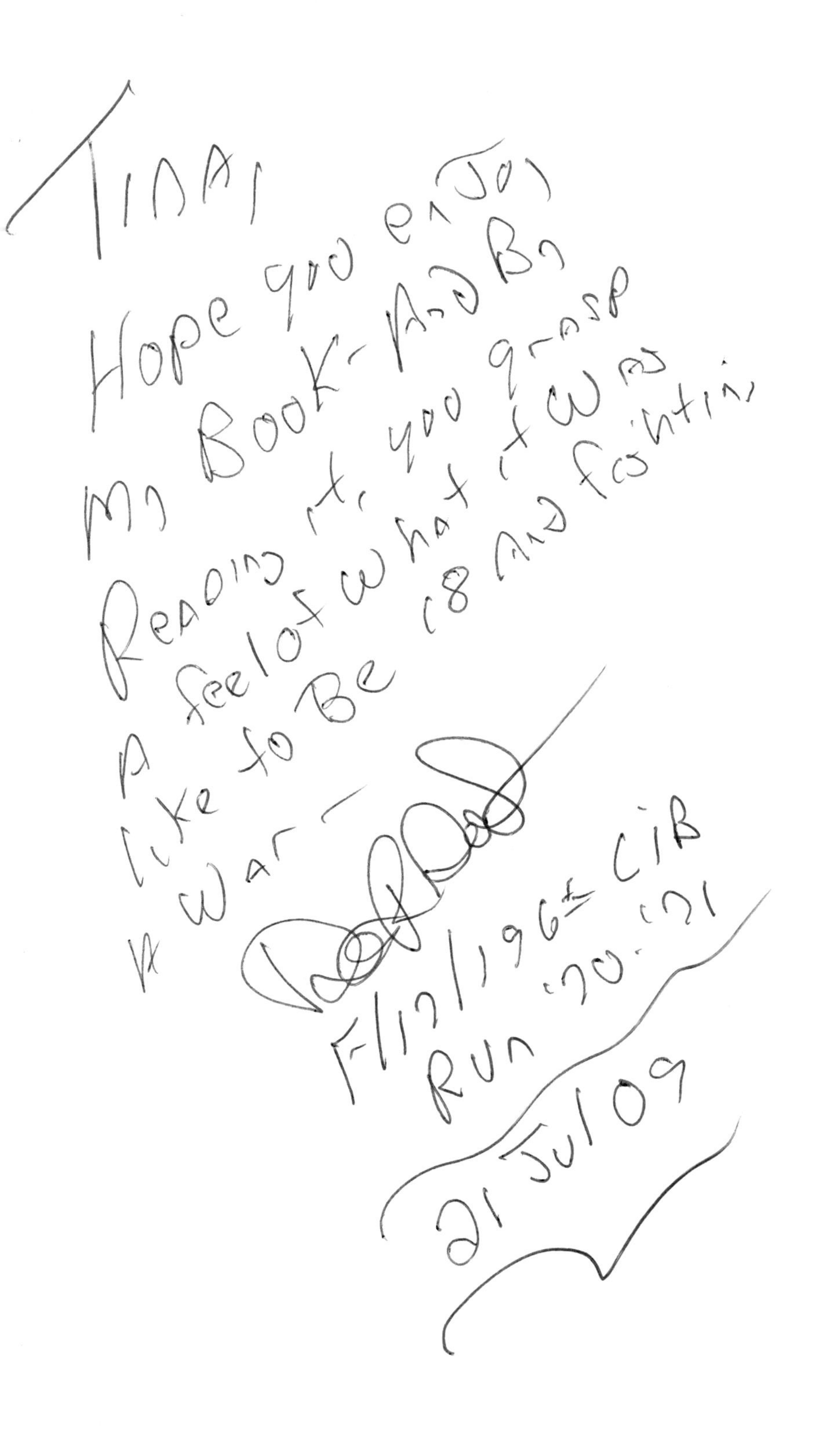

Tina,
Hope you enjoy
my Book - And By
Reading it, you grasp
a feel of what it was
like to be 18 and fightin'
a war -

F/1/2/196th CIB
'70-'71
Run
21 Jul 09

Three Fifty-nine and a Wake Up

By Dennis R. Daniels

Cover design by Dave Stabley,
BCO Printing, Tonawanda, New York, USA.

ISBN 978-1-60458-043-3

Printed in the United States of America by
Fundcraft Publishing Company.

Dedication

This book is dedicated to my uncle, 2Lt Ralph T. Clapps, who was killed in action while serving as a copilot on a B-24 Liberator with the Eighth Air Force in England during WW II.

On February 24, 1944, his ship was on a mission to Gotha, Germany, when a rocket fired from a German fighter hit the nose of his Liberator. My uncle and the pilot fought the controls of their plane long enough for the surviving crewmembers to bail out. In contacting the survivors of that ill-fated crew almost 60 years after the event, they said there was never a day they did not think of the heroic efforts of my uncle and the pilot, 1Lt Sidney Swanson.

The book is also dedicated to 1Lt Douglas Mabee who was killed in action on April 10, 1970, in Quang Tinh Province, Vietnam. He was the epitome of what all young officers should be.

Finally, it is dedicated to all those who served with the 196th Light Infantry Brigade in Vietnam and especially those in F Troop, 17th Cavalry.

Foreword

I grew up in a small rural town in Western New York. At a very young age I was so intrigued by the military that I devoured every book I could get on the Civil War and the role of the Navy and Air Force during WW II.

I envisioned a military career; and to prepare for that, I went to Miami Military Academy in Miami, Florida. My biggest concern back then was that the Vietnam War would be over before I graduated. During my junior year, a graduate from two years earlier had just completed a tour in Vietnam and came to talk to our third year ROTC class. He had been wounded several times and told us about his year in Vietnam. For many of us it was a sobering experience but something at least some of us hoped to experience, despite the risks.

Soon after graduation, I entered the U. S. Army; and after completing basic and advanced training, went to Vietnam. I was assigned to the 196th Light Infantry Brigade, which was located in the northern part of the country, designated as I-Corps. Although the War was starting to slow in many parts of Vietnam, I-Corps was still a very active area for Viet Cong and the North Vietnamese Army. Contact with these forces was frequent and at times heavy.

This book is not an attempt to portray any actual events of the war, but instead focuses on three characters whose backgrounds closely resemble the majority of those who served in the War.

The 1960s and early 1970s was a very turbulent period for America. Opposition to the War was strong, not only from liberal politicians, but from a great many college and high school students as well. As the war dragged on with little progress, the unrest grew. College students were well organized in their efforts to oppose the War and relentless in their approach. This tension eventually led to events such as what occurred at Kent State University in 1970 when members of the Army National Guard shot and killed four college students during a demonstration protesting the war.

Caught in the middle of this political upheaval were the soldiers who served in Vietnam. Many volunteered their services, while others were drafted into the Army. The result was an army that was difficult to manage and lead, and for the soldier presented a tug-of-war as to who was right.

It has been said that we failed in our bid to win the War, but I don't agree. I vividly remember air raid drills in grammar school and the near panic that occurred during the Cuban Missile Crisis. Vietnam was considered a stepping-stone for communism; and to stop communism, we needed to keep South Vietnam a free country. Although we may have failed in that, the threat of communism is no longer a concern, nor is the fear of nuclear holocaust.

Sadly, the soldier who served in Vietnam faced a host of problems. It was a strange war that few fully endorsed and was fought in a manner that was far different from previous wars. Returning home was a bittersweet experience that other veterans of more glamorous wars didn't face. There were issues of acceptance, health concerns, a shortage of jobs, and the daily nagging of whether or not what they did was worth the sacrifices.

The typical soldier in Vietnam either enlisted and was proud to serve or was drafted and either opposed the war or simply didn't want to face the consequences of combat. There was also the professional soldier who had to somehow lead troops in combat who were not totally committed to their mission. And then there were the officers, who somehow straddled the line between wanting to be there and realizing what they hoped to accomplish was probably impossible.

I have attempted in this book to tell the story of three soldiers. One, a professional soldier, Jack Peterson, who returns to Vietnam for his second tour; John Whalen, who protested the war during college and was drafted into the army, and Brian Calhoun, a recent graduate of West Point who finds himself leading men in combat for a war he doesn't necessarily believe in.

War is about people. It is the very young who fight and give up their lives. The Vietnam War took a terrible toll on human lives and left a scar on the American soul that still exists today. In terms of combat casualties, Vietnam cost us more lives than the American Revolution, the War of 1812, the Mexican War, the Spanish American War, and the Korean War combined, and it was about on a par with WW I.

It is my hope that after reading this book the reader will have a better understanding of what it was like to be a soldier in Vietnam. I have tried my best to give you the feeling of what it was like. All who lived and were of the age in that era could have served. Some did; most did not.

To believe in America, to value its principles, to harvest its wealth and freedom, we must always turn to the soldiers who for different reasons found themselves defending our country's name. Some did it for the glory, others because they had to; but in reality most weren't sure of the reason. It is for these soldiers we write books and create movies. If we ever forget what they did, or if we forget the role of the soldier, we will have forgotten what America is. There is no board room in America, no body of men and women who have ever met that will ever be as challenged as those who face an enemy in combat whose sole purpose is to eliminate you. If war is anything, it is the greatest equalizer of all. Bullets and land mines find their way to the smart, the handsome, and the best athletes, as well as those who aren't as fortunate. It is the most non-discriminating occupation of all.

For those who served in Vietnam this book will bring back a lot of memories. It is a novel; and although many of the events portrayed did occur while I served in Vietnam, it is a work of fiction.

Chapter 1

The tick-tock of the Baby Ben clock echoed through the small room with a monotone redundancy. John Whalen stared at the hands, which seemed to move slower each minute. "Only 2:30 AM," John thought as he sighed and swung his legs over the box spring and mattress set directly on the floor. He was careful not to disturb Natalie who was sleeping beside him. The eight-track player continued to hum in the corner of the room, quietly playing *San Francisco Nights* for what seemed to be the hundredth time.

There would be no sleep tonight. John picked up the dime bag of grass laying on the makeshift nightstand and started to roll a joint. He expertly held the two Top papers, licking them together as he put just the right amount of pot in the cupped papers. Licking them again, he rolled the papers together, finishing by tightly rolling the ends. Lighting the joint, he inhaled deeply, holding the smoke deep into his lungs before blowing the cloud of smoke toward the burning jasmine incense.

Standing up, John stretched his 6' 2" frame and slowly walked over to the window. Lying on the chair next to the window were his jeans and in the back pocket was the reason for his insomnia—a notice from the draft board asking him to report to the Armed Forces Examining and Entrance Station in Cleveland for testing to determine his eligibility for the Armed Forces. Staring out the window he thought, "How can the war still be going on after all these years?" It was now 1969; all through college he thought that the war he opposed would be over before he could get caught up in it.

The window faced north, toward Canada, where he had helped many go to avoid the war. He thought of the protest marches, the hours and hours working on campus helping others to avoid a war that he thought was wrong. Now it had caught up to him and he was afraid. Afraid not of the war, but more afraid of what his family and friends would think of him back in Sandusky if he became a draft dodger. He thought of his father and the stories he told of landing at Omaha Beach on D-Day. He thought of his uncle, who had served in submarines, fighting the

Japanese on what he called pigboats. How could he face them, or his friends back home, or his high school football coach?

Dragging deeply on the joint, he felt the exhilaration of the high peak briefly before the tug-of-war with his conscience brought him back to reality.

And then there was Natalie. He met her when they were both sophomores and were inseparable ever since. Last summer after graduation, they set out with their friends in an old Ford van and toured the country, winding up at Woodstock. They returned to Columbus, she to continue graduate school, him to work and find himself, or as Natalie had said, "To mellow out."

She didn't know about the draft notice, but he would have to tell her in the morning. She wouldn't like the news, or his decision. He would have to go for the exams and knew that he would be found fit for duty. It was something he had to do.

Lying back down, he felt a sense of relief in finally making a decision. Slowly he drifted off to a drugged sleep.

Chapter 2

Sergeant First Class Jack Peterson sat down at the dinner table and watched as his wife Janet tried to get their two boys to settle down. Aged seven and five, it wasn't an easy task. "They had some really nice steaks at the commissary today, so I bought a couple for us. The kids are having spaghetti."

Peterson thought of how lucky he was to have an army wife, a wife who understood what it took to live within the rules and regulations that the army imposed. Setting the plates on the table, Janet noticed that her husband was quiet. Too quiet. "What's wrong?" she asked. "Bad day on the range?"

"No, the trainees did well today. Some of them even hit the pop ups," Peterson answered while cutting his steak.

Sensing something was wrong, Janet sent the boys to the living room, each with a plate of canned spaghetti. Jack looked at his wife admiring her beauty. Her auburn hair was long, hanging down well past her shoulders offset by soft green eyes and just enough freckles to give her a forever-young look. Before they were married, his friend, Kevin Linhardt, had tabbed her as always having a "fresh out of the shower look."

Piercing another piece of steak, Jack slowly rubbed it through a small puddle of steak sauce while he continued, "You remember Sergeant Michalski, the guy that handles C Range? He's the guy who came to Fort Jackson a few weeks before us."

"I remember him. I see his wife Barbara all the time. Her kids are about the same age as ours."

"Well," it was hard saying it; Jack sighed, put the fork down on his plate, looked at Janet and continued, "His orders came in today. You know it's been three years. Stateside tours are usually three years." Janet sat down, beginning to comprehend. "He's going back to 'Nam," Jack said. "My orders are probably just a few weeks away. I'm eleven bush; I don't think they'll be sending me to Hawaii."

"You don't know for sure, honey," Janet answered, reaching her hand across the table and grasping his hand. "You already did a tour there, maybe we'll get orders for Germany again."

"No, the war is still going on. I have a feeling it's going to be 'Nam, and I think we need to start to prepare. I'll take my 30 days before I go. You should stay here in Columbia. You know Fort Jackson. There's a good support group for the wives here and the kids like the schools. I'm sorry honey, but that's the life we chose. I need to count on you while I'm there. I need to put all my energy and attention into my platoon. I wish there was another way." Holding Janet's hand, he watched her face as it slowly absorbed the reality of war. The freshness was gone; she seemed tired, the strain already beginning to show on her young face.

"It's hard Jack, every phone call, every knock on the door, you never know what the news is going to be. It was terrible last time and now the boys are older. I don't know if I can do it again."

"You must have known that this could happen," Jack said as he pushed the plate away and reached for a cigarette. "The war is still going on; you read the papers. It's only a year tour; the turnover is high, and there aren't that many non-coms. I've been in 11 years, I'm sure this will be the last combat tour. I've been thinking of putting in for DI school when I'm in 'Nam. I'm sure I'll get it. Two combat tours, and my duty here with trainees. That would ensure stateside duty for a while. Maybe I could even get Fort Jackson again. It's my job, honey; I'm a soldier; soldiers have to fight." Moving the chair away from the table, he slowly pulled Janet toward him. She seemed to fold onto his lap, wrapping her arms around him tightly in an embrace that told him she was afraid.

Chapter 3

John woke up to the smell of coffee. Turning over, he saw Natalie dressed only in one of his t-shirts as she bent over the small hot plate that was sizzling with the sound of bacon. He watched as she cracked two eggs in a small pan and cooked the eggs in the bacon fat. She was a vegetarian and would never eat bacon, but she knew he liked it. Getting up, he softly walked over to her and wrapped his hands around her small frame.

"You got stoned again last night, didn't you?" she said turning around. "Why didn't you wake me? We could have balled again."

"No, I just couldn't sleep," John answered while sitting down at the worn card table that served as their table. Reaching for the pack of cigarettes on the table, he started to open the flip top box, but changed his mind when Natalie put the plate of eggs down in front of him. The sunny-side-up eggs were cooked perfectly, nestled neatly on the plate with two slices of toast and a stack of crisply fried bacon. Picking up the salt and pepper shakers, John carefully seasoned the eggs, while Natalie put a steaming cup of coffee down in front of him and sat down beside him.

Sensing that John was troubled, Natalie reached out and touched his arm, "What's the matter, did you have a bad trip last night?"

John looked at her brown eyes beckoning him to say what was on his mind. Sighing, John decided this would have to be the time. He put the fork down on his plate and took her hand in his. "Natalie, I got my draft notice last week. I'm supposed to report for testing in Cleveland next week."

Natalie stared at John for a moment in disbelief. A slow anger started inside her that she quickly quelled. "But John, we talked about this; we helped hundreds when we were in college. There are a lot of ways to fight this. If we have to, there is always Canada. Remember when we used to take protesters to Canada?" Natalie began to feel uneasy as she looked at her lover of the past three years. She thought she knew him better than anyone, but now there was a different look in his eyes and face.

It was an expression she had never seen before. "You're not thinking of going are you?"

John, sensing her anger, stood up from the table, slowly taking a cigarette from the pack and lighting it. Drawing deeply on the cigarette, John went over to the window and stared out at the busy street below. "I have to go Natalie, I...I just can't…"

Natalie stood up and moved to the window, grabbing John's arm and turning him toward her she said, "Don't say you can't; you know the war is wrong. Nixon is an asshole, a fucking asshole. The war is wrong. What did we do all those years in college? We informed thousands of the truth."

John put the cigarette in the ashtray and put his arms around Natalie. "It's not that easy, Natalie, it's not right for me. I never thought the war would last this long. I never dreamed I would get caught up in it. There's my dad, my uncle, my younger brother, I don't know if they would understand. I don't know if I could do this to them."

"We'll talk to them; I'm sure they don't want you to fight in a war that isn't even ours. I'm shocked. I don't know what to say."

"Natalie, they would think I'm a coward, afraid to fight. They don't give a damn about the politics of it. That's not the way older people think."

Just then the door opened; it was never locked, always open to their friends. Natalie and John looked as Benjamin walked in carrying a small bota bag and obviously still high from the night before. Benjamin was slight in build with incredibly long hair and a beard to match. He was wearing wide flared jeans and a flowered shirt buttoned only on the bottom. Bare foot, he walked over to the couch and sat down. Looking up at Natalie and John, he smiled and nodded in their direction.

"Need a place to crash; I really got fucked up last night. Did some acid, balled a girl...I think she was an angel, an angel with big boobs, is that possible?" He looked over at the eight track, still playing Eric Burdon and the Animals, "You need some new tapes, the Doors, Zeppelin, man even Glen Campbell would be an improvement. I smell food, man. Hey look if you ain't eatin' those eggs, pass 'em this way."

Natalie walked to the table, picked up the untouched plate and gave it to Benjamin. He ate hungrily, occasionally stopping to take a hit off the bota bag. "Eggs and wine are what you need after the night I had."

Natalie moved over to the couch where Benjamin was eating and sat down. "Does Benjamin know of your decision?" she asked, looking up at John.

"No, I haven't told anyone." Turning to Benjamin, John said, "I just got my draft notice, and I'm taking my physical next week in Cleveland. Some shit, huh. Never thought it would happen, Ben, not to me. How the fuck long can the war last?"

"Aw shit man. What a downer. What are you gonna do?"

"I'm not going to do anything. I'm going to Cleveland and see what happens," answered John.

"Wow. That's some really bad shit, man. Fuckin' Nam man. They're killing everything that moves over there man, but I did hear the dope is good, if that's any consolation. Imagine that, from Woodstock a few weeks ago, to the fucking 'Nam. Ain't that a trip? What was that song they were singin' at Woodstock, you know by Country Joe and the Fish? *Two, Four, Six, Eight, what are we fighting for, now I don't give a damn, next stop is Vietnam,*" Benjamin croaked.

"Look, there are some really bad vibes here, and you guys got some real bad stuff to talk about, so I'm gonna split, man. Peace, brother. I hope you change your mind. You don't believe all this government, John Wayne, Green Beret shit do you? We don't belong there, you know that." Benjamin turned, giving John and Natalie the peace sign and walked toward the door. Putting a hand on the doorknob, he stopped and said, "Canada, man, that's what I'd do. Fuck the army, FTA all the way."

"I'm going home to Sandusky for a couple of days," John announced to Natalie. "I need to think about this whole thing, really think. I'm supposed to be in Cleveland for testing next week. It doesn't give me much time."

Chapter 4

Newly commissioned 2Lt Brian Calhoun sat on his duffel bag and gazed at the sprawling campus of West Point from his barrack's window. He had just graduated and had stopped by the barracks one last time. Spotting his friend, Mike Swanson, he called to him and offered his good luck wishes. "Well, I guess after we complete basic infantry training we'll be seeing each other in Vietnam. It looks like that's where everyone will be headed."

"Fucking 'ay," answered Swanson, while lighting a cigarette, "and that's where I want to be, out there killing some gooks. What do 'ya think? We'll kick their ass, you know. This class of 1969 is tough; we'll put an end to the war by this time next year. What do 'ya think, Calhoun?"

"I think you're crazy. The war has been going on for a lot of years and probably will continue for a lot more; but what the hell, if anyone can do it, it'll be the class of '69. Good luck, Swanson, and don't get too fucking gung ho over there."

Chapter 5

Sergeant Peterson sat at the end of rifle range B-2 and shaded his eyes from the rising sun, squinting to look at the pop up targets 300 yards away from the rifle pits. Sergeant Will Stodson, warming his hands on a steaming cup of coffee, looked up and said, "Well, Jack, we've got bravo-three-one coming in today. They can't shoot worth a damn, and they only got a week to go."

Jack reached into his fatigue shirt and pulled out a pack of cigarettes in the box. Taking a cigarette out, he carefully lit it with his Zippo lighter. Turning the lighter over, he looked at the engraved Big Red One. The First Infantry Division was his unit during his first tour in Vietnam. He wondered if he would go back there; or if he did go back to Vietnam, if he would be assigned a new unit. "It's them fucking M-16s," Jack offered while lighting his cigarette. "If we were using M-14s, they'd be OK, but what the hell, this is what we have to deal with."

Turning his head, Jack watched as several deuce and a halves started up the dirt road leading to the range. They came to an abrupt stop just as the booming deep voice of Drill Sergeant Jacob Miller could be heard through the clear, cool morning air. "Un-ass those god damn trucks and form up, you fuckers. Get your asses going, god damn it, there's a war going on."

Jack and Will both laughed, as Will said, "Hell, every other DI brings them right here, but not that fucker, he makes 'em march in." Jack watched as the solid green ranks quickly formed up. The guidon bearer stood at attention at the front of the first platoon, company colors and banners flapping in the gentle breeze. A muffled "forward march" floated through the air as the three platoons began their trek down the dusty road.

Sergeant Miller wasted no time in calling cadence. *"I know a woman who wears black, she does her work on her back. Am I right or wrong?"*

Three platoons quickly answered in practiced unison, *"You're right."*

"Sound off."

"One, two."

"Sound again."

"Three four."

"Bring it on down."

"One, two, three, four, one-two, three-four!"

Miller wasted no time in starting the next cadence, "*If I die in a combat zone, put me in a box and ship me home. Pin those medals on my chest; tell my folks I done my best. Am I right or wrong?"*

"You're right."

"Are we going strong?"

"You're right."

"They look good," Will said as he put his coffee cup down on the faded green bleachers. "Too bad they can't shoot worth a damn."

Jack, lost in thought, watched as the three platoons were dismissed and began clamoring up the steps of the bleachers. He wondered if any of those boys would be in his unit and how many wouldn't make it home from Vietnam.

"What are 'ya thinking, Jack?" asked Will. "It looks like you got a lot going on."

"Ah, I was just thinking about these boys and if I'll see any of them in the 'Nam."

"Probably will, but, what difference does it make? Our job is to train 'em, not worry about the fuckers."

Sergeant Peterson moved to the center of the bleacher area and yelled "At ease, men. Listen up. You have only a couple of days left on the range before you qualify, and you ain't shootin' for shit. Too many of you fuckers ain't squeezing the goddamn trigger; you're jerkin' it, and you're aiming too low at the 50 meter pop ups. All you're hittin' is dirt. And remember to police up your brass. Now, let's unass those bleachers and kick some ass today."

Chapter 6

Brian Calhoun sat nervously in the chair, periodically rubbing his clammy hands together. He could feel a small bead of sweat form on the back of his neck. He looked casually around the hotel room his parents had rented to attend his graduation from West Point. His father, a Brigadier General, was also a graduate of the Point, as was his father. His father, always the taskmaster, had given him little choice in what he wanted to do. He would represent the third generation of Calhouns to attend the prestigious military academy.

Hearing a car pull up to the motel, he could feel his stomach start to turn. From the window he watched as his father, impeccably dressed is his uniform, leaned over and told his mother to wait in the car.

Entering the room, his father removed his hat and sat on the corner of the bed. "I'll make this short son. Your mother and I are proud of you, and I know you will give the Calhoun name honor. You are an infantry officer, so I don't have to tell you that after you complete basic infantry school, you will be going to Vietnam. You'll have some boys you will be responsible for, but the Point has trained you well. Do your duty and come home. Don't ever show your men that you are afraid, and you will be. So afraid that your knees will knock and you'll piss yourself. But you can't show it. Remember, you're third generation military. We have been in all the wars serving our country, and I expect nothing less from you. Your mother wants to say good-by, and we have to get back to Washington today." His father stood up, held out his hand and offered a short "good luck" before putting his hat back on and exiting the door.

Brian watched his father as he opened the door for his mother. He could see that she had been crying. Holding the door open for his mother, she came in and hugged her son in a long embrace. Backing away, she said, "I never wanted this for you, and I have never been sure it is what you wanted. I hope it is, but I know my son, and I don't think your heart is in it."

"I'll be fine, Mom," Brian answered, "You know I didn't have much choice. Dad would have sent me to the dog pound.

Remember when I suggested I go to Annapolis instead of the Point?"

His mother let out a short laugh and smiled, "I'll never forget that. He didn't talk to you for a week."

His father, always impatient, beeped the horn as a signal that the meeting between mother and son would have to come to a close. Embracing her son once more, she looked at him and again let out a small laugh, "It's not like when you went off to summer camp this time is it? Please be careful; write when you can, and we will be waiting for you when you get home."

"I'll be careful, Mom."

She slipped out of his arms as she moved toward the door. Opening the door slowly, she glanced at her son. How handsome he looked in his uniform. She smiled, another tear beginning to form, as she once again bid her son farewell. "Write when you can, and we will see you when you get back."

"OK, Mom, don't worry."

Chapter 7

John looked down at the gas gauge as he cruised north on I-71 and wondered if had enough gas to make it to Sandusky. The 1964 Ford Falcon had well over 100,000 miles on it and was no longer very dependable, but it had served him well over the last few years at Ohio State University in Columbus. Natalie had a 1965 Pontiac that she had received as a High School graduation gift. They used that car anytime they had to have more dependable transportation. John, his decision made, would tell his parents about the draft notice and see how they reacted. His father, never happy with his dress or his anti-war stance, would be surprised to hear his decision.

The miles flew by as John thought over and over about his fate. Maybe the army would give him a job as a clerk or something. Or maybe they wouldn't want him at all. John turned up the radio and tried to tune in a rock station from Cleveland that was playing *Peace Train*, one of his favorite songs by Cat Stevens.

The house was quiet as John entered through the kitchen door. Walking down the small hallway to the living room, John saw his father and his younger brother Mike watching a movie on television. His father, hearing him come in, turned and smiled, "Well, lookie here, Mike, your brother is paying us a visit."

Mike jumped from his spot on the couch and ran to his brother, "John, I got a new football, do you want to play catch?"

"We'll do that later, Mike. Right now I want to chill out. It's a long drive from Columbus."

"So, what brings you home, son? Your mother is shopping, but she'll be back soon."

"I got my draft notice in the mail, and I wanted to tell you about that. I have to go for my physical and testing next week in Cleveland."

John's father rubbed his forehead as he often did when lost in thought. "What are you going to do? I know how you feel about the Army and the Vietnam War."

"I don't know Dad. I never thought this day would come. I protested the war in college and helped a lot of guys avoid the draft. Now that it's my turn, well I just don't know. I think I'm going to have to go. If I went to Canada, it may be years before I could come back. I know that wouldn't sit well with Mom, you, Mike and everyone else. I don't think I can do that to the family."

His father, John, Sr., sighed and said, "It's your decision, John. I know it's tough, but whatever you decide, we'll stand behind you. You know I don't agree with everything going on, but it's been a tough war, and everyone is starting to get tired of it. What about Natalie?"

"She's bummed out, Dad. If I go, I don't think she'll stand by me. She doesn't understand and I guess I can see her point." John desperately wanted a cigarette, but smoking was not an option in the house and the situation was difficult enough.

"How long are you going to stay?" asked John's father.

"Just until tomorrow. I want to go back to Columbus and spend a few days there before going for my physical. If I'm going to get drafted, I want to get in as soon as possible. I know that if I qualify, and it looks like I will, I can volunteer for the draft. I don't want this thing hanging over me. It's only two years, and the time will go by fast."

"A lot of the boys are going to Vietnam. I know at the plant there are a bunch of the guys with boys over there. Maybe it won't come to that for you. Have you thought of the Navy or the Reserves?" offered John, Sr.

"I thought of both Dad, but it's hard to get in the Reserves; and if you do, it's six years of summer camps and weekends. The Navy, well, I don't know, it's four years and I don't know if I would do well on a ship. I think the best thing to do is go and get the two years over with. Not everyone goes to Vietnam. I hear that only about 10 or 20 percent actually go to 'Nam, but I guess I'll find out."

John's father walked over, put his arm on John's shoulder and said, "Well, you'll look different, that's for sure. I guess it will be goodbye for the hair, huh son? Let's wait until tomorrow to tell your mom. I know she'll be excited about seeing you, and I don't want to spoil that for her."

Chapter 8

John quietly entered his apartment thinking Natalie would be sleeping. It was late, and the drive back from Sandusky had worn him down. His mother had taken the news hard, and he could see the worry on her face. She had a friend whose son had been killed in Vietnam a year earlier and that weighed heavily on her mind. Slowly closing the door, John could see Natalie lying on the couch with an open book across her stomach. She obviously had fallen asleep while reading. Walking over he looked at her innocent beauty and knew that she was struggling with his draft notice as much as he was.

Natalie woke up and saw him standing in front of her. Sitting up, she yawned, reached for a glass of wine on the table and took a sip. “How did it go?” she asked.

“As well as can be expected. We can talk about it tomorrow.”

“No, now is fine, I just dozed off while reading. How did your mom and dad take the news?”

“Dad’s not surprised. He said a lot of the guys at work have sons who have been drafted; and I think he knew that since I lost my student exemption it was only a matter of time. Mom, of course, is worried.”

“John,” Natalie said while reaching out and pulling John toward the couch, “we need to talk about this. I think you should try to fuck up your physical. Take something to raise your blood pressure. We’ve helped a lot of people avoid the draft. It’s wrong John. This isn’t WW II. We didn’t get bombed.” Natalie put her arms around John and whispered, “I can’t bear life without you, John, and I thought we would be together forever. This isn’t right.”

Standing up, John went to the window and stared outside. “I know the war isn’t right, but if I don’t go, I have to live with myself Natalie. This is a decision that doesn’t just affect me; it affects my family too. I have to go do this.”

****

John arrived at the Armed Forces Examining and Entrance Station in Cleveland where a large group of possible recruits were herded into a large assembly area. They were broken into two groups, one for mental testing and one for physicals. John's group went for mental testing first. He completed the Armed Forces Qualification Test with ease and wondered how in the world anyone could fail. He thought of some of the bright college students who had taken the test and purposely failed. Moving on to the physical, John was amazed as approximately 50 of them stood in a large room where two doctors hurriedly went from recruit to recruit checking their blood pressure, heart, extremities, and so forth. As the line slowly moved along, John spotted one of his classmates at Ohio State leaving the audio booths used to check hearing.

"Hey John," Mark called out, "you get your notice too?"

"Yeah, I'm afraid so," answered John. "Feels funny shaking a guys hand dressed only in underwear," laughed John. "What are you going to do, Mark?" John asked as the line slowly shuffled along.

"I think I'll be okay," answered Mark. "I have a heart murmur. Had it since I was a kid. I think that should keep me out. Well, I gotta move on. Good luck John." After another quick handshake, Mark moved on to the next station to have his eyes examined.

Chapter 9

Sergeant Jack Peterson sat on a footlocker in the orderly room where the clerk had just handed him his orders. He read slowly as they ordered him to report to Oakland Army Base, Oakland, California, for further processing to Long Binh Air Base, Republic of Vietnam, for further processing to his ultimate unit. He would get 30 days leave enroute. The clerk, a sandy haired young man from Minot, North Dakota, asked, “Is there anything I can do for you, Sergeant?”

“No, Mitchell, I’ll get things wrapped up here in the next few days. When is my replacement coming?”

“He’s due here in two days. I’m sure the Captain will let you go now.”

“Naw,” answered Peterson, “we’ve got a couple of units qualifying on the range. I’ll finish that up, start packing and moving my family. I’ll probably go home for a few days. Fuck, Mitchell, it’s hard to sit here and spend 30 days enjoying yourself. They should just put your ass on a plane and send you over right away.”

“It’s the army, Sergeant; you know nothing makes sense,” Mitchell added.

Chapter 10

John listened as a sergeant talked to the group of draftees. He told them that they would certainly be drafted, and it could be at anytime. They could volunteer for the draft, which meant they would go to basic right away, avoiding the anxiety of not knowing when they would go. An Army recruiter talked to them about enlistment options. If they enlisted, they could have a school of their choice, but they would have to enlist for three years. John thought about it, thinking that maybe he could pick some job that would keep him from Vietnam, or at least having to fight in the war. After mulling it over, he decided to go in immediately, keeping his service time to two years.

John sat impatiently in a small cubical and watched as a young woman, not much younger than him, typed up paper after paper. Occasionally, she would look up from her typewriter and smile at him. She had a cute round face with large brown eyes and perfect teeth. Each time she smiled her nose would wrinkle. She reached over and pulled the last paper he had to sign from the typewriter. She smiled again and explained, "This states that you will arrive at the Armed Forces Examining and Entrance Station on September 15th at 6:00 AM for processing to your basic training unit. Everything you need to bring is listed here. Do you understand?"

John nodded as he looked over the last form he had to sign. "I guess I do." Changing the subject, he asked, "You're a civilian, aren't you?"

Brushing her hair back, she smiled and answered, "I went to secretarial school after high school and took the civil service exam. They offered me a couple of jobs, but I thought this would be the most interesting." Looking at John quizzically, she asked, "You don't agree with the draft or war do you?"

Shaking his head, John replied, "No, not really, but I just can't bring myself to go to Canada or do something that isn't truthful. I'm not afraid; I just don't believe we have any business in Vietnam."

Slowly she picked up the papers and pushed her chair back, swiveling until she was in front of a filing cabinet. John saw that she had a short skirt on, revealing a very nice pair of legs. John couldn't help but stare at her. Turning, she caught him staring and in an embarrassed laugh said, "I wish the fashion would change, so that the skirts would get longer, but I guess you wouldn't like that, would you?"

"No, I guess we wouldn't. I didn't mean to stare, but, well, you have nice legs. Back at college, not many of the girls wore mini-skirts. You must get asked out a lot."

Rotating the chair back to the desk, she uncrossed her legs and slid them under the desk. "No, not really, at least by guys that I would consider going out with. Most are going in one of the services; and if they're not, it usually means something is wrong with them. Anyway, I still live at home. I guess I'm boring." Wrapping the bundle of papers in a rubber band, she handed them to John and smiling wished him good luck.

Standing up to leave, John stopped and asked, "Do you have a name?"

"Of course, I do, we all have a name. Did you want it for some reason?"

"I do. I want to call you when I get back, you know after my two years. Do you think you would remember me?"

She looked at him for a long moment and a strange rush came over her. It was as if she had known him for a long time, although she had just met him moments ago. Smiling again, she answered, "Well, Whalen, why don't you just call me in two years and find out. My name is simple to remember; it's Debbie, Debbie Fisher."

Whalen smiled at her and said, "Okay, Fisher, I'll remember."

The drive back to Columbus seemed to take John forever. He dreaded the thought of telling Natalie he had volunteered to go right away, but he just wanted to get it over with. He would take his chances. Maybe, just maybe, he would get some sort of job that would keep him here in the states.

Finding a spot to park on the street, John locked the car and took the papers Debbie had given him. He walked across the street and up the stairs to his apartment. Opening the door, he could smell the combination of incense and marijuana. Walking into their small living room, John saw Natalie sitting on a beanbag chair totally mellowed out while Jefferson Airplane played softly on their record player. Hearing him come in, she turned and looked up. Somewhat expressionless she asked, "So you did it didn't you?"

John sat down taking her hand and simply answered, "I hope you'll wait for me. I leave in a week. I want you to be here when I get back. I want us to have a life together. I know you don't want this and neither do I, but I love you; and if you love me, then you'll help me through this."

Natalie turned away, stood up and moved to the window, and answered, "I'll try, John, but no guarantees." She turned back to him, tears welling in her eyes, "I don't know if I can ever forgive you for this. It's not who we are."

"Maybe not," John answered, "but I have to do what I think is right. For me, it's going. I hate the war. It's wrong, but so is leaving my family and turning my back on everything I love here. Let's just see what happens." Walking to the window, he put his hands around her waist and pulled her toward him. He kissed her deeply and could feel the passion rise inside of him. In moments they were on the floor, twisting and caressing each other as they made love more passionately than they had in weeks.

Chapter 11

John Whalen sat in the middle of an army bus as it headed down the interstate toward Fort Gordon, Georgia, near Augusta. He had just completed a week of reception at Fort Jackson, South Carolina, where he had been given a horde of shots, physicals, watched what seemed like a dozen movies which were all written and filmed at a fifth grade level, and now he was enroute to basic training. So far, the experience had reminded him a little of the football camps he attended while in high school. His long hair that had hung to his shoulders was now gone; and looking at himself in the mirror, he wondered what Natalie would say. She was not happy with his decision to go, and John had a strong feeling she would not be with him for long. She promised to write, but he knew she was too opposed to what he was doing to wait for him for long. They made no promises, and he left with an understanding that they would see what happens when he finished training. Who knows, not everyone went to Vietnam. There was a lot of talk at Fort Jackson about getting stationed in Germany. If that happened, Natalie could come over with him. She spoke a little German and had visited there while in college. They could share an apartment and maybe continue their life together. Everyone on the bus started shouting as they entered the main gate of Fort Gordon, interrupting his thoughts. Getting waived through, they weaved through the base, which was home to the Signal Corps and the Military Police. Most of the Fort appeared relatively new, but as they headed through the complex of new buildings, they ended up at an area of sand and two-story wood frame buildings painted dull white that appeared to be built during WW II. Stopping in front of one, the driver stood up, turned, and said in a sarcastic snicker, "Everyone stay seated, your Drill Sergeant wants to welcome you to Fort Gordon."

Just as everyone on the bus started to move, a very suntanned, Sergeant First Class, impeccably dressed in his fatigues and wearing sunglasses, and a Drill Sergeant, hat perched on his head, climbed on the bus. Glaring at his new recruits, he yelled, "Well what are you going to do, sit on your asses all day? I want this bus unassed in ten seconds. Pick up your duffel bag and get off this bus. Where the fuck you going, asshole?" he yelled at a tall, thin recruit sitting in the second row who had started to get up. "I'll tell you when to start unassing this bus. When you get off this bus, you run, not walk, between these two barracks and form up behind the building on your left. Now, unass this bus and all I want to see are assholes and elbows."

Between the two barracks, two drill sergeants sat at opposite ends with a small rope buried in the sand. DI Hess stood to the side as the recruits pushed and shoved their way off the bus and ran through the sand with duffel bags filled to the top. As the trainees got to the rope, the two DIs in training pulled it, sending the first dozen recruits sprawling in different directions. Sergeant Hess, suppressing a laugh, went over and grabbed one of the recruits by his collar, "What the fuck, are you clumsy? Can't you run without tripping yourself? Get your asses up out of that sand and form up."

John, being one of those who had fallen, started to get an uneasy feeling in his stomach. With all the ineptitude of new recruits, they lined up in a very ugly formation, three lines across.

Sergeant Hess, climbing up a small podium, glared at them again. Out of the corner of his eye, John could see the other two platoons going through the same ritual to the left of him. Hess stared at them for a moment before speaking, "My name is Drill Sergeant Hess, and I will be your drill sergeant. I will be with you morning and night for the next eight weeks. My job is to take you spoiled, rotten, lazy shitheads and turn you into soldiers; and not just regular soldiers, but the best goddamn soldiers in the world. Right now, you look like shit to me. What the fuck have all of you been doing out there, smoking dope, fucking fat girls, and jerking off? How the fuck does this man's army expect me to turn you shitheads into soldiers? Well, that's my job and goddamn it, I'm going to do it."

With that Hess stepped off the podium and headed for the first rank. Stopping in front of a very over weight young man, he looked at him and said, " Holy shit, son, are you a pig or a soldier? How the hell did you pass the physical to get in this man's army? You are one fat fuck, did you know that?"

The trainee, sweat popping up on his forehead answered, "Yes sir."

Sergeant Hess, turning red, took off his DI hat, threw it to the ground and pushed his face to within an inch of the trainee. "Now goddamn it let me get one thing straight. Never, ever call me 'sir' again. I work for my living. You only call the officers 'sir.' With me, it's either, 'Yes, Drill Sergeant,' 'No, Drill Sergeant,' or 'No excuse, Drill Sergeant.' You got that fat boy?"

"Yes sir," the trainee answered.

"God damn it boy, you're not only fat, and you're dumb as dirt. What the hell did I just tell you? Now get your ass on the ground and give me 20 pushups." Motioning to Sergeant Thompson, he asked him to count them out.

Moving down he stopped in front of John. Putting his DI hat back on, he pushed his face to within an inch of John's and bellowed, "You're a little older than the rest of my trainees, so that must mean you went to college. You were a fucking hippie in college, weren't you? Are you a commie too? Did you burn your draft card? I'll bet you were a goddamn war protesting, draft burning, pot smoking, hippie, weren't you?"

John simply stood at attention and decided to let Sergeant Hess continue his hazing. "I asked you a question, Hippie. Were you a goddamn draft dodging, pot smoking whore fucking, hippie?"

John, starting to shake a little, answered, "I was in college, Drill Sergeant, I don't know if I was a hippie, I'm not sure what that is."

"Well, hell, you must have been one. How much acid did you take? Spend any time in Haight Ashbury? I'll bet you're real glad to be here, Hippie. I don't give a damn what your name is. From now on I'll call you 'Hippie' and the fat kid is 'Pig.' Got that, hippie?"

"Yes, Drill Sergeant," said John.

Moving back down the rank, Sergeant Hess stopped at the last trainee in line. A short kid, only 17, with a face only a mother could love. "Well, what the fuck do we have here?" Hess said while letting out a small surprise laugh. "Where you from, boy?"

"Tennessee," answered the nervous trainee.

"How old are you, boy?"

"Seventeen, Drill Sergeant," he answered.

"So you joined the army to become a man, did you?"

"No, I joined to serve my country."

"Well, Tennessee, you got the biggest ears I have ever seen in this man's army. I'm going to call you 'Dumbo.' Now, where did you get those ears? Did your daddy have big ears?"

"No, Drill Sergeant."

"You mean to tell me your mama has ears that big?"

"No, Drill Sergeant, she doesn't either," Tennessee answered.

"Well, that must mean the mailman or the milkman had big ears, huh, boy. That means you're a bastard, I guess. Did you ever think of that, Dumbo?"

"No, Drill Sergeant."

Returning to the podium, Sergeant Hess said, "When I say dismissed, I want everyone to get your asses in the barracks and find a bunk. When the first floor is filled, get your asses up to the second floor. Sit on your bunk until myself or one of the other DIs gets up there. We're going to show you how to pack your shit in your footlocker and how to make up your rack. And there is no smoking in the billets. In fact, there is no smoking until I tell you. Dismissed."

Whalen turned and ran to the door that led to the barracks. Running to the second floor, he threw his duffel bag on one of the upper bunks at the rear of the billets. No sooner had he done this, when Sergeant Hess arrived at the top of the stairs and began shouting, "Quit the goddamn grab ass and stand in front of your racks. Now shut the fuck up. You don't have time to talk." Hess walked to the center of the room looking at the green linoleum floor. "I hope none of you are tired, because this fucking place isn't fit for pigs. I want to be able to see my face in the floor, and that is going to take some work. We had the boys that were here before you strip the wax before they left. There is no smoking in these billets. These structures were built as temporary barracks during WW II. The wood is dry; and if one of these billets catches on fire, they'll go up in flames in seconds."

Whalen watched as Sergeant Hess walked over to one of the bunks, grabbed a duffel bag, carried it to the center of the floor and dumped it out on the floor. "None of you better have anything in your bag that the army didn't give you, or that you can buy at the PX." Hess rummaged through the pile on the floor until he came to a small black bag containing shaving articles. Picking through it he pulled out a bottle of cologne and a foil wrapped condom. Standing up, Hess walked over to the soldier who was now standing in front of his bunk. "What the fuck boy, are you a fag?"

"No, Drill Sergeant, I'm not a fag. I like women."

"Well, who are you trying to smell good for? And what about this?" Hess asked while holding up the condom. A few snickers started coming from the other men watching, prompting Hess to shout, "You fuckers that are laughing better dump your bags out right now. I'm sure to find some shit in each one."

"I was hoping my girl friend could come here on the weekends, Drill Sergeant, and I never fuck her without a rubber," the trainee answered.

"You got a picture of this bitch?" asked the Drill Sergeant.

"I sure do," he said as he opened up his wallet and handed Hess a wallet-sized color picture of a young woman sitting on a bicycle in a skimpy two-piece bathing suit.

"Well, goddamn, who did you steal this picture from? There is no girl that looks this good that would be caught dead with you, asshole."

"No, she's mine, Sergeant. She loves me."

"And you think she's just gonna be waiting for you when you get home? She's already nailed half your town, boy." Hess handed the picture back and began showing the trainees how to make up their bunks and how to put everything in their footlocker.

The trainees had barely finished their work in the barracks when Sergeant Hess had them form up in the company area outside the barracks.

"It's chow time. When we get to the chow line, I don't want to see any grab ass. A few of you are going to serve as KPs or Dining Room Orderlies, or what we call DROs. Your job is to take care of all the DIs. When we yell out that we need something, you better get your ass moving. You'll also be doing some other shit too, depending on what the cooks need. The chow we have here is damn good, and I don't want to hear any bitching.

Whalen was moving through the chow line, when Sergeant Hess appeared between him and the recruit he called Pig.

"Why, excuse me, Hippie, I want to help our overweight trainee." Beckoning to one of the KPs ladling out food, Hess motioned to one of them, "Now you need to give this boy more food than that. Look at the size of him. We don't want him writing home to his mama saying that we aren't feeding him enough, do we?" The KP looked curiously at Hess and filled his ladle with a heaping portion of mashed potatoes and plopped it on the fat boys tray.

"Now that is more like it," smiled Hess. Moving down the line, he instructed the KPs to heap it on. Whalen watched curiously as the big trainee whose name was Kishner smiled from ear to ear. As they rounded the corner of the mess line, Hess picked up two milk cartons and set them on Kishner's tray. Just as Kishner was about to pick up the tray and carry it to his seat, Hess stopped him.

"Now, boy, that's a big tray of food there, why don't you let me help you," offered Hess. Kishner looked at Hess a bit suspiciously, but set the tray down. Hess picked up the tray and started to follow Kishner. Stopping by the garbage cans used for trash after the recruits were finished eating, he called out to Kishner. "Hey Pig, on second thought, you don't need any of this food. As big as you are, you should be okay for about a month." Hess then turned the tray full of food on its side and let the contents slide into the garbage can. Handing the empty tray back to Kishner, he said, "Well, Pig, I guess you already had your dinner."

Whalen looked at Kishner who was on the verge of tears. A slow anger built up, and for a brief second he wanted to pound the crap out of Hess. He felt a real hatred and was just about to say something when Hess turned toward him.

"You got a problem, Hippie?" You don't like the way I run my platoon? If you feel sorry for Pig, give him some of your food, but you better hope this guy isn't in the 'Nam with you and he has to move fast, cause he sure as hell can't do that now." Hess then went back to his table, sat down and bellowed, "DRO, I need juice."

Whalen turned to Kishner and said, "Sit with me, I'll share my food with you."

Kishner followed Whalen back to his table, sat down and said, "I joined the army to get in shape. I hate being this way."

Whalen put half his food on Kishner's empty tray and said, "Don't let him get to you. It's a game with them. They have to take the spirit out of us first. This isn't much different than some of the football camps I've been to."

Kishner's eyes lit up when Whalen mentioned football. "Hey, I played ball; offensive line in high school. I was always big, but I wasn't this fat. After I graduated, I went to college, ate and drank too much and fucked myself up a bit. This is going to be tough, isn't it, Whalen?" asked Kishner.

"Naw," answered Whalen, his mouth full, "a day at a time, Kishner, a day at a time."

****

With a giant thud, Sergeant Hess picked up a highly polished black boot that was sitting on top of a footlocker and threw it against the floor. "Everybody get out of those racks! Get your asses at attention in front of your rack."

Whalen looked at his watch and saw it was only 5:30 AM. He glanced at Hess and was surprised by his appearance. His uniform was neat and his eyes fresh and alert. "When does this fucker sleep?" thought Whalen to himself.

Hess cleared his throat and stated what would become a daily ritual. "I want your asses dressed and in formation in twenty minutes. Boots shined, clean-shaven and ready to go for the day. We'll have a police call, chow, and then march your asses to some training. Twenty minutes, you got that? I can't hear you!"

"Yes Drill Sergeant," the barracks erupted.

"Good, now get your asses going. I have only eight fucking weeks to turn you shitheads into soldiers, and it's going to take every goddamn minute of it," said Hess.

After chow, Hess paced in front of his platoon. "This morning we are going to march to an assembly area where you are going to watch a few movies on various topics that are vital to your welfare. After that, we will have noon chow, form up again and go to the armory where you will be issued your M-16 rifle. Before we go, I need to pick three squad leaders from you shitheads. Whoever I pick will be responsible for your squad." Motioning to a big kid with broad shoulders and a quick smile, Hess waved him to the front of the rank. "What's your name, boy?" Hess asked.

"Kraus, Drill Sergeant," he said while standing at perfect attention.

"You'll take the first squad; get your ass to the head of the rank." Walking to the second column, Hess pointed to a short, stocky kid with brilliantly shined shoes and brass. "You think you can be squad leader?" Hess asked.

"I know I can Drill Sergeant," he answered.

"Well, get your ass up at the head of the rank," ordered Hess.

Walking back to the front of the platoon, Hess took off his DI hat and squinted into the platoon. "Hippie, get your ass over to the third squad, you'll be their leader."

Whalen started to say something when Hess spoke again, "Hippie, don't give me any shit, get your ass over there."

Putting his DI hat back on, Hess addressed the platoon. "I want you squad leaders to make goddamn sure your squad is looking stract each morning. Their footlockers better be locked, their racks made up properly, and their weapons clean. It will be your ass if they are not. In a minute your Senior Drill Instructor is going to get our asses moving, and this platoon better do the best marching."

Whalen looked down the rank of his squad and wondered to himself, "Why the hell did he pick me? I couldn't give a rat's ass less about the army." Then it occurred to him that was probably the reason Hess did it. Take a potential troublemaker, give him some responsibility and it removes a threat. Whalen looked over at Hess who was waiting for the Senior Drill Instructor to start moving the company out. "The fucker is smarter than I thought," Whalen mused to himself.

****

It was almost time for dinner and once again the platoon was formed up in the sand of their company area. Everyone was clumsily getting the feel of his newly issued M-16. After receiving them, they spent the next few hours learning how to disassemble and maintain them. Hess ordered them to memorize the serial number and reminded them that they would be asked the number and they better get it right. Seeing one trainee fumbling with his rifle, Hess moved with the quickness of a cat until he was at the classic DI position, two inches from the trainee's face. With rain dripping down the bill of his DI hat, Hess bellowed, "What the fuck is the problem, soldier?"

"The safety seems to be stuck on my gun, Drill Sergeant."

Hess grabbed the M-16 from the trainee and screamed, "What the fuck did you call this weapon, soldier? Did you call it a gun?"

The soldier, turning red, started to answer, when Hess held the M-16 over his head with his left hand, and said, "This is my rifle," pausing briefly, he took his right hand, dropped it quickly to the soldier's crotch, and with all his might squeezed as hard as he could and said, "this is my gun." Shaking the M-16 again with his left hand, he continued, "This is for fighting," and again squeezing the boy's crotch said, "and this is for fun." The trainee, wincing in pain, doubled over as Hess handed the M-16 back to him. Moving to the head of the platoon, Hess ordered everyone to repeat after him. "Now everyone, follow me."

Holding a mock M-16 in the air, everyone followed his cadence:

"This is my rifle, this is my gun, this is for fighting, and this is for fun."

"Now goddamn it, why aren't you guys grabbing yourself? Hell, you play with yourself every night; now one more time and this time put some balls into it."

"This is my rifle, this is my gun, this is for fighting, and this is for fun."

"A lot of you are going to 'Nam, so you better learn to respect your weapon. Tonight you're going to sleep with your M-16, and you will be carrying it to the mess hall for chow too. In the 'Nam you won't go anywhere without it. It will become part of you, and it will save your life many times over. Squad leaders, dismiss your squads."

Whalen sat on the steps leading to the barracks trying to write a letter to Natalie when Kishner sat down beside him. "Hey Whalen, what did you think of the low crawl mats today? Fuck those are hard."

Whalen thought of the rough canvas mats the DIs laid out on the sand of the company area. The trainees had to crawl as rapidly as possible down and back for a total of 40 yards. Few could do it, causing the DIs to scream at them as to how inept they were physically. Already Whalen could see his fatigue shirt starting to fray from the low crawl mats and knew by the end of basic training his pockets would be literally worn away. "They're tough, Kishner, but I think the 150 yard man carry is harder."

"We need a 300 on the PT test to graduate. I hope I can make it. The overhead bars are hard for me, too, but I'm getting better," said Kishner. "Did you hear about the gas training we have to do?" asked Kishner.

"No, Pig, I didn't," answered Whalen. "What about it?" he asked curiously.

"I heard from a guy in one of the other companies that they are going to put us in a room with our gas masks on and fire up some CS gas. Then they make us take the masks off until we start to puke before they let us leave the room."

"I didn't hear that," responded Whalen, thinking about it. "No kidding, they make us do that?"

"That's what I heard. Comes in about our sixth week, and hell that's coming up in a couple of weeks. I'll let you get back to your letter; I'm going to walk down to the PX with some of the guys. They're starting to give us more privileges, now. Hey, Whalen, they're giving us a pass pretty soon, probably after the gas training. You're going aren't you?"

"Fucking 'ay, I am," answered Whalen as he put down his pen. Kishner shuffled off toward the PX as Whalen turned back to his letter. Natalie had written him once since basic started. The letter was uninspiring and John knew that any attempt to keep the relationship going was futile. It was a shame, as mail call and letters from home took on a much greater importance in basic. It was your only contact with the real world and those trainees getting letters and pictures from their girlfriends back home were the envy of everyone.

Whalen heard someone approaching and looked up to see who it was. Startled, he watched as Sergeant Hess approached him. Whalen stood up and was about to say something when Hess spoke first, "Hippie, one of your men showed up for guard duty with a dirty rifle and boots that looked like shit. I'm not going to do anything about it, but he's in your squad; and if he ever looks like that again, I'm going to hold you personally responsible."

Whalen, knowing who it was, nodded and simply said, "I'll deal with it, Sergeant."

"Good," answered Hess as he walked back toward the orderly room.

The next morning, Whalen waited for those who served on guard to return. Hearing them come in, he approached the one he was sure was the trainee Hess had talked about last night. "How was guard duty last night, Ziemer?"

"What do you think? It sucked. We walked around the fucking post for two hours at a time, lugging this fucking M-16. Why?"

"Because your boots and brass look like shit, and I don't like being chewed out by Hess."

Ziemer looked at him and said angrily, "Well, fuck Whalen, what gave you a case of the ass? It's no shit off your ass. This fucking army bullshit sucks. I didn't ask for this."

Whalen looked at him and said, "Ziemer, you better get your ass straightened out because I just want to get this fucking basic over with and Hess out of my fucking life. You got KP in the mess hall this afternoon, so be there after noon chow."

"What the fuck you talking about? Pig has KP tonight," Ziemer angrily responded.

"Not anymore. You got it now," answered Whalen. About to walk away, Whalen turned back to Ziemer, put his finger in Ziemer's chest saying, "You don't want to fuck with me Ziemer, but if you decide to, I will be ready. Now do the fucking KP. When you get back this evening, I'll help you clean your M-16; and if I have to, I'll help you shine your brass and boots. Everyone else is looking great except you. You make the whole squad look like shit. Now go find Kishner and tell him your taking his place."

****

The Senior Drill Instructor stood on the podium and casually took out a smoke grenade. Popping the arming lever he tossed it in the sand in front of the company. The DIs yelled gas and within an instant everyone donned his gas mask.

"Good work, men," the SDI said. "Today you are going to gain confidence in your gas masks. You are all going to enter a building with gas masks in place. The building will have active CS gas. Your DI will ask you some questions and after answering them correctly, you will be allowed to leave the area. We will have juice available for you. This evening you will be given a pass to go into Augusta. Your DI will talk to you a little about that before you leave."

Sergeant Hess looked at his trainees and said, "I don't know if you deserve this pass, but you're getting it, so go into town and enjoy yourself. A few words of caution. Stay in a group; don't go wandering off by yourself. There are a lot of civilians out there who will be trying to sell you stuff. Stay away from them. None of you have the money at $80 bucks per month to waste on those rip-off civilians. Now, I know you all want to get laid and some of you have probably heard of the Shirley Hotel.

They have women there; but if you go there, you'll probably be coming back with a case of the clap. If that happens, you'll be starting this training over. So, stay the fuck out of the Shirley Hotel. I know some of you will end up there anyway, but at least I warned you. And make sure you get your asses back here by 1800 tomorrow. We will have a roll call and your asses better be here. Any questions?"

One trainee yelled from the back of the platoon, "Yeah, Drill Sergeant, do you have the address of that Shirley Hotel?" A chorus of laughter erupted.

"No Phillips, but you're so ugly, those whores wouldn't even have you," Hess retorted.

Whalen watched as the line of trainees grew shorter and shorter. Two at a time they entered the small building with gas masks on only to come out on their hands and knees sputtering, coughing, puking, and with tears streaming out of their eyes. The laughs that echoed through the company after the first few had come crawling out had died, and now everyone shuffled forward in quiet fear. When John's turn came, he entered the building and saw Hess and one of the other DIs motioning to him.

"Do you have confidence in your gas mask?" Hess asked.

"Yes, Drill Sergeant," Whalen and the other trainee answered.

"Well, take them off," Hess ordered. Whalen and the other trainee removed their masks and immediately began choking and coughing. Whalen felt like his lungs were going to explode when he heard Hess asking him for his serial number? John attempted to give it to him and did manage the first three numbers before going down on his knees.

Hess bent over, grabbed him by the collar and half dragged him to the door. Once out in the fresh air, both Whalen and the other trainee began gulping the fresh air while rubbing the back of their necks, now burning from exposure to the CS gas.

"Holy fuck," said the other trainee, "no way I'm going in there again."

One of the DIs came over and ordered, "Get over there and get some juice. It will help you clear the CS gas from your system."

****

Pig and Dumbo sat on their footlockers giving their shoes one last buffing. The trainees were running around the billets like wild men in anticipation of their pass into Augusta. All dressed in their army greens for the first time, the uniforms looked bare with no insignia.

Pig turned to Dumbo and said, "I sure wish I had some of the ribbons and shit these guys have that have been to 'Nam. Our uniforms look kind of naked."

Dumbo gave him a glance as he tried for the fourth time to get his tie on right. "That will come in time, right now we're only trainees."

Whalen walked over and asked if they wanted to team up. "Fuck yes," answered Kishner. "We'll have the best time of anybody in Bravo Company. Maybe even get laid, huh, Whalen?"

"I don't know about that," thought John, thinking about Natalie and all the sex they had had.

****

Natalie sat in her apartment and looked at John's last letter. She had just finished smoking a joint, when she heard a quiet knock on her door. She glanced at the letter one more time, crumpled it and placed it in her wastebasket. Getting up, she went to the door, opened it, and saw her friend, Christopher, at the door holding a bottle of wine and a bag of Chinese food from one of her favorite restaurants. Christopher set the bag down and held her in an embrace as he whispered gently, "I am so happy you invited me over. It's going to be a terrific night." She closed the door, smiled, tossed her hair back, and answered, "I'm happy, too, very happy."

****

Whalen, Tennessee and Kishner climbed off the bus and stared down the main street of Augusta. "Shit," Kishner observed, "it's just trainees by the thousands."

John looked down the street jammed with other soldiers, not a girl in sight. Since he was the only one old enough to drink, going to any of the bars would be difficult.

"Well, let's get going," Tennessee said.

After a few minutes of walking, a man of about 40 approached them and asked, "Why, you boys look like you could use a drink." Opening up a brown bag, he pulled out an unopened bottle of Seagrams 7 Crown. "Twenty dollars is all," he said, squinting at the trainees.

Tennessee looked at Whalen, smiled and exclaimed, "Well, son-of-a-bitch, things are starting to look up." With that he reached in his pocket and pulled out $10 saying, "I've got half of it covered."

Kishner, reaching in his pocket, retorted, "Well hell, you'll be drinking half of it, so you should pay that much."

"Let's get something to mix with it and find a place to stay for the night. Fuck, if nothing else, we'll get hammered," Tennessee said.

Turning down a side street, they found a small store and bought a couple bottles of mixers and some snack food. Walking out they stopped in their tracks as they stared at an old building, obviously built at the turn of the century with a simple lighted sign that proclaimed they had found the famous, at least at Fort Gordon, *Shirley Hotel.*

Whalen started to laugh, "Well boys, there you have it, the famous Shirley Hotel. Clap City, the DIs call it." Opening the bottle of 7 Crown, Whalen took a large gulp, feeling the whisky burn as it traveled to his stomach.

About to walk back to the main street, Tennessee stopped and said, "You know, I hate to say this, but I've never been laid."

Kishner looked at Whalen and both started laughing. "You mean, a country boy like you never got laid?"

"No, I'm only 17, I never had a girl. Well, the hell with it, I guess this ain't the place for the first time."

"Now wait a minute, boys," Whalen said, "let's get old Tennessee here laid." Whalen led the group across the street and opened the glass door that was badly in need of cleaning. They entered the lobby with carpet worn thin from age and walked up to the main desk that obviously at one time was considered ornate. Standing behind the desk was a thin, balding man of about 50 with piercing eyes. Looking up, he stopped what he was doing and asked in a thin voice. "You boys want a room?"

Whalen answered, "We do. How much?"

"Thirty dollars," the man responded while going back to his work.

Whalen continued, "How much with a girl?"

"That's up to the girls. You book a room, and then you can talk to the girls. They're in Room 108 down the hall. But first you need a room."

Whalen turned to the others and said, "All right, let's chip in, and I'll see what I can do for Tennessee."

The room was poorly furnished, smelled of liquor and smoke and had two single beds with well worn mattresses. In the closet they found a rollaway, which Kishner set up.

Whalen announced he would go down and talk to the girls. "What do you want me to do for you Kishner, you want in too?"

"I don't know. I don't have much money, but what the hell, see what you can do."

Whalen went down the elevator, passed the desk clerk who was still lost in his work and headed for Room 108. Finding it, he saw the door was open, so he simply walked in. A heavy-set woman of about 30 with bleached reddish blonde hair and a nice smile was sitting at a table playing solitaire when Whalen walked in. Standing, she smiled and said, "Well there soldier, welcome to the *Shirley Hotel*. Now what can we do for you?"

Whalen looked at the other girls in the room who were now giggling softly. "Well, ma'am, we've got three of us here and we were wondering what you can do for us. We're recruits and we don't have much money."

"They all young like you?" the woman asked, moving closer.

"Yes, they are. One's only 17," offered Whalen.

"Well, that's good, because that means it won't take long. You see Ginger over there? She hasn't had a customer all evening so she'll do the three of you for $60. In and out, no touching, grabbing, or feeling. Just stick your dick in and go."

Whalen nodded, thinking he really didn't want to do this, but then again, it had been some time and Ginger didn't look too bad. "Okay," he said. "What do we do now?"

The girls laughed as the big redhead said, "Well, you got to pay and follow Ginger."

Whalen gave the woman $60 and followed Ginger to another room. She promptly took off a pair of silky black pants revealing very shapely legs. Whalen thought, "How does a girl this pretty get involved in something like this?"

Ginger looked at Whalen and said, "Well, don't just stand there, I have to wash your dick off." She grabbed his arm and led him into a small bathroom where he removed his pants as she started to scrub him. From there it was to the bed and in just seconds the whole thing was over.

Ginger laughed, "I guess you needed this, huh?"

Whalen got out of the bed, put his pants on and then thought to himself that he hadn't used a condom. Reading his mind, Ginger shook her head, saying, "I know what you're thinking, but don't worry about all that crap you hear at Fort Gordon. I don't have the clap." Walking over, she kissed him lightly on the cheeks and murmured, "Your girl back home is lucky, now go get the other boys."

Whalen walked into their room and said to Kishner and Tennessee, "I got the deal set. I paid $60 for the three of us, so you guys owe me $20 each. The girl's name is Ginger. Brown hair, kind of petite, maybe 22-23 years old. She's pretty good, but you gotta get your rocks off fast. You got that?"

Tennessee walked into the room and Ginger eyed him closely. "How old are you? You don't look 17, and I know you have to be 17 to join the army."

"I don't turn 18 until December," answered Tennessee nervously. His hands started shaking and he could feel his knees starting to knock. Sensing his nervousness, Ginger moved closer, took his hand and led him to the bed where they both sat down.

"You ever been with a girl?" Ginger asked softly.

"No, I haven't, but I'm ready. As ready as I'll ever be, I guess."

Ginger smiled and said, "Well I am honored to be your first, and I'm going to make sure it is an experience you'll remember."

Kishner paced the room back and forth waiting for Tennessee. Hearing him come, he scowled, "Where the fuck you been, Tennessee? What did you do, pay her extra?"

"No, we just got to talking," smiled Tennessee. "She's very sweet."

Kishner sneered at Tennessee, left the room and headed down to the elevator. Walking into the room, he saw Ginger sitting on the end of the bed.

"Now, my, my, you are a big one, aren't you? Thing is, all you big boys have small dicks. Isn't that true?" asked Ginger as she stood and walked over to Kishner and led him to the bathroom. Ginger giggled as she exclaimed, "Well, you know, they say there is an exception to every rule."

Chapter 12

Sunday evening came quickly and B Company was once again ordered to fall in behind their barracks. The Senior Drill Instructor climbed to the podium, stared at his troops and bellowed, "Now that you got all that horseshit out of your systems, it's back to work. Rifle range tomorrow, and you better shoot the hell out of them M-16s. Any of you go to the *Shirley Hotel*?" A few snickers came out of the platoons, but no hands were raised.

"I hope not, but we'll find out in a few days when you piss and it feels like glass coming out.

****

Whalen sat on the steps of the billets with his duffel bag packed. He looked glum as he fingered his orders one more time. He was to report to Fort Polk, Louisiana, for advanced training at their infantry school. Pig, running down the stairs of the billet, smiled for a brief second until he saw Whalen. Sitting down next to Whalen, John noticed how much weight he had lost and remarked, "Kishner, the army has been good to you. You must have been a helluva football player. You look good, damn good."

Kishner nodded and stammered as he tried to find the right words, "I'm, well, I'm sorry to hear that you're going to Fort Polk for infantry. I'm staying right here to go to Military Police School. Fuck, Whalen, I know how to break the law, but upholding it, hell, how do they figure out who does what? They got Tennessee going to Combat Engineer School someplace in Missouri."

Whalen lit a cigarette lost in thought. Maybe he should have gone to Canada. Maybe there was still time. He looked at his orders again. About a dozen or so from his company were headed to infantry school where they would be trained for the military occupation designated as 11 Bravo, or what many called 11 Bush.

Kishner, realizing that Whalen wasn't going to talk, simply stuck out his hand and said, "Good luck, Whalen, and thanks for everything. I wouldn't be graduating if it weren't for you. And congratulations on getting E-2, you deserved it."

Whalen stood up and took Kishner's hand. Smiling, he gripped it firmly and said, "Good luck to you too, Kishner, I know you'll make a helluva military cop."

About to go into the billets for one last time, Whalen turned to go through the door when he saw Hess standing in the doorway with his arms crossed. Staring at Whalen, he took off his sunglasses and said, "I took that hippie shit out of you, Whalen. It's gone. You're a soldier now and a part of you will always be a soldier. You were never a hippie, not really. Years from now, you'll still remember what we did here. You were a damn good squad leader, the best I had. I knew you would be. Leaders stand out, and you need to know that at Fort Polk and when you go to Vietnam. The boys will look up to you. Don't disappoint them." Whalen started to say something when Hess brushed him aside and said, "Nothing for you to say, Whalen. You better grab your duffel bag, your bus is leaving for the airport."

Chapter 13

Whalen stood in the company area of F Company at Fort Polk, Louisiana. The billets were virtually the same as Fort Gordon, but the post was not as modern, nor did it have the facilities of Fort Gordon. Whalen waited as the SDI climbed the podium and began speaking to the trainees.

"Welcome to Fort Polk. My name is Sergeant Wilson and I will be your Senior Drill Instructor. You are here to earn the military occupation specialty of infantryman. Most, if not all, of you will be going to Vietnam. It is my job to train you to not only help us defeat the enemy, but to give you the skills you need to survive."

Whalen watched in amazement as Wilson chewed a giant wad of tobacco. As he chewed, he would spit a stream of yellow juice out between his teeth every few words, without stopping or even slowing down.

"During the course of your training," Wilson continued, "you will learn tactics, how to stay alive in the field, and you will learn a number of new weapons, including more with the M-16, which most of you had in basic. We'll instruct you on the M-79 grenade launcher, the M60 machine gun, claymore mines, recoilless rifles, the LAWs rocket, and a number of other weapons. I don't expect to have to treat you men as recruits, I expect you to act like soldiers and pay attention. I will train you, so you don't get your shit blown away. So, pay attention. In just a few weeks, you'll be in Vietnam and I won't be there to help you."

Chapter 14

Sergeant Jack Peterson listened as they called for final boarding of his flight to Atlanta, which was the first stop on his way to Oakland Army Base and then to Vietnam. He turned to his wife Janet, who came to the airport without their kids. It was too traumatic for the boys and Janet wasn't sure how she would react. Peterson looked at Janet's upturned face and knew that she was trying to put on a brave front. "The year will be over before you know it and I'll be home. The boys will keep you busy and so will the other wives. I'll write and make MARS calls when I can."

Janet nodded, but couldn't get any words to come out. Somehow she had a bad feeling. She sensed something deep inside her was telling her something bad would happen to her husband. As a military wife she couldn't let that emotion show. She had to be strong and brave. Janet thought of their love and how it had grown so much during their stay at Fort Jackson. She wasn't all that sure that she could handle the next year.

"You know, it's only a few months and we will be on R&R in Hawaii," offered Jack as a consolation.

Janet managed a weak laugh, smiled a little and said, "I'll make up a short timers calendar like you guys do."

Jack pulled Janet close to him and embraced her firmly. As he held her, he let out a long breath and whispered, "I'll be back as good as ever and I promise I'll never leave you again."

Janet pushed him away, smiled and said, "Well Sergeant Peterson, you better get on that plane or you'll be AWOL, and I don't want to be writing you at Leavenworth."

Jack picked up his carry-on bag, turned and with a boyish smile answered, "I won't be AWOL. I have the most beautiful wife in the world and I'm going to come home to her soon. I love you. Say goodbye again to the boys for me."

Jack entered the plane and sat down next to another sergeant on his way to Vietnam. Glancing over, he noticed by his insignia that he was in Supply and probably would have a relatively secure job in a rear area somewhere. REMFs were what the troops called those who served in the rear. Not a very glamorous expression considering it meant Rear Echelon Mother Fucker. The Supply Sergeant catching his gaze asked Peterson, "How many tours have you had in 'Nam?"

"This will be my second," answered Peterson.

The Supply Sergeant pulled out a fresh pack of cigarettes and offered one to Peterson, which he accepted. "This will be my third. Well, actually, two and half. When I made my first tour, I was 11 Echo, cavalry. We caught some shit and I got my ass wounded. I said to myself while I was recuperating, "Steve, if you are going to stay in this man's army, goddamn it, you better get a different MOS." So, when I re-enlisted, I switched to Supply. The only problem was, when I went to 'Nam for my second tour, I was stationed on an LZ that was damn near overrun and shit if I didn't get my ass wounded again. Minor wound. I guess I was lucky."

"I didn't think the Army would send someone to 'Nam three times," commented Peterson.

"Uh, well, I volunteered this time. I play poker and last tour there I put away about ten grand, so I decided it was time to go back," answered the supply sergeant.

"You must be a helluva poker play," deadpanned Peterson.

"I'm the best," smiled Steve.

Chapter 15

Captain James Murphy had barely started to unwind from a grueling three weeks in the field when he heard the company jeep head his way while on the way to his hootch. Stopping, Murphy watched as the driver, Buck Sergeant Scott Jervis, skidded to a halt barely six feet from him, kicking up a cloud of dirt and dust that covered LZ Hawk Hill. Jervis was now driving the company jeep after receiving three purple hearts for wounds received in the field.

"Sir, they want to see you down at Brigade Headquarters. Top says they want to talk to you about the patrol."

Murphy threw his cigarette in the sand and angrily stomped it out. "Fuck, they don't give you a minute, do they Jervis?"

Taking off his boonie hat and rubbing his hand through his long non-regulation hair, Jervis laughed, "Guess not, sir. Same shit you know. May as well get in and let me drive you there sir." Jervis threw the jeep into gear and headed off in the direction of Brigade Headquarters. "I heard it was a tough patrol, sir, not many gooks, huh?"

Murphy, lighting another cigarette, let out a small, nervous laugh, "Well fuck, Jervis, that would be the understatement of the year. Naw, the gooks are out there, but the fuckers are holed up some place. I got a feeling they're getting ready for something big somewhere, you know, a big push. Fucking rice caches in a lot of the villes ain't a good sign. But what the fuck, the old man here at Brigade, well, he's probably gonna kick my ass. All he wants is body count. By the way, do you know anything about Hutchinson and McDivers? You know the two who were wounded last week?"

"Hutchinson will be okay. He'll probably be back in another week. McDivers? I don't know, sir, it doesn't look good. If he makes it, he'll be going to the hospital in Japan. He took three AK rounds. Those shells rip you apart inside, but we'll see. He's a tough fucker, so we'll just see."

Murphy stared at the dirt and dust road ahead of him thinking about the brief firefight that caused the wounds to his men. A small tree line and out of nowhere a burst of AK fire.

They returned fire, but after five minutes or so, the gooks disappeared, leaving his two men wounded. They searched the tree line, but found no evidence that they had killed or even wounded them. "Fucking gooks," thought Murphy.

Jervis skidded the jeep to a halt in front of Brigade Headquarters. The building consisted of heavy wood timbers set deeply in the ground with dirt piled high around the outside and several layers of sand bags packed on the roof.

"Want me to wait, sir?" asked Jervis.

"Naw, you can go back. Who the hell knows how long I'll be. I'll hoof it back."

Murphy entered Brigade and walked down a hallway to a small office. He watched as a clerk sat on a chair typing a report. Murphy casually noticed a Combat Infantry Man's badge sewn on his fatigue shirt and wondered how he was fortunate to get a job in the rear.

The Specialist looked up from his typing and in a polite southern drawl said, "Ah, sir, the Colonel will be out shortly. He has Captain Tillman from Echo Company in his office right now, but I'm sure he's about done."

Murphy nodded and was about to sit down on a folding wood chair when Tillman and the Colonel came out of his office. Colonel Stafford Hewitt, Brigade Commander, was a short, stocky man of about 40, who literally filled the doorway. Briskly gripping Captain Tillman's hand, he shook it vigorously while biding him farewell.

"Excellent patrol, Tillman, you helped shorten the war. I will have my people arrange a helluva stand down for your boys. I want them to know they did a good job."

"I'll tell them," answered Tillman, who, as he passed Murphy, gave him a slight nod.

"Well Murphy, get your ass in here and let's talk," boomed Hewitt. Murphy entered his office and sat down next to Colonel Hewitt's desk, removing his boonie hat and nervously holding it in his hands. "How do you rate your patrol Murphy?" asked Hewitt, while fingering a pencil that he had picked up from his desk.

"Not good sir. We flushed out some gooks, but not many. Burned a lot of rice, but didn't see much of the enemy. Charlie is holing up, maybe getting ready for a big push." Murphy watched as Hewitt's big hands fiddled with a pencil. On his right ring finger, he wore his West Point ring.

Hewitt, catching his gaze, held up his ring hand. "I'm third generation West Point. Neither my daddy or granddaddy made general rank, but I am going to end that Murphy, and I need your help." Standing up, Hewitt walked around his desk to a small table where he had several pictures of his family. Picking one up, he handed it to Murphy. "That's my daddy, me, and my granddaddy at my graduation from the Point. My grandfather died a few years ago, but my daddy is still alive. This is my second tour here, and I know that with a good tour I can get general rank. To do that, Murphy, I need body count. That's all this war is about." Sitting back down, Hewitt clasped his hands together and stared at Murphy. "What are we going to do about that, Murphy? The body count, that is. Do you have any ideas?"

"Well, sir, first we've got to find the gooks. Our Kit Carson scouts told us there are some NVA moving in, and I think the VC are working with them somehow."

Hewitt picked up the pencil again. "S-2 believes something is in the works, too, they just don't know what. I've got some Ranger units out to do some probing, but hell, if Charlie doesn't want to be found, he won't be. Those fuckers are getting aggressive. We caught some gooks in the wire two nights ago. You know what they did, Murphy? They turned the claymores around. If those men on guard had set them off, they would have blown their own shit away."

"They've been turning claymores around on ambush for quite awhile," answered Murphy. "And on ambush, it's tough to see. Those starlight scopes aren't that good.

"Murphy, I know you don't want to hear this, but I'm going to send you back on patrol in three days. We've got to find out what the hell is going on, and I need as many units as I can get out in the field. You get me some body count, and I'll give your men a stand down in Chu Lai they'll be telling their grandkids about. I know you just got back and all, so I'll keep the patrol short, maybe about four or five days or so."

"Sir, the men are bone tired. I don't know if they will be ready."

"Well, hell, get 'em ready Murphy. This is your second tour here, isn't it? You served as a platoon leader with the Big Red One, didn't you?" asked Hewitt.

"Yes sir," answered Murphy, "but it was different then. That was a couple of years ago and not much progress has been made, sir. And hell, sir, you know what it's like back home. There's not much support for the war. It's tough on these boys, sir."

"Murphy, the best way for us to end the war is to kill enough of these NVA and VC off so they don't have the heart anymore. We're still the best goddamn army in the world, and we need to kick these gooks asses back to wherever they came from. I'm going to put you in an area where S-2 believes the NVA are holed up. We'll give you plenty of support should you catch some shit. I'm going to have a cav unit in the area and fire support from Chu Lai and here. I don't like this war either; it's tearing the country apart. Thank God for Nixon, he'll get this mess straightened out. But the best way for us to save American lives later is to sacrifice some now so we can get these boys home where they belong."

Murphy wondered how long it had been since Hewitt had been in the field. It was different during his first tour. There was hope. Now, it seemed as if nothing had changed. Sensing the meeting was over, Murphy began to stand up when Hewitt asked him, "How are your officers, Murphy? Don't you have a young man, Calhoun? He graduated from the Point last spring. I served with his father. He comes from good stock. He's third generation West Point too."

Murphy thought of young Lt. Brian Calhoun. He was popular with his men, but certainly not a career officer. His heart wasn't in it. Nevertheless, Murphy nodded, "Good man; good with his men; he's fine."

"What about the others?" Hewitt asked. Murphy shrugged his shoulders, "Okay, I guess. Bromley is a little laid back; nuts at times, but the men like and respect him. Hathaway is an

ROTC officer. He's a little aggressive at times. I have damn good platoon sergeants. For the second platoon I have Jack Peterson, he served with me in the Big Red One. He's a good man. Sir, we'll do our best. I'll have the boys ready."

"One more thing before you leave, Murphy," Hewitt said, as he ruffled through a stack of papers on his desk. "I have a memo here from S-2 on a kid you're bringing in today. Let's see, here it is. You have a Private E-2, 11 Bravo, coming in today as one of three replacements. College kid, graduated from Ohio State last spring. Intelligence says he was very active in anti-war demonstrations. His name is Whalen, John Whalen. Went through basic at Fort Gordon and AIT at Fort Polk with no problems, but I guess he bears watching. I suggest you assign him to Calhoun's platoon. I don't want an issue made of this, just keep an eye on him."

"Yes, sir," answered Murphy. Saluting more for tradition than respect, Murphy turned and left. No handshake like Tillman thought Murphy as he walked outside to the sweltering heat. Shading his eyes from the sun, he began walking back to his company area. He felt like he was 60 years old, yet he was barely 26. Lighting a cigarette, Murphy, thought, "How the hell do you get body count when the dinks are holed up. You can't shoot at what you don't see." Disgusted, he thought of how the men will react when he tells them they'll be heading back out to the bush in just a couple of days.

Arriving at the company orderly room, Murphy entered and noticed the only one who was there was the First Sergeant, Gary McClure. "Well Top," Murphy announced, "the old man ain't happy and won't be until we shoot us some more gooks. And we gotta go back out in a couple of days. The men are really going to have a case of the ass now. How do like that shit?"

"The boys won't like it a bit. They just got back figuring they would have a week or so," answered the first sergeant while shuffling through some papers on his desk.

Captain Murphy sat down and said, "Top, I need to talk to the platoon leaders. Is Jervis still around?"

"He's in the TOC bunker. Do you want him for anything?" asked Top.

"Yeah, I do, I want him to round up the platoon leaders. I may as well tell them what the hell is going on. But first, I understand we have three FNGs that came in today. I want to talk to them first, so if you could get them in here, I'll get that done, then we'll let the platoon leaders know what's going on."

Top got up from his chair and left the small orderly room that housed his office, an area for the company clerk, and a small office for the company commander. Walking out in the hot sun, he saw Jervis, who was leaving the Tactical Operations Center, or TOC. "Hey Jervis," Top called out, "get your ass over here."

"What's up, Top?" asked Jervis.

"The Captain wants you to get the three FNGs over to the orderly room, then when he's through with them, he wants the platoon leaders. See if you can find these guys, and I hope none of them are getting laid or smoking dope.

Jervis laughed as he said, "Top, those FNGs are so nervous I doubt they are doing anything but getting the shit scared out of them by the guys. And as far as the officers, other than Bromley, I don't think they ever smoked a joint. I'll find 'em, Top. It may take a few minutes, but I'll find 'em."

Jervis had no trouble finding the three FNGs. New fatigues were easy to spot. As he predicted, they were in one of the hoochs listening to war stories from some of the seasoned troops. Jervis laughed as he heard one of them, Specialist Fourth Class Bob Scarcelli, bragging to the FNGs on how short he was. "Hey, FNGs how short are you guys? What have you got, 359 and a wake-up? Man, you fuckers got some time to do. Me; I'm down to 24 and a wake-up; and you know what I'm doing after I get done with you fuckers? I'm going to see this Captain we have and tell him, "Hey, you know what Murph? I'm too short for the field. I'm so short; I don't think I can hit a pistoon anymore, unless I stand on your shoulders. I'm gonna have to piss in my boots."

Seeing Jervis walk in, Scarcelli stood and mocked a salute, "Oh man, should we stand and salute, or get the hell out of the way, 'cause this guy attracts Charlie like ants at a picnic." Turning to the FNGs, Scarcelli said, "This fuckers got three purple hearts and you did it in what, Jervis, a couple of weeks?"

“Naw, it took two and a half months of putting up with you shitheads.” deadpanned Jervis.

“They took his ass out of the bush because no one would get near him,” laughed Scarcelli. Jervis turned to the FNGs and said, “The captain wants to see you in the orderly room, so why don’t you guys head over there. I’ve got to run a couple more errands.”

Walking over to the orderly room, the three FNGs walked in and stood nervously at a high, simple makeshift counter. The first sergeant sent them in one at a time to talk to the captain. His talk was brief and to the point. They were at war and their job was to perform search and destroy missions, or what they were now told were reconnaissance missions. When Whalen’s time came, he nervously walked into the Captain’s office.

Captain Murphy looked up at Whalen and managed a weak smile. “Welcome to B Company Whalen; have a seat.” He motioned to a small folding chair where Whalen quickly sat down. “Whalen, we are here to destroy the enemy, and we will do everything we can to achieve that goal. It is also my job to get you back to The World safely. I know the first few weeks are going to be tough, but before you know it, you’ll be a short timer. Brigade told me you were active in protesting the war in college. I don’t care about that. What you did before the army nailed your ass is your business. But I will tell you we are a team here, and when we get into some shit, you better fight. That means firing your weapon and following the orders of your platoon sergeant and platoon leader. I can promise you, if you don’t shoot to kill and fully engage these gooks out there, then one of your own men will put a bullet in your ass during a firefight sure as hell and no one will say a word about it. So go out and do your job, as I know you will; pay attention, stay alert and you’ll be going home. You got that?”

Whalen nodded his head and answered simply, “Yes sir.”

“What the hell,” Whalen thought as he left the orderly room, “the government had its nose in everything. How did they know about college and his involvement in the anti-war movement?”

Seeing Whalen coming out of the orderly room, one of the other FNGs stopped and asked, “What did the Captain ask you, Whalen?

"He said 'Welcome to the 'Nam;' and I answered, 'I'm glad to be here. Now, when do start killing gooks?'"

"Fuck you, Whalen, you didn't say that shit."

While they were walking back to their hootch, a short, stocky, very well built sergeant with the name Matt Berner stopped them. "Hey, you FNGs, I need you at the armory so I can issue your M-16s, rucks, and some other shit. After that, Top says you guys gotta burn shit tonight. You guys ever burn shit before?"

Whalen looked at him and answered, "No, what the fuck are you talking about?"

With a laugh, he answered, "You'll see."

As they headed to the armory, Berner started talking as they walked along. "The M-16s I'm giving you are good. I checked 'em out myself. Thing is, here in 'Nam, they get fouled up quick. I'm gonna give you guys a few bottles of LSA. If that M-16 jams up on you, don't be afraid to squirt the hell out of it with the stuff. I can give you about a dozen ammunition clips, but you'll need more. Pick 'em up when you can. You need to talk to some of the guys who been out in the bush. They'll tell you how to pack your ruck. Got all that? Oh, one other thing, remove the web belts from those rifles and replace it with a piece of rawhide. Those metal buckles on the webbing clang like hell and Charlie will hear it a mile away."

Arriving at the simple armory, Berner unlocked the door as the FNGs waited outside. Leaving the door open, Berner began by tossing a few lengths of rawhide at them. Moments later he started flinging items on the ground in front of them—entrenching tool, ruck, canteen, heat tabs, cases of C-rations, two towels, a poncho, poncho liner. The stuff kept piling up. "The trick is to pack it right," offered Berner with a smile. "I did six months in the bush, then I got this gig. You guys keep your noses clean and you can get a REMF job, too. Ain't so bad here on the hill. Sure as hell beats the bush."

Just as Whalen started to pick everything up, Whalen's platoon leader, Lt. Brian Calhoun, walked up to the three of them.

"Which one of you guys is Whalen?" the L. T. asked.

"I am," Whalen answered, without looking up.

"I'm Lieutenant Calhoun, your platoon leader. When you have a minute, I want to talk to you. We'll be leaving for the bush in a couple of days, and I want to make sure you know what to expect."

Calhoun looked at Whalen quizzically. "You go to college?" he asked.

Whalen, taking out a cigarette, answered, "I did. I went to Ohio State and graduated in '69. I got drafted; otherwise I would be back home. Where did you go to school?" Whalen asked.

Calhoun laughed, "I'm afraid West Point. I have a military family, so there really weren't a lot of choices for me. I've been here for a couple of months now. I really wanted to be a lawyer and go to a regular college. I'm sure you have a lot of stories about Ohio State."

"Well, I guess I do, but I'm not sure being a military man and all you would appreciate them," laughed Whalen.

"I have stories, too," smiled Calhoun, but they would be boring compared to yours. I bet you did Woodstock didn't, you?"

Whalen thought for a moment about Woodstock. The rain, the drugs, making love to Natalie, the music, the huge unexpected crowd, and for some reason didn't want to talk or even think about it. Shrugging his shoulders, he let out a short laugh, "No, missed that one," he lied.

Chapter 16

Sergeant Jack Peterson sat on the corner of his cot and slowly opened one of the letters he received from his wife that morning. He read the letter and knew that she was having a tough time without him. The boys were hard for her to handle, but she was careful not to let him know too much. He started to put it away when he saw the motor pool sergeant, Roger Harrelson, enter the hootch.

"Hey Jack, they got a deuce and a half running to Chu Lai this afternoon. How about we get on it and hit the NCO Club there. Hell, we can get drunk, play some cards and get out of here for a couple of days. What do you think?"

Jack thought about his offer, but shook his head no. "I don't think so, Roger. Fuck, I need to stay here. I'm not sure when we're going back out. Rumor is the old man at Brigade has a case of the ass. We didn't do a fuckin' thing out there on this last patrol, so I don't know. I better hang around here."

Harrelson stood there for a moment, not sure what to say. "Well, suit yourself, but sometimes you just need to get away."

As he started to leave, Peterson asked, "Hey, is it true you were in the infantry in WW II?"

Harrelson stopped, smiled and answered, "Sure as hell is. Went in when I was 17. Ended up in Germany fighting the Krauts. It was a whole lot different. Fucking thousands of men, tanks, and air support. What an operation. After the war, I got out, but there were no jobs, nothing to do, so I re-enlisted and was able to get them to send me to mechanic's school. I got the time to retire, but I never married; all I know is the army. Helluva thing isn't it?"

"I think you're lucky. It's a lot of worry having a family back home. It's a long year for them, and I sure as hell wouldn't want to do it."

Harrelson stared through the open door of the hootch listening to the outgoing artillery that was a constant on Hawk Hill. "This is a different war, Jack. Back then we didn't want to be there, but we were a team. These soldiers today couldn't do what we did. These kids don't give a rat's ass. We marched through Germany winter, spring and summer. Our rations were terrible. We had Patton over there, Jack, what a fighter he was. Did you know his kid has a cavalry unit down south?"

"No I didn't, but I don't agree with you about our boys compared to back then," argued Peterson, "I think these soldiers are just as good, if not better, but they don't know what this war is all about. They need a reason to fight and a reason to get their shit blown away. It ain't easy for them. But they can fight. Maybe they ain't as pretty as you WW II guys, but they got guts, I'll give them that."

"Maybe so, but I'll take the WW II guys any day. So, you sure you don't want to come Jack?" asked Harrelson one more time.

"Naw, you go ahead. I'm gonna just hang out here, maybe make a MARS call."

"Okay Jack, you take it easy. I'll see you when I get back."

Peterson watched him walk out of the hootch. His whole life was the army; he didn't know anything else. He had to be in his mid 40s, thought Jack, not old for a job in The World, but to be in 'Nam? Well, shrugged Jack, he didn't want to end up like that.

He reached down and picked up Janet's letter and read it again. He missed her so and thought for a moment about R&R. He would put in for it as soon as he was eligible. Maybe he should start planning now. After a few moments, he put the thought aside and lay down.

Chapter 17

Captain Murphy sat at his desk and motioned for his three platoon leaders to sit down. Grabbing folding chairs they all sat in a circle around the Captain's desk. Clearing his throat, Murphy yelled, "Top, I want you in on this too."

The first sergeant walked in and sat down awkwardly on an overturned garbage can.

Murphy, lighting a cigarette, looked at the platoon leaders. Calhoun was a West Point graduate, Bromley from Officer's Candidates School, and Hathaway from an ROTC program at some small mid-western college. All were young and inexperienced but were doing their best to lead their men. "I don't have good news for you men. I went to see the old man today and he has a case of the ass against us. Wants more body count. He did confirm what we talked about in the field though. He says S-2 believes that there is a build-up of NVA troops taking place in I Corps somewhere. He wants our asses out there again in just a couple of days. Wants us to probe and look for the gooks. Although he didn't say as much, I think he has an idea where they are. I know our boys aren't ready, but what can we do? I want you to tell your sergeants about this and get the men ready. On the bright side, the old man said if we can get some body count, he'll get us a stand down in Chu Lai."

Bromley, slowly shaking his head, glanced at the other platoon leaders before he replied, "Captain, I think it's a mistake going out again so soon. These guys are beat. We got shot up a couple of those days, took some casualties. We need to get that out of our systems. Can't we let 'em unwind for a week, get 'em drunk and laid, and then maybe head out? Those gooks will be milling around out there for a month. Why don't they send some Ranger units out to find 'em?"

"They did," replied Murphy, "but hell, they can't go against Charlie. They're going to send a cav unit with us, so I think we'll have some good support. What about you, Calhoun, what do you think?"

"I'm with Bromley, sir, the men are tired, and I think we'll be hard pressed to get them to respond. In a few days, it would be better, but I doubt we have much choice."

Nodding toward Hathaway for his thoughts, Murphy was surprised at his answer, "Aw, fuck it Captain, let's get back out there. My platoon took the hits and I think my men would like to re-pay Charlie. You know, give him some shit. Ain't nothing going on here, and they been getting gooks in the wire and mortar rounds at night. I don't know about you guys, but I would rather be out there fighting Charlie than inside this wire. Hell, the food sucks and artillery is being fired off around the clock. I say we go out there and get some body count, come back and have one helluva a stand down."

Bromley looked at Hathaway in some disbelief and asked, "What the hell has gotten into you? You been smoking some shit we don't know about?"

"It ain't that Bromley. I've been over here a few months and all we do is let these gooks peck away at us, knocking us off one by one. Let's get those bastards in a real firefight and kick their ass. It's about time we do that."

Murphy reached for his pack of cigarettes, and took a cigarette out, carefully lighting it. Blowing a large inhaled puff of smoke into the air, he finished the meeting by saying, "Well, it's Tuesday. Let's plan on moving the boys out on Friday. At least that gives them a couple of days." Turning to the First Sergeant, he said, "Top, make sure we have everything ready to go and I want to talk to your clerk. I have a couple of awards I want him to put in and I know some of the men have earned the Combat Infantryman's Badge. Hathaway, write something up for the two men who got our boys in that dustoff chopper under heavy fire. Put 'em in for a silver star. They'll downgrade it to a bronze with "V" device, but they at least deserve that."

"Yes sir," Hathaway answered.

"One other thing," mentioned Murphy as he butted out his cigarette, "we got some FNGs, so make sure we get them squared away. You each got one in your platoon. We'll talk again tomorrow, so be here about 1600."

As they were leaving, Murphy motioned to Calhoun to stay. Sitting back down, Calhoun waited for Murphy to talk.

"The old man at Brigade wants us to keep an eye on one of the FNGs, a kid named Whalen. They say he was active in protesting the war. I put him in your platoon. I don't think there is anything to it, but let me know if you see anything, okay?"

"I already met him sir. He looks okay, but I'll keep an eye on him sir. I'll talk to him a little tonight."

After they left, Murphy motioned to the first sergeant, who came and sat down next to the captain. Opening the bottom drawer of his desk, Murphy pulled out a bottle of bourbon and two glasses. Pouring some into each glass, he handed one to his First Sergeant. Taking a large gulp, he set the glass down and looked at Top. "Fuckin' war sucks, doesn't it Top?"

"It sure does Captain, but that's why we're in this man's army for, isn't it sir?"

"I don't know anymore Top. I really don't. We're fighting this war with one hand tied behind our backs. The gooks, they ain't gonna engage us anymore." Twirling his bourbon around in the glass, Murphy looked up at Top and asked, "Do you remember reading about a guy they called the Swamp Fox during the American Revolution? His name was Francis Marion and he terrorized the hell out of the British with guerilla tactics down in Georgia. That is what the gooks are doing to us. Top, we can't win fighting that way. This is their homeland. They can hit and run all day. We need to catch the fuckers out in the open. We used to do that a couple of years ago when I was with the Big Red One, but they ain't gonna let us do that anymore. You served as a platoon sergeant here, didn't you Top?"

Top reached over and poured another inch or two of bourbon in his glass. "My MOS is 11E, Armor. I served in a cavalry unit near Pleiku. Not good terrain for tracked vehicles and we didn't have the M-551 Sheridans then. Had the old M-48s, not very good for this type of country."

Murphy was about to say something when the company clerk stuck his head in the door. Looking up, the first sergeant asked, "Do you need something Simmons?"

"Yeah, Top. Scarcelli is here. Says he wants to talk to the Captain."

"Do you know what it's about?" Top asked.

"Naw Top, he didn't say."

Top looked at Murphy, who shrugged his shoulders and said, "Bring him in I guess."

Scarcelli entered the small office and nodded to Top. Turning to Captain Murphy, he said, "Sir, I don't want to bother you, but I want to see if I can do something here on Hawk Hill. I'm short, real short. I got only about three weeks left and then I go back to The World. Most of the other guys with a lot more time left than me stay on the Hill or in Chu Lai."

Murphy looked at Top and asked, "He have his orders yet?"

"Yeah, came in a couple of days ago," Top answered.

"Scarcelli, I don't have a problem with that, but you should have talked to your sergeant and your platoon leader first."

"I know sir, but Calhoun, well, he's green sir, and so is Sergeant Peterson, at least with our unit. I don't know if they would understand. I just don't want to get my shit blown away with a couple weeks left sir, and you've been in the bush with us a long time. I thought you would understand." Scarcelli looked on nervously, not sure what the answer would be.

"Well, Scarcelli, I guess we can arrange something for you here. Tell Peterson, on second thought, I'll talk to Peterson. Don't tell him about our conversation. In the meantime, I want you to take the FNGs that came in and work with them tomorrow. And don't give 'em the shit I know you guys do. Help get their rucks squared away. You meet these guys yet?"

Scarcelli grinned as he answered, "I have sir, and I'm just the guy to do that. I'll talk to them tonight and I'll have 'em ready for the bush tomorrow." Turning, Scarcelli left and felt a huge sense of relief as he went outside in the hot Vietnam sun. Seeing one of his friends from his platoon, he yelled, "Hey, dude, not only am I short, but I'm out of the bush. The Captain called me in his office and said, 'You know Scarcelli, you've done your work here, so we're gonna let you stay on the Hill until you sky up for The World.' And you know what I said? I said, 'Murphy, I don't know if you can get by without me, but if you insist, I'll stay here and get ready to get my ass back home.'"

His friend, dubbed Bongo Man, laughed, "Fuck Scarcelli, you're full of shit. The whole company knows you were gonna talk to the Captain. So he got you out of the bush? Well, I'm happy for you. And did you hear? We gotta go back out in just a couple of days; at least that's the rumor. Hell, man, these lifers are fucked up, Scarcelli."

Bongo Man took off his boonie hat and scratched his head. Setting down a five gallon can of water, Scarcelli could see he was getting ready to take a shower in one of the so-called shower facilities put together by Navy Sea Bee units. They consisted of nothing more than a wood structure with a 55-gallon drum perched on top. To use it meant collecting five gallons of water, climbing a set of wood rungs to the top, dumping the water in the drum and finally standing underneath the drum while you opened and closed a simple valve that let the cold water out.

Scarcelli, getting serious for a moment, looked over at the shower and the drum perched on top. "Hey, Bongo, you ever wonder why this whole fucking country is green and dense and yet this Hill is barren like a planet? How the hell did they get rid of all the foliage? I heard they dumped chemicals by the thousands of gallons to clear everything up. See that drum on top of that shower, the orange one? Well, these guys say that the shit they used was in those drums. Fuck, man, it makes me nervous. If that shit is strong enough to permanently destroy everything that grows, what the fuck is it doing to us?"

Bongo glanced at the drum and laughed, "Scarcelli, the last thing I'm worried about is that old drum up there on the shower. Old Charlie and his AK-47 machine are what worry me, not some weed killer. Well, I'm gonna get me a shower and drink some beers tonight. That's real good news Scarcelli; I'm glad you're out of the bush."

Scarcelli watched, squinting his eyes in the sun as Bongo picked up the can and sauntered off to the makeshift shower. He was totally naked with a cigarette dangling from his mouth, boonie hat perched on his head, and a towel and drum of water in his hands.

Scarcelli was about to move off to one of the hoochs to tell everyone that they would have to fight the war without him, when out of the corner of his eye, he saw one of the FNGs walking toward the mess hall. Yelling at him, Scarcelli set off toward him in a trot. Catching up to him, he said, "Hey, I saw you guys earlier in one of the hoochs. My name is Scarcelli." Scarcelli looked at the sewed-on name tag and continued, "Whalen, get the other new guys and meet me over by the armory at 0800 tomorrow right after morning chow is down. The old man wants me to help you guys get ready for the field. And don't be late; I don't wanna spend all day with you fuckers. Got that?"

Whalen nodded, thinking this is the same guy that was just giving them shit about having 359 days and a wake-up left in 'Nam and now he's gonna help us?

****

Major Nguyen of the 4th Regiment, North Vietnamese Army, sat on his haunches and looked down from his hiding spot in a heavily wooded tree line less than a klick from an American Ranger unit. He watched as they slowly moved through the area, ignoring the tree line above them. Smiling to himself, Nguyen thought of how easy it would be to eliminate them. His men, a company of about 180 seasoned North Vietnamese Regulars, were scattered through an area the Americans called the Pineapple Forest. Nguyen watched and hoped the Ranger unit would stop for the night. He had a surprise in store for them. Nguyen liked surprises. In Hanoi last year his leaders had told them they must be patient. Hit the Americans frequently, but do not engage fully. Bring about casualties; break their spirit; that was their mission. Back in America, the people were restless. Nguyen thought of one of their actresses, Jane Fonda, as she taunted the Americans for their bombing of Hanoi when visiting there. He watched as the Ranger unit passed from his view, moving on through the valley below him. That is all right, thought Nguyen; we will wait for another night. Patience, he thought, we must be patient.

Chapter 18

Lt. Bromley expertly shuffled the deck of cards and with a deft motion carefully dealt out the entire deck. He watched as Calhoun, Hathaway, and the Executive Officer, Timothy Miraball, arranged their cards by suit. Looking to his left Calhoun shook his head and exclaimed, "I got nothing again, Bromley, what the hell you doing to me?"

His partner, Lt. Hathaway, looked up from his cards and asked, "Can you nil?"

"Fuck no," retorted, Calhoun, "I guess I'll bid three."

Bromley glanced at Hathaway who smiled and said, "Hell, I guess I'll have to bid six."

Miraball, looking again at his cards, complained, "Fuck, Hathaway, you got all the spades again don't you?"

"Well, that is the name of the game, isn't it?" smiled Hathaway.

"Hell, I'll bid two," growled Miraball.

Bromley sighed, scratched his chin and stared at his cards for a long moment. "I'll nil, but you better cover my ass Hathaway."

The cards darted out on the table as Calhoun and Miraball worked to spoil Bromley's nil. Unsuccessful, they did manage to keep them from getting their six tricks.

A bit in mock anger, Bromley threw the cards on the floor, and exclaimed, "You fuckers sandbagged your hands."

About to pick up the cards, Bromley stopped as he heard the whine and boom of artillery, only this time the whine and boom were backwards. Jumping up, he headed for the door of the hootch, realizing they had incoming mortar rounds. Stepping outside, the officers headed for their respective battle station. Climbing on top of the TOC hootch, Bromley realized he didn't have his weapon, flak jacket, or helmet.

Seeing the Lieutenant in their bunker, Top laughed and said, "Sir, what the hell are you gonna do like that should these VC decide to try and overrun us?"

"Well Top, if you were any kind of first sergeant, you would have brought me a goddamn rifle to shoot the sons a bitches with."

Back in the enlisted men's hootchs, the mortar rounds were heard, as most of the men were playing cards, drinking beer, or involved in a bull session. John Whalen, caught by surprise, started for the door when one of the men stopped him. "Where the hell you going? This hootch has six layers of sand bags on top and is buried in good old Vietnamese dirt. Charlie is just sending in a few rounds, he'll stop in a minute."

Whalen nervously waited for the sound of another incoming round, but none came. In moments everyone was back to doing what they were before. Someone turned up the radio and once again Radio Saigon filled the room. Whalen nervously lit a cigarette and sat on the edge of his cot. A buck sergeant named Manrique came over and handed him a cold beer he had dug out from his makeshift cooler.

"First time is a little scary, but it's a whole lot worse in the bush. In time, you'll get used to it. That's all for Charlie tonight. He won't fire any more. He doesn't want us to get a bead on him. Notice our artillery has picked up?"

Whalen listened and could hear the 105 mm cannons roar in the background sending rounds out as fast as they could be loaded. "I guess I'm just not used to this. Didn't get many mortar rounds back at Ohio State."

Manrique sat on the edge of the cot next to Whalen, opened a rusty can of Falstaff beer and slowly lit a cigarette. "I guess I'm your squad leader. My name is Manrique and I'm from Miami. I got drafted and after Infantry at Benning they sent me to Shake and Bake School. Got my stripes at the end of it and here I am. We have a good platoon. The L. T., Calhoun, is all right and our Platoon Sergeant, Sergeant Peterson, he's all right too. Peterson is on his second tour here and Calhoun is a ring knocker. You know what that is Whalen?"

Shaking his head, Whalen said, "No, I don't."

"Well, it's a dude that went to West Point. He's young and from what I seen, not all that gung-ho, which is good. Scarcelli, I guess you met him, is gonna work with you and the other new guys tomorrow. He's a bullshitter, but the fucker has survived a year in the bush and did what he had to do. Listen to him tomorrow and then come see me. I'll help you where I can, but fuck, man, once we get in the bush and shit starts happening, it's tough for me to keep an eye on everybody."

Getting up, Manrique looked at Whalen and said, "Write home. Your folks are probably worried. We're headed back out in a couple of days. Get to the PX and get what you need tomorrow." With that, Manrique went back to the rear of the hootch where he and the other E-5 buck sergeants had partitioned off a section of their hootch with poncho liners.

Whalen, taking Manrique's advice, sat down on the edge of his cot and tried writing his first letter home. Although he had been in Vietnam less than two weeks, things had been so hectic he hadn't had time to write. After training at Fort Polk was over, he received ten days leave. Going home was hard. He had been home a few weeks earlier at Christmas. Although he saw Natalie, she was very distant and didn't seem to want to continue their relationship. When he went home from Fort Polk after getting his orders for Vietnam, he sat down with Natalie for the last time and they agreed to wait until he got back from Vietnam. It would be too hard to try to continue their relationship, and any promises they made to each other would likely be broken. Natalie was obviously disturbed over his decision to go in the army and she could not accept his decision.

Friends had told John that Natalie had been seeing other men while he was in training. Most of the men were younger Ohio State students who were active in protesting the war.

Enroute to Vietnam, John had orders to Oakland Army Base and from there a private jet took them to Vietnam with stops at Honolulu, Wake Island, and Manila. Someone had a couple bottles of liquor on the plane and proceeded to get drunk on the last leg from Manila to Vietnam. The plane was rollicking with laughter as could be expected from 18 and 19 year old soldiers on their way to fight a war. When the plane landed at Bien Hoa Air Base, the entire plane quieted down. Everyone peered out the windows at their first glance of Vietnam. Artillery could be heard in the distance and a group of Cobra Gun Ships continued their lazy circling of the air base. As the plane came to the end of the runway, a pretty flight attendant picked up the microphone and said that they would all exit the aircraft from the front of the plane. She ended the conversation with a sobering, "God bless you."

Exiting the airplane, John could feel the heat of Vietnam as it hit him hard. Sultry, hot, humid, it was all there. What followed were a couple of days of processing. Then his orders came for the Americal Division, I-Corps. John asked the clerk what he knew about the Americal. The clerk, without even looking up, simply said, "It's bad up there, man, real bad."

Once at Chu Lai, Headquarters for the Americal Division, John went through three more days of training before his assignment to the 196th Light Infantry Brigade headquartered on LZ Hawk Hill, which was some 20 miles or so north of Chu Lai. While at Chu Lai, John learned that the Americal Division was where the My Lai massacre had occurred some years earlier, giving the Division a tainted reputation.

John returned to his letter and decided to keep his first letter short, simply stating that he was okay and that he was at his unit and would write again when he had more to say. He made sure that he included a note to his younger brother. Sealing the envelope, he wrote the word "FREE" in the upper right hand corner of the envelope and put the letter aside. He would mail it tomorrow. He thought for a moment about writing to Natalie and decided it wouldn't be a good idea. Nothing would come of it.

About to stretch out on his cot, Whalen heard someone enter the hootch and looking up saw it was Lt. Calhoun. Sitting back up, Whalen said, "Sir, what brings you here?"

"No one uses 'Sir' over here much, just call me L. T. I wanted to make sure you got squared away. Did you meet Manrique?"

"I did," answered John. "He seems okay. I think I'll be all right. One of the guys getting ready to go home, I think his name is Scarcelli, is gonna work with us tomorrow over at the armory. I'll see what he says."

Calhoun nodded his head. Looking uncomfortable in the enlisted men's hootch, Calhoun said to John, "Let's climb on top of the hootch and watch the war."

Following Calhoun outside, they climbed up the mountain of dirt piled on the side of the hootch and stepped on top of the sand bagged roof. Sitting down they lit cigarettes and watched the red tracer rounds off in the distance, the sound of artillery booming from the Arty Company next to them and the white star shells being fired from their perimeter. In the background was the steady drone of a generator running to provide some minimal power to the base.

"Have you been here long sir, I mean L. T.?"

"No, a couple of months is all. I got a long time to go yet. You have a girl back home?"

Whalen let out a short nervous laugh, "No, not now. I had a girl. Loved her; loved her with everything I had, but after I got drafted, well we didn't get along after that. No sense in trying to save what wasn't there. I loved her; at least I think I did. But I'll see, maybe we can get things going again when I get back, but that's dreaming isn't it?"

"Whalen, from what I've seen, you're better off. So many of these guys get letters every day. Then after a couple of months it's down to one a week, then one every couple of weeks. Then they either stop all together, or they'll get a letter from a friend telling them their girl is with someone else. I doubt more than ten percent still have their girls when they get home. And hell, that includes the ones that are married. There's enough to think about here in the 'Nam without worrying about a girl back home."

"How about you, L. T., you got anyone?"

"Whalen, at the Point, that was hard to do. I dated a lot. There were girls all over that get off on dating cadets from the Point. A lot of them were easy to get in bed, too, but none of them would be anyone you would want permanently. Scags, really, lots of mileage."

"I can't imagine going to West Point," commented John. "It must be like basic for four years?"

"Naw, we have summer camp, then plebe year, but after that it's not too bad. The academics are a bitch. It's a tough school. I had some good times there. It wasn't my first choice. My Dad, well, he's what guys over here call a lifer. He's a Brigadier General. His Dad graduated from the Point too. So I never had much choice. I always wanted to be a lawyer. I can still remember watching Perry Mason on TV. He always won his cases. Other kids would be playing cowboys and Indians, and my sister and I would set up a court in the basement and try pretend cases. Screwed up isn't it?"

Whalen shook his head, "Oh, I don't know. Doesn't the army need lawyers?"

"Yeah, but most come from law schools, not West Point. I might look into it when this year is over, I don't know, we'll see."

"I don't want to sound out of place L. T., but from what I have seen of the Army, not many officers talk to the enlisted men. Aren't you going to catch hell for this?"

"Ah, it's not that strict here, besides we're the same age. Most of the men in this unit are 18-19 years old. The other platoon leaders, well, they're a bit strange. Bromley, he got drafted, and then he went to OCS. Never went to college, but he's smart, a little wild, but smart. The men love him. And Hathaway, he's an ROTC guy. He's getting more gung-ho every day."

Standing up, Calhoun smiled and mused, "Beautiful country here, it's a shame it's all torn up over war. They've been fighting here forever it seems."

"I noticed it's awfully primitive," added John. "Water Buffalo running the streets and just hootchs everywhere. It's hard to believe it's the 20th Century here."

"That's what war does, Whalen, it halts progress." Calhoun stared off at the sky and watched as a white star shell arced its way skyward from one of the guard towers.

"I don't think we'll ever win, Whalen. I just don't think we will." Shaking his head, Calhoun slowly stepped off the sandbagged roof and started walking back to the officer's hootch.

Whalen sat on the roof for a while and smoked another cigarette. He started thinking about Natalie and realized that it was almost impossible to be any further away from her. He was literally on the opposite side of the world.

About to climb down from the hootch, two of the men from his platoon climbed up and sat down on the opposite side. Opening a small bag, they took out some local marijuana and rolled a joint. Lighting it, they turned to Whalen and motioned to him, “Do you want a hit? It’s good shit, man; the best.”

Whalen, not sure what to do, walked over and took the joint. He hadn’t smoked any dope since his leave before coming to Vietnam. Taking the joint, he inhaled deeply holding the smoke in his lungs before letting it out. He thought of Benjamin when he said they had good shit in Vietnam and he was right. Handing the joint back, he thanked them and headed back down.

The one hit of the joint helped Whalen go to sleep. Waking at 7:00 AM, he washed as best he could in a plastic bowl of cold water and shaved. Putting on the same fatigues he had on the day before, he walked over to the mess hall for breakfast. Grabbing a tray, he stopped at the first station and was given some powdered eggs. After taking some bread, canned fruit and coffee, Whalen sat down. He looked cautiously at the two malaria pills that he took from bowls stationed at the beginning of the chow line. There were two different strains of malaria in this area of Vietnam and failure to take the pills could result in being infected. One was small and white and had no side affects. The other, a large pink pill, was reputed to cause stomach cramping and diarrhea. Taking them both in one gulp, John took a large drink of an orange Kool Aid type drink that was given in lieu of real orange juice. The coffee tasted terrible, but knowing that the local water was contaminated, the Army was forced to treat it heavily with iodine, giving the water a reddish color and altering its taste considerably.

Picking up his tray, Whalen saw the two other new guys at another table. Walking over, he sat down and took out a cigarette. Lighting it, he asked if they were ready for what Scarcelli had to offer.

Both looked at each other and said they weren’t sure. “Hell, all he’s gonna do is tell us how short he is,” one of them remarked.

“Well,” Whalen said, “we won’t know until we see what he has to say. So let’s get over there; it’s almost 0800.”

Walking over to the armory, they could see Scarcelli talking to Jervis and the First Sergeant.

"About time you showed up," complained Scarcelli. "Let's get going. You guys sit down and I'll show you how to pack your ruck. In a pile next to Scarcelli were the contents of what he took to the field. Taking the ruck and placing it in the aluminum frame, he first picked up some C-ration cans. "Put the Cs in first, and not too goddamn many. You get re-supplied damn near every evening; so don't waste space on Cs, save it for other shit." Next he put in some bandages. "Get some bandages from one of the medics. You never know what could happen. At some point you may have to stop some bleeding on you or someone else." Next he put in some star shells, plastic bowl, writing supplies, towels, insect repellent, LSA, an entrenching tool, soap, razor, foot powder, extra boots, fatigue pants, shirt, socks, poncho liner, and an extra boonie hat. On top he put a dozen or so clips, each loaded with 18 rounds of ammo. "You guys should know that these fucking M-16s jam when you try to put more than 18 rounds in a clip." He threw in some P-38 can openers, heat tabs for the C-rations, and a mess kit, finishing by folding up a gas mask and putting it on top.

"If someone pops some CS, you need to get the mask on quick. That shit will fuck you up. Some of the guys use C-4, the plastic explosive, to heat up their rations. It works, but you gotta be careful with it. You can get the C-4 from the guys on the mortar squad. Now, one or two of you may be asked to carry some claymore mines. You used them at AIT, so I won't get into that. You'll set 'em up every night along with trip flares, so make sure you take care of them. Charlie is scared shitless of the claymores. If you see what happens to one of those gooks when they get blasted with one, you'll know why. You guys will be issued grenades out in the bush. You'll probably get a couple each. I never took 'em. Fuck if Charlie is that close, he's too close, but it's up to you. Each man will also have to carry 200 rounds of ammo for the M-60. A couple guys will have to lug a spare barrel. As you guys probably found out in AIT, those barrels heat up fast when you don't use short bursts. At night after setting up your perimeter, if the area is not too hot, the choppers will bring in a meal, your mail, ammo, and some other stuff. They'll also take any outgoing mail you have. Keep writing letters, the more you write, the more you get back. Write everyone you know back in The World, even if you didn't like them. Those letters are damn important."

Nodding their heads, Whalen and the others listened as Scarcelli talked to them about a range of subjects.

Blowing out of his mouth, Scarcelli stopped and stared off in space before talking again. "I don't know how to put this, but there are some weird fucks out in the bush. Stay friendly with everyone. A lot of these guys are high and after a while they lose sense of what's right and wrong. You get on the wrong side of someone, and they get a bad enough case of the ass, they'll shoot your ass during a firefight. And be damn careful you don't turn up chicken shit out there, 'cause you'll get an M-16 round up your butt for sure. The trouble with 'Nam is Charlie isn't your only enemy. Make some friends, hang with 'em and don't trust nobody. Got that? Nobody."

Looking at his watch, Whalen noticed it was already noon. Scarcelli, looking over at the mess hall, told everyone to get some chow and meet back at 1400 hours. Going into the orderly room, Scarcelli saw Top sitting at his desk reading the most recent issue of Stars and Stripes.

Looking up from his paper, Top asked, "How did it go?

"Okay, I guess. Top, the fuckers are green, but they all listened. The one guy, Whalen, I think can be a squad leader in a couple of months. Pretty smart, big guy, you might want to mention it to Peterson."

Top nodded his head, thinking of what Brigade had said about him being a war protester. "Did he say much about the war?" Top asked.

Scarcelli shook his head, "No Top, he didn't. No one wants to be here. Anyway, I told them I'd get with them at about 1400. Top, I want to thank you for letting me stay in the rear. Anything you need over the next few weeks, I'll be happy to help you with."

"No need for that Scarcelli. You did your duty here. It was Murphy's decision anyway; he's the Company Commander."

"Ah hell Top, who you fooling? Everyone knows you run things here."

Chapter 19

Back at Brigade Headquarters, Colonel Hewitt sat at his desk and listened intently to Major Reynolds and Lt. Saban as they unfolded a military topographical map of I-Corps. "Sir," Major Reynolds said, "the Ranger Units we sent out believe that there are two companies of NVA regulars holed up in this heavily dense area we call the Pineapple Forest. One company is located to the south in this area, and the other is just north on the other side of this narrow valley. The Rangers captured a VC and he told the Kit Carson scout about them. Trouble is sir, we don't know what the hell they are up to, and we are certain the VC don't know either. Best guess is they are waiting for one of our units to go through this valley; and with infantry on both sides, they could easily crush us."

Hewitt looked at the map and muttered to himself, "Damn good area they have, tough to flush 'em out. During the Civil War, they would call that good ground. That's what won the battle of Gettysburg for the Federal army, the ground, you know. They had the high ground; Lee had shit. General Ewell, of the Confederate Army had a chance to take the high ground the first day but didn't. Could have changed the war if he had."

"Sir, pardon me, but this isn't Gettysburg," muttered Reynolds. You're getting ready to send a couple of companies in there and they could get their ass kicked. These NVA are dug in waiting for something. We don't like it. I say we hit 'em with an air strike, get some napalm in there. It will save a lot of lives sir."

Hewitt sat back in his chair and shook his head. "Napalm won't work; it's too dense. We could fire artillery in there all day and Charlie would just climb into their tunnels and wait it out. No, we gotta flush 'em out the old fashioned way, with infantry and maybe some cavalry support. They aren't as smart as they think, Reynolds. If the Ranger units are right, the gooks could be caught in a trap."

Standing up, Hewitt reached over and tapped the area just to the south of where the NVA were. "If we could place some heavy fire here, it might push these gooks to the northern part of this first dense area of jungle. My guess is if we made it hot enough for them, they would have to move north to the extreme northern end of their heavily wooded area. We could then move our fire gradually up, forcing them to cross the valley to join forces with the other company north of their position. If we could get an infantry unit in the western edge of this tree line, we could catch them out in the open and destroy them as they cross the valley to join forces. Are the Rangers sure there is another company of gooks in this area to the north?" Hewitt asked.

"They're sure, sir, but who knows; tomorrow is a different day."

"I'll think on this, Reynolds. Let's talk tomorrow morning," Hewitt said.

Rolling up his map, Reynolds offered it to Hewitt. Declining his offer, Reynolds stuck the map in a folder and started to leave Hewitt's office. "Sir, as you know, I'm being transferred to DaNang. Lt. Saban will be taking over my duties." Hewitt, nodded, as he answered, "Yes, I know. I'm sure the Lieutenant will do well."

Walking slowly back to his office, Reynolds opened the door and sat down at his desk. "Body count," he muttered to himself. "Who the hell is he kidding? Can't get body count with an air strike or Napalm, at least body count that you can get credit for. You can only get that with infantry and getting your own men blown to shit."

****

Janet Peterson opened the door to her small apartment in Columbia, South Carolina, and set the grocery bags on the kitchen counter. Her knees were wobbling and she felt another wave of nausea come over her. Knowing she couldn't make the bathroom, she reached under the kitchen sink and pulled out the small garbage can she kept there. Leaning over it she threw up for the third time that morning. Sitting down on the floor, she felt small beads of sweat forming on her back, neck and forehead. She could no longer ignore the signs. She had missed her period and although she thought it might be just due to nerves, she was now certain she was pregnant. Jack had always wanted a daughter, but who knows what sex the baby is? She didn't know if she should tell Jack. He had enough to deal with. Getting up, she started to put the groceries away.

****

Colonel Hewitt stood in the darkened room with an overhead projector running on a large screen with a topographical map of I-Corps. Squinting, he looked at the men sitting in front of him. Two company commanders, their platoon leaders, and platoon sergeants stared at the image in front of them.

"Gentlemen, what we have here are two NVA companies located in this area of dense foliage. The company to the south is spread out in dense jungle over an area covering about 200 meters. The other company is sandwiched in a smaller area just to the north where the tree line ends and joins the valley that extends between the area of dense foliage to the south and this area to the north. What we want to do is press the gooks to the south and force them to cross this valley that separates their two companies. We believe if pushed, they will try to move to this large area here," Colonel Hewitt said placing his pointer on the large area of dense jungle to the north.

"Our Rangers report there is one infantry company to the south and one to the north. Both areas are riddled with tunnels. They discovered caches of ammunition and supplies, so it is apparent that Charlie wants to use that area, but for what reason, we don't know. Most likely they want to catch us moving troops through the valley; but if we move quickly, we can catch them at their own game, so to speak."

Captain Bitterman of C Troop, an armored cavalry unit, cleared his throat, "Colonel, how do you propose to use my unit? It's too dense to get any APCs or Sheridan tanks in there to flush those gooks out sir."

"Captain, what we'll do is move Murphy's infantry unit down this ridge. He'll concentrate some fire into the tree line. That should draw some fire. We're going to have some Cobra gunships ready to move when that happens, and we're going to blast the hell out of this area just to the south of where the NVA are. We will slowly direct the fire from south to north, moving Charlie closer and closer to this valley. We believe Charlie will move up to join the other company here in this area of dense jungle. We'll then place heavy artillery and gunship action to the south, squeezing them into this small area, which has less cover. Your unit will be hidden behind the fish hook here, so when Charlie decides to leave the area to the south to join his forces to the north, he'll have to cross this valley. At that time you'll wheel your tracks and Sheridans out; and at the same time Murphy can get his infantry into position here, and we should have them cold. What you don't get, the gunships will."

As Hewitt finished, Murphy looked at his officers who sat in stoic silence staring at the map in front of them. Standing, he looked at Hewitt and commented firmly, "Sir, this is my second tour here, as you know, and although this plan may work, I think all Charlie will do is hide out in the jungle. If he moves north, it will be at night. These are NVA troops, sir, not VC. They're good soldiers, and I don't think they will allow themselves to get caught in that position. I know you want to squeeze them north so we can catch them in the open, but I think it's going to be tough sir."

Hewitt stared at Murphy and a sense of anger started to come over him. "Murphy, I'm tired of letting these gooks get away with the crap they have been up to lately. We need to destroy these two companies, or at least one of them. It's damn rare to catch more than a squad of NVA at any one time. We're going to squeeze them out in the open. Your men will be positioned here, so they can't move west and Bitterman will be here, preventing them from moving north to join their other company. This ridge will keep them from moving east; and if they move south, our artillery will pound the daylights out of them."

Murphy sat back down and noticed Bitterman looking at him in disbelief.

"That is all, men. Get ready to move on Friday. My S-2 officer will meet with you later today to go over some final details." Hewitt turned off the projector and left the room not looking back at his officers.

Bitterman walked over to the wall and turned the lights on. "What do you think Murphy?"

"I don't know, it seems possible, but they got RPGs, mortars, machine guns, and when I move in to push them, I'm going to be out in the open. It's hard moving those NVA. The air strikes will be the key. Well, we don't have much choice, so let's go and get it done."

Chapter 20

Scarcelli wiped the sweat from his forehead as he continued training the FNGs. "Fucking hot here," he muttered. "Okay, let's talk about going out on ambush. You guys are going to hole up somewhere for the night. Charlie is sure as hell going to know where you are. So, to make it a bit tougher for him to sneak in on you after dark, we send a few of you boys out on what we call ambush. You sneak out at night, find some good spot to hide, set up some claymores and trip flares and wait for Charlie. He knows we do this; and if we can keep him from knowing where the ambush points are, it will generally keep his ass away from the company."

Whalen asked how many men are usually out on ambush.

"Not many," answered Scarcelli, "enough so you got a couple guys up and a couple sleeping. Just hope Charlie doesn't start poking around and use the starlight scopes, otherwise he'll be on your ass before you know it. Things are getting a bit quieter these days, so you guys should have it a little easier. When I first got here, it was a lot tougher."

Scarcelli sat down, took off his boonie hat and started again. "Big thing for you to worry about are mines and booby traps. Not much you can do about either, except keep your eyes peeled for them. When you hit the bush, you'll run across some APCs and Sheridans that have hit mines and are blown to pieces. So you can imagine what would happen to you should you step on one. Fucking Charlie is setting 'em up every night, too. That's why they had you put a dog tag in your boot. Sometimes that's all we find for the body bag. I know you don't like hearing this shit, but that's the way it is. About your flak jacket and helmet. You'll see a lot of guys wearing boonie hats, but when you get in a firefight, that boonie hat won't stop a damn thing. Your fatigue shirt won't help stop an AK round either. The flak jacket and helmet can save you from getting your shit blown away, so I suggest your wear 'em. You got that?"

The FNGs nodded their heads in unison.

****

Sergeant Peterson listened to Lt. Calhoun as he told him about the plan he heard earlier that morning at Brigade. "Jack, you've done a tour here before, what do you think?"

"I think the old man at Headquarters is crazy, sir, that's what I think. If Charlie has two companies in there, they have close to 300, maybe 400, men. And they have good cover. Even with air support and artillery, we'll be damn lucky to get a lick or two in."

Calhoun sighed and said, "It turns out Hewitt knows my old man. Served with him once I guess. I think he is counting on me to be like him, you know aggressive and all that. I don't know, Jack, it seems we're putting these men through a lot without much hope of getting much back. I'm more cautious. But if it did work, we would really put a hurt on the NVA wouldn't we?"

Peterson smiled, "That we would, L. T., that we would."

****

The night before the company was to move out on patrol, Whalen was unable to sleep. Finally getting up, he went outside and walked over to the mess hall. Entering, he watched the night cooks baking cakes and bread for the next day. Sitting at a small table in the kitchen, he watched as the cooks worked oil-fired field stoves, struggling to get the temperature right to bake the bread.

One of the cooks looked over at Whalen and nodded toward the corner of the kitchen. "We got coffee over there if you want. Also some leftover apple pie from dinner."

Whalen wasn't hungry so he simply shook his head. "No thanks, I just can't sleep. I'm new here. I'm going on my first patrol tomorrow. I guess I'm a little nervous is all."

The cook opened the door of the oven, stuck his hand in and started counting. Pulling his hand out after a few seconds, he determined that he had the right temperature and slid the tray of bread dough in.

The cook leaned against a crude plywood counter and asked Whalen to keep his eyes open for rats. Rats were everywhere on

Hawk Hill. They were in the hootchs, orderly room, TOC, armory, and mess hall. Whalen had one run across his cot the evening before.

"I'll watch for them," Whalen answered.

After about a half hour, Whalen went back to his hootch and lay down. He eventually drifted off to an uneasy sleep, waking up at 0500.

****

Jack Peterson stood at the edge of the main gate to Hawk Hill. He took off his rucksack and rummaged around for a new pack of cigarettes. Removing a hard pack, he tossed it to one of the Vietnamese boys begging for cigarettes around the main gate. Just as a few more Vietnamese boys started to gather around, his squad leaders came up to him. Manrique took off his helmet and said, "Sergeant, we've got everyone accounted for. I think we can move out. It looks like we're a good klick or two behind the first platoon."

Peterson nodded his reply and asked Manrique to make sure everyone had a clip of ammunition loaded in their M-16 and another clip handy.

Looking around, Manrique wondered where Lt. Calhoun was. "Where's the L. T.?" he asked.

"He'll be here in a minute. He's bringing in a forward observer from Artillery and checking to make sure we have a medic assigned to us."

Moments later a jeep pulled up with Sergeant Jervis driving. In the truck were Calhoun, a forward observer, a medic and Scarcelli.

Seeing Scarcelli, a chorus of cheers erupted from the platoon. "Hey Scarcelli, changed your mind, huh. I knew you couldn't stay back on the Hill when we were out."

Scarcelli jumped out of the jeep laughing, "Fuck you. I'm just dropping by to wish you guys good luck. I'm not sure you can fight the gooks without me, but we'll see." Scarcelli moved along the platoon thumping backs and wishing everyone good luck. Coming to Whalen, he stopped, grasped his hand and said,

"Stay cool, be alert, listen, and get your ass back here safe. Just think, Whalen, when you get back you won't be an FNG anymore, and you'll be down to what, maybe 350 and a wake up? See," Scarcelli held his thumb and forefinger about a ¼" apart, taunting Whalen, "this is how short I am." Smiling and laughing, Scarcelli turned and walked back to the jeep, sitting down next to Jervis.

Whalen smiled and yelled back, "You bet your ass I'll be back. Thanks Scarcelli, I appreciate your help."

Whalen, about to light another cigarette, was interrupted by Sergeant Peterson who told everyone to form up and move out. The men put their rucks on and gave their M-16 rifles a final look over, then headed out in two staggered columns keeping several yards between men. Whalen stepped off and in minutes they had left the security of Hawk Hill. Looking over his shoulder, he was surprised how insignificant the Hill looked and how vulnerable to attack it seemed to be. Squinting ahead, Whalen could barely make out the platoon ahead of him and could see the third platoon behind him just beginning to form up. Although it was just after 0800, Whalen could already feel the heat as the Vietnamese sun bore its way inside his body. He had two canteens of water, but he knew that it would hardly be enough.

After an hour or so, the terrain changed, as they seemed to be going higher and were in an area that had a dense overgrowth of heavy bush. After another hour, they passed the first platoon, as they were sitting down having a smoke, eating a few C-rations and resting. Whalen knew in an hour or so it would be their turn to take a break and allow the third platoon to catch and pass them.

The hour passed quickly and soon they were resting on the side of what appeared to be an old path that led to a small village. Until now, Whalen had seen little signs of life. Gazing at the small basic shacks, now abandoned, Manrique who was sitting next to him read his thoughts.

"You'll see a lot of that Whalen. Lot of different reasons the Vietnamese move on. Sometimes it's because of the VC, other times it's because of us. The Vietnamese people are caught between us and the VC, so it's tough for them to choose sides."

Sergeant Peterson walked up to Lt. Calhoun and asked, "L. T., why are we moving due west? I thought we were going to rouse the gooks up north."

Calhoun, looking at a map, shook his head, "Not right away. They want us to give them a diversion first. We know Charlie will be keeping an eye on us, so we're going to move west for a day. What good it will do, I don't know." Unfolding the map, Calhoun pointed out where they would be that evening.

Peterson didn't like the location or the terrain. "Not much of a spot to lay up for the night. Where the hell we gonna set up the ambush?"

Calhoun folded the map and simply shook his head. "I don't know. It's pretty wide open, but I guess they want us to be seen."

Annoyed, Peterson said, "Sir, if we lay there that wide open, Charlie's gonna pepper the hell out of us all night, and there won't be a thing we can do about it."

Calhoun looked at Jack, smiled and said, "Now Sergeant, don't tell me a career man like you has his doubts about the men back on the Hill making these decisions?"

"Hell yes. I don't trust 'em. Let's get their asses out in the bush and see how they like their decisions."

Word came to move out and everyone got up and adjusted their rucks as best they could. The first day marching was the worst; and before long, the rucks seemed to weigh much more than they actually did.

As they started out, the L. T. motioned to his RTO and had him call ahead to Captain Murphy who was with the first platoon. Calhoun gave him a status report and they continued to move on.

Sergeant Peterson plodded ahead keeping his platoon back about one klick from the first platoon ahead of him. Watching a tree line off to his left, he had a strange feeling that either the NVA or some VC were watching him. Jogging ahead, he caught up to the men on point and cautioned them to be alert for any activity. No sooner had he stopped to allow the rest of the platoon to catch up, when he heard the pop, pop, pop from several AK-47s. The steady stream of fire seemed to be directed toward the center of his platoon. Motioning for everyone to get down, he signaled for the RTO. Lt. Calhoun crawled on his belly and in effort to get a little closer to the ground, took off his helmet. Moving alongside Peterson, he looked at the tree line but could see no movement. His platoon was raking the tree line with M-16 fire. Within seconds an M-60 machine gun was set up and started spewing out its deadly rounds. Signaling for the platoon to slow their fire, Calhoun said to Peterson, "I think it's probably just a few VC stirring some shit up, but you never know. If it were any more, they would have come down with a lot more fire. Were there any casualties?"

"Negative," answered Peterson.

The RTO, with his PRC 25 radio ready, asked the L. T. what he wanted transmitted. "Tell them we took some AK fire from the tree line due south of us, but they have stopped firing. Tell them we have no casualties and we will move out momentarily."

****

Sergeant Luong Ba Vanh signaled for his men to halt their firing on the American platoon. Well entrenched, the counter fire had not been accurate and he sustained no casualties. He knew had he continued firing, artillery and air support could have devastated his small squad of Viet Cong.

His orders were to harass the American troops with sporadic gunfire and he did that. He hoped he had caused some casualties, but he knew that it was unlikely. Short periods of fire in a spread out formation rarely produced much, but he smiled knowing that the Americans will be very uneasy. Signaling one of his young scouts, he told him to report the Americans' position and ask for his orders. Strange, he thought, the Americans were heading in a direction opposite of what Major Nguyen had suggested.

****

John Whalen nervously stood up, reached down and wrapped his hands around his knees. They were shaking uncontrollably. With the sound of the first rounds being fired, Whalen had thrown himself flat on the ground only to have several AK-47 rounds cut off the blades of tall grass not two feet from his head. Drawing himself into an almost fetal position, he heard the sound of other rounds hit a small clump of trees behind him. Somewhere behind him, he heard Manrique order his men to return fire and direct it at the base of the tree line. Reaching down, Whalen felt for his M-16 and nervously moved it in front of him so he could fire. Not wanting to raise up much, he tried aiming from as low to the ground as possible but soon realized it couldn't be done. He heard the men around him firing, yet he had not got a round off. Rolling over, he cradled the M-16 in front of him, moved the safety to the off position and started squeezing off rounds in the general direction of the tree line. With some comfort he heard their own fire increase and the enemy's dwindle. As soon as their M-60 swung into action, the fire from the tree line stopped.

"Okay, hold your fire," Peterson yelled. "No sense wasting anymore ammunition on Charlie. He's either dug in or moved out." Peterson, in a half squat, peered at the tree line through binoculars seeing nothing.

Manrique half crawled over and asked if they were going to go into the tree line.

"I don't think so, Manrique, we would take boucoup casualties and not find the gooks. Chances are we'll hear from them again. They'll be waiting up ahead for us, or maybe they'll pick on another platoon." Putting his binoculars away, he heard Lt. Calhoun say they would be moving out in three minutes.

Manrique, checking on his men, asked Whalen how he felt.

"A little shook up, I guess. First time is tough."

Manrique gave him a bit of a punch on the shoulder and told him he had time for a cigarette. He watched as Whalen, still shaking, removed a cigarette from a crushed pack that he had in his fatigue shirt pocket.

Lighting it, he looked at Manrique, "I did get off some shots."

"Fuck yeah, you did. You know, you've earned your Combat Infantryman's Badge. What about that?" Manrique said.

"Hell, that's an award I could do without," deadpanned Whalen.

"By the way, Whalen, my nickname is Loco. When we know you a bit better, we'll pick one for you too. Most everyone in the bush goes by a nickname. If you don't get one, it means no one likes you."

****

Natalie was just putting the finishing touches on a term paper due for a graduate school course she had registered for when the phone rang. Somewhat annoyed at the interruption, Natalie reached down on the floor and picked up the receiver, answering it with a less than enthusiastic, "Hello."

"Natalie?" the familiar voice asked on the other end of the line. Sighing, Natalie realized it was John's mother. Hesitating for a moment, Natalie finally answered, "Mrs. Whalen, how are you?" Reaching down again to the floor, Natalie turned down the radio.

"I'm fine," Mrs. Whalen answered, "I just wanted to see if you have heard much from John. We've received only one letter so far and although he said he is fine, we are a little concerned."

Natalie had not heard from John and really didn't expect to. She thought of their last night together before he left when they agreed that they would let things slide until he returned. Natalie, realizing that John's mother was worried enough, decided it was not the time to tell her that John and her had decided to break up.

"No, Mrs. Whalen, I haven't, but I told John before he left to concentrate on what he was doing and not to worry about writing me. I'm sure that the first few weeks are hard. I'm sure he's fine. Please don't worry."

"Well, I wish we could phone him. We talked to some of the parents in the area who have boys in Vietnam and they said that most of the boys write every few days. The letter we received took over a week to get here."

Natalie, switching the receiver to her other ear, started to feel guilty. Not so much over her decision to end her relationship with John, but because they hadn't told his parents. She had been close to them for over two years and now she had to lie to them. "Mrs. Whalen, I'll let you know if I hear anything, but John is really tough and he is awfully smart. If I know him, he is probably holed up somewhere drinking beer."

Mrs. Whalen, feeling a little relieved, simply said, "I hope so dear. Well, let me know if you hear from him."

"I will, Mrs. Whalen, I will." Hanging up the phone, Natalie sat back down and for a brief moment thought of writing John. Her heart ached for him, but she couldn't forgive him for what he did. She found the war distasteful. No matter how she tried to envision some redeeming quality for it, she couldn't.

Laughing for a moment to herself, she thought of some of the times she and John had together. Well, who knows, she thought, maybe he'll just walk in the door and say, "Natalie, you were right, war is wrong. I told them that, and they sent me home to you." Natalie again laughed silently to herself, thinking she had been reading too many J. R. Tolkien books.

Chapter 21

Whalen was surprised to find that when they stopped for the night, they did so separately from the other platoons. Seeing Manrique, he asked him about it. "Hey, Manri... I mean Loco, how come we aren't with the other platoons? It seems the more men we have the better."

"Naw, it doesn't work that way. Trying to set up any kind of night perimeter with the whole company would be a bitch. By the way, I'm not going to send you on ambush tonight. It's tough enough being your first night. But I'm probably gonna send you out tomorrow. Did Scarcelli tell you about ambush?"

"Yeah, he did," nodded Whalen, "I think I know what to do."

"Well, ask if you don't. The entire platoon is depending on you."

Whalen sat down and looked around. Some of the men were using their entrenching tool to dig a slit trench in the ground for cover. Whalen started digging while he watched one of the men in his squad, a heavy set, short kid who looked no more than 18, open up a can of C-rations. Whalen remembered that Scarcelli had said they would usually get a hot meal at night sent out by chopper. "Hey Stinson," Whalen asked, "don't they send hot chow out in the evening?"

Stinson looked up and laughed. "Who told you that shit?"

"Scarcelli," Whalen answered.

"Scarcelli? He was fuckin' with you, man. Sometimes they do, but it ain't the SOP." Grab yourself a C-ration from your ruck and heat it up. I have some C-4 you can use if you want to save some time."

Whalen wasn't hungry and decided to wait a bit. "Thanks for filling me in. It sucks being new out here."

Sitting down, Stinson looked up and said, "If you ever see any Ranger outfits, see if you can get them to give you some LURPS. They're real good. All they are is freeze dried food. Real light to carry too. You mix 'em with some water and heat 'em up. They got spaghetti, beef stroganoff, stews. Hey, look, you want my cigarettes? I don't smoke."

Whalen watched as Stinson reached into the box the C-rations came in and handed him the little four pack of cigarettes. Whalen nodded his thanks and shoved the cigarettes in his shirt pocket.

"Where you from?" Whalen asked.

"Pennsylvania, Harrisburg actually. Never thought much of it, but I miss it now. I was drafted. I went to Penn State for a year and quit. They drafted me after that. Funny thing is, when I went for my physical, they thought I had lied about my age 'cause I don't look old enough, but hell I'm 20. How about you?"

"Drafted, went to Ohio State, and I'm from Sandusky, Ohio."

Stinson smiled and said, "Well, I'm damn glad you ain't from Virginia, West, by God."

They both laughed as they thought of the men from West Virginia who always answered when asked where they were from by stating "Virginia, West, by God."

Stinson, putting his empty cans in the box, looked up at the sky and commented, "Sure is beautiful here at times, but it can be hell once the shit hits. I hope to hell we get some body count. Murphy says if we do, we're going to get a stand down in Chu Lai. You ain't been on one yet, but they are one good fucking time."

"You been on R&R yet?" Whalen asked.

Stinson, rummaging through his ruck, pulled out his well-worn poncho liner and laid it down in his slit trench. "Yeah. Went to Bangkok a couple weeks ago. Had a helluva time. The women were unbelievable. Can you believe it? Twenty-five dollars for 24 hours of non-stop fucking. The bars were great and so were the hotels. Think about it when the time comes. Another good thing about Bangkok, the plane ride ain't long." Stinson returned to his ruck and pulled out a Three Musketeer's candy bar. Breaking some off, he handed it to Whalen, simply saying, "Care package from home. My mom sends me candy bars and stuff once a week. Hell, I got a five pound bag of M&Ms for Christmas."

Thinking of Christmas, Whalen thought it must have been a bitch to be in 'Nam during Christmas. He had arrived a few weeks after the holiday period was over.

Reading his thoughts, Stinson said, "We were lucky. We spent the time on Hawk Hill. It's hard to believe, but the cooks turned out a pretty good meal."

Hearing someone approach, Stinson in a mock tone said, "Shit, here comes the L. T. better hide the candy."

Laughing, Calhoun sat down by Whalen and Stinson. "Stinson, did you get another care package? Don't you know that candy rots your teeth and the last thing you want here in the 'Nam is a toothache."

"Fuck it L. T., as long as my mother sends it, I'm gonna eat it."

"Did your squad leader tell you that we want all the candy and cigarette wrappers you can muster up?"

Whalen and Stinson both nodded. "What do they want that shit for? We gonna get fined for littering, L. T.?" Stinson joked.

"Just something we're gonna try, Stinson. You'll see tomorrow."

Calhoun and Whalen both laughed as Stinson got up, grabbed a few sheets of toilet paper out of his ruck and disappeared.

"How you holding up Whalen?" Calhoun asked seriously.

"Fine, I guess sir. I was pretty scared today, but I guess everyone was. I never have been shot at and those rounds came close. Awfully close."

"We're gonna move out early tomorrow. There's a ville a few klicks from here. We're gonna check it out. A lot of time the gooks lay caches of rice and weapons in these villes so they can retrieve the stuff later. It's their supply line. When we find it, we destroy it; and they go that much hungrier and that much shorter on ammunition."

"I was talking to Stinson about R&R. Have you been yet?" asked Whalen.

"No, I haven't. I don't have enough time in yet. I'm not looking forward to it. My parents want me to go to Hawaii, which is all right for the married guys, but not if you're single. I would just as soon go to Bangkok, or maybe Hong Kong. Where you going to go?"

"It's so far off, I don't know. I'll worry about it when I get a bit shorter."

Calhoun looked around the platoon and seemed satisfied. "You should heat up some C-rations, Whalen, it gets dark early and we don't want any light. If you smoke, smoke under your poncho liner. Make a tent with it. Charlie can pick out the glow of a cigarette from the bush and lay an AK round dead nuts on your forehead. That's a bad way to go."

"Hey L. T., how about the supply bird? Scarcelli said they usually come every night with mail and some hot chow."

"Naw, a few nights each week maybe. When they come, they telegraph our position. Not that Charlie doesn't know we're here, but we at least make it a bit tougher on him."

Calhoun bid Whalen good night and left to check on the rest of the platoon. Whalen watched him move off and thought he was awfully easygoing for a West Point officer. Going back to his ruck, Whalen pulled out a writing pad and a pencil and began writing a letter home to his parents. He kept the letter brief, simply telling them that he was on his first patrol and that everything was going well. He didn't mention taking small arms fire earlier in the day. No sense worrying them even more than they were.

Wakeup at 0500 hours came early, and Sergeant Peterson was busy getting everyone up and ready to move out. Most of the men were ready in just a few minutes. A little water from their canteens would be poured into their plastic tubs, a simple shave, change of socks and boots and they were ready.

Peterson went over to Calhoun, lit a cigarette and said casually, "Big day today sir. If we're gonna make this work, we gotta get our asses moving. The men are gonna be wondering why we're turning around."

"Doesn't matter if they know Sergeant, its Charlie we want to confuse. We need to get back to the valley where S-2 says the gooks are holed up. Fuck, they say there are two companies of them in there. With the cover they have, they could lay a big hurt on us if we don't do everything right." Calhoun removed his steel helmet and wiped a towel through his hair. "Hot already sergeant. Hot as hell and the sun isn't even up. You got an RTO picked for the day?"

Peterson nodded and said, "Yeah, it's gonna be Linsinberg today, L. T. He's done it before."

"In 15 minutes check the whole AO. Make sure everything is in order to move out. I'm going to call Murphy and let him know that we're ready."

The platoon started moving out before the sun had risen over the horizon. Whalen wondered if this wasn't dangerous, as they had no chance of picking out any mines or other booby traps. Before he had much of a chance to worry, the platoon was stopped in an area of dense underbrush. There they waited until the sun was up and then they moved out again. It was a feint, Whalen thought, simply a ruse to throw Charlie off.

****

Lt. Truong was heating up his breakfast over a small fire when he heard one of his scouts approach. "Lt. Truong, the Americans moved during the night. Their perimeter was empty this morning."

Lt. Truong set his small pan down on the ground and thought of what Private Phan had just said, "How could that be? The Americans never move at night. They must have a specific plan in mind." Picking up his pan and carefully placing it over the fire, he said, "Find out where they went and report back to me. Take a runner with you, but I must know as soon as possible. Is that clear?"

Private Phan saluted and left at a fast walk knowing that it would be easy to see where they went. The Americans always leave a trail of cigarette butts, candy wrappers, and other litter. Phan smiled as he thought of how happy Lt. Truong will be when he comes back with their location.

****

Sergeant Peterson stopped and squinted at the small village ahead. Consisting of not more than 20 shacks scattered in a semi-circle, it was typical for this region of Vietnam. Turning around, he motioned to his men that he wanted four men to go to the left of the village to cut off any VC or NVA who may decide to make a run for it when they arrived.

"We're gonna go in loud. I want to let 'em know we're coming. So make some noise, okay?"

The squad leaders nodded and headed back to their men. Peterson tugged on Manrique's sleeve giving him a quick thumbs up. Manrique removed a smoke grenade from his belt, pulled the pin and threw it toward the village. The grenade hit with a dull thud and rolled toward the door of the second hootch on the left. In seconds it fired and green smoke quickly spread through the village. Downwind of the smoke, Peterson gave the sign for his men to begin to move in, with the second squad entering first.

Peterson started to yell, "Di Di Mau, Di Di Mau. Get out. Let's go, get out of your god damn huts, let's go."

His men quickly moved in and chased the Vietnamese out of their huts, herding them into a central area. Most of the occupants were women, children and a few old men. Seeing one of the old men acting suspiciously, Peterson went over to see why he was acting strangely. "Papa San," Peterson shouted, "what are you hiding?"

"No VC. No VC," Papa San shouted back.

"Oh, come on now," Peterson said, "when did they leave?"

"No bic," the old man answered.

"Fuck," growled Peterson. "Where the hell is our Kit Carson scout?"

"He's coming Sergeant. He'll be here in a second."

The Papa San started walking away when Peterson, moving quickly, caught him by the sleeve, "Not so fast, Papa San, not so fast, you sit down." Peterson pushed the old man backwards until he was next to a log where he sat down looking up at Peterson with a worried look on his face.

Peterson watched as one of his squad leaders, Sergeant Michalski, came rushing up, "Sergeant, you better come and see what we found." Signaling to Manrique to watch the Papa San, Peterson followed Michalski through the village to the last hootch. Entering, he saw where a table made up of old ammo boxes had been pushed aside revealing a large earthen dug out. Peering into it, he saw two of his men lifting ammo boxes out and setting them by the edge of the dug out. Along with the ammunition were four RPG launchers, several AK47s, two M-16s, cases of C-rations, six claymore mines and several M-79 grenade launchers with a case of 40 mm ammunition for them.

"Sergeant, how did they get the claymores and grenade launchers? They look new."

Shaking his head, Peterson knew exactly how. "The black market Michalski, crooked GIs. Get this crap out of here and pile it up outside. It's too much to blow. I think we need to call for a chopper and have them fly the shit out of here. Fuck, this is a big find." Leaving the hootch, Peterson saw Calhoun standing by the growing pile of ammo. Several men were grunting as they carried the ammo boxes out of the hootch and arranged them according to the type of ammunition each one held.

Calhoun slowly shook his head as he looked at Peterson and said, "Peterson, they must be planning something big. This is a shitload of ammo, a lot of it American. I don't like it. The whole fucking NVA army could be a klick or two away, and we could be in the middle of a trap. Let's find out if that Papa San of yours knows anything."

Walking back to the end of the village, they watched as the Kit Carson scout grilled the Pap San. Calhoun asked him if he had given him any information. The Kit Carson scout, a former VC who had been captured and converted, shook his head and angrily spit on the ground. "No L. T., he say he know nothing. He liar." Taking the butt of his rifle he reared back and speared the old man in the right shoulder. Wincing in pain, he fell backwards off the tree stump he was sitting on. "Maybe his memory be jogged now sir," the Kit Carson scout said. Getting back up, the old man looked defiantly at the Kit Carson scout and rambled off a hurried exchange of words that ended with another violent butt thrust, this time to his opposite shoulder. Getting back up again he stared at the scout before sitting back down. Again the Kit Carson scout asked him a series of questions, only this time just getting a blank stare back. Meanwhile, others in the platoon reported finding medical supplies and large caches of rice. "What should we do with the shit sir?" a young Specialist Fourth Class asked. "Manrique wants to know L. T."

"Tell him to burn the rice, but make sure it's far enough away from the ammo. I'm going to call for a chopper to get the ammo out of here. Signaling for his RTO, he had him call the TOC back at Hawk Hill and report his findings. Peterson unfolded a chart and quickly calculated the coordinates. In minutes he was told a chopper would be out.

Calhoun ordered Peterson to set up a perimeter in case the NVA moved in. Nervously, he sat down and wondered why there was so much ammo.

Walking over to where the women and children were corralled, Calhoun heard one of his men shouting and waving his rifle at a Vietnamese boy about 14 years old. Getting closer, he heard him yelling, "Where did you place the mines around here you fuck? You're a goddamn VC aren't you?" Placing the muzzle of his weapon on his cheek, he started to yell at him again when Calhoun moved in and yelled, "What the hell is going on here?" The soldier, red-faced with rage, looked at Calhoun and answered, "L. T. this fucker is a VC. I'm sure of it. Look at the shit we found. I saw him trying to hide that AK over there. He's a fuckin' VC. Let's fuckin' waste this place sir. These fuckers are all in on it."

Calhoun shook his head, "No one is going to waste anyone. This isn't going to be another My Lai. If you think this kid is a VC, and maybe he is, we'll send him to Chu Lai, but we aren't going to do anything more. Take him over to where the Papa San is; we'll watch 'em both."

The soldier, a wiry kid, maybe 20 years old with a quick temper and a hatred for the Vietnamese, shook his head, "No fucking way, L. T., this fucker is gonna tell us what the hell is going on or I'm going to blow his shit away."

Calhoun, his mind racing, thought of his days at West Point and how ill trained they were for some of the situations they encountered. Standing fast, he glared back at the soldier they called Hammer and ordered him to put his M-16 down. Waving to one of the other men standing nearby, he told him to escort the Vietnamese boy over to where the Papa San was.

Slowly lowering his M-16, Hammer stared back at Calhoun, "Is that what they teach at West Point L. T., to let these sons-a-bitches stay out here so they can kill more of us? This is a fuckin' VC village. If Hathaway was here, he woulda wasted it."

"I'm not Hathaway, and we aren't wasting the village. The best thing you can do is sit down and cool off. We'll be moving out after the chopper loads the ammo and weapons we found." About to leave, Calhoun saw Peterson walking up to them.

"What the hell is going on?" he asked. Hammer, seeing Peterson and sensing that he would see it his way, responded, "Sergeant, this fuckin' kid was sneaking around with an AK. He's a fuckin' VC and this whole village should be wasted. The L. T. won't let us do shit."

Peterson looked at the kid who was now starting to show some welts from an obvious beating. "No one is going to set this place on fire or waste any civilians. We got what we came for. If Brigade wants to waste this place, they can do so, but we're not. Chances are they will, but even if we did, they would rebuild these shacks in a week and we would be no better off."

Walking back to the head of the village, Calhoun asked Peterson if they should put Hammer on the chopper and send him back to Chu-Lai.

"I don't know sir, he's a good soldier, fights like a lion. I'll talk to him. Most of the time we would burn the village, but we don't want to get any more attention drawn to us than we have to, especially since we don't know where the NVA are."

Chapter 22

Colonel Hewitt leaned back in his chair and listened intently to Lt. Saban from S-2 who told him of the large ammo and rice cache. "Sir, I think this is proof that Charlie is going to launch a major attack on some element of our Brigade. Maybe one of the LZs, maybe they just want to take out a platoon or two, but with that much ammo and what we know about the two companies holed up in the Pineapple Forest, maybe that isn't all that's there. Hell, maybe they have a whole Brigade out there."

Hewitt put his arms behind his head and clasped them together. He rocked back and forth in his chair before sighing deeply and staring at the map spread out on his desk. He didn't like it either. What was bothering him the most was the company that seemed in the midst of the danger. He silently wished that Captain Tillman were there instead of Murphy. Murphy was too timid he thought. Shaking those thoughts from his head, he looked at the map again. "Lieutenant, I think we're good for now. Charlie would have moved in to save their ammo and food if they knew we were there. Let's stay with the plan, but alert the chopper boys on the hard stand that we might need them quick. If our boys get in some shit, I want to get some fire support out there."

The Lieutenant, rolling up his map, stood up, saluted crisply and left the room with the nagging feeling that something wasn't right.

Hewitt stared at the wall and smiled. He felt better now. Catching the NVA would be a major coup for him and the brigade.

****

Private Phan slowly walked through the area the infantry platoon had set up the night before. Empty Cration cans and boxes were strewn everywhere. He quickly followed the trail of litter out of the camp, but something just wasn't right. Phan picked up an empty box of Marlboro cigarettes and turned it over in his hand. "The Americans," he thought, "simply threw the boxes and empty soft packs of cigarettes out, they never crumpled them." Continuing down the trail, the litter suddenly stopped. Phan smiled and began to see what had happened. The Americans had deliberately tried to guide them in the wrong direction. He quickly retraced his steps, arriving back at the campsite; he set off in a new direction that seemed more logical.

****

"L. T., chopper coming in," someone yelled. Shading his eyes from the sun, Calhoun looked up and saw the chopper as it began its descent. Landing a short distance from the village, Peterson and Calhoun had the men start moving the ammo and weapons to the chopper. One of the door gunners jumped out and whistled under his breath, "Holy shit, that's a lot of ammo. It's gonna be a load for us, but we'll get it in."

In minutes everything was on the chopper, including the boy and the Papa San, and it lifted back off the ground. Calhoun grabbed his M-16 and growled at Peterson, "Let's get the hell out of here before Charlie moves in."

Whalen turned back to look at the village as they moved out. All the Vietnamese belongings that had been strewn around the village were being picked up and moved back to their hootchs. He started thinking about his anti-war protests back at Ohio State. "Baby killers" they preached to anyone who would listen. That is all the Army was. Baby killers. Now Whalen could see the other side of it. A village teeming with ammunition that would have killed American lives. What do you do? Off to his right and several paces ahead was Hammer. Whalen didn't like him. He was brash and cocky and seemed to like the whole business of fighting way too much, but Whalen knew it was important not to make any enemies. As if reading his mind, Hammer, whose real name was, Brian Cummings, shouted over his shoulder to Whalen, "What did you think, Whalen, we should have trashed the fucking village, don't you think?"

Evading the question, Whalen answered, "Lot of shit there. It's good we found it."

“Fucking ay it is, whole fuckin’ AO was filled with shit. Old Charlie is going to have a real case of the ass when he finds out his cache is gone.”

****

Private Phan reported back to Lt. Truong, who listened to his report. Removing a well-worn map from his sack, he unfolded it and pointed out several areas to Phan. He saw that the Americans appeared headed away from the area where two large companies of NVA were concentrated. Major Nguyen would be happy. They had been placed there with intentions to overrun two isolated LZs located not far from their position and to possibly trap an American unit that attempted to go through a valley that stretched between the two companies of NVA troops. Lt. Truong turned to Phan and thanked him for his fine work.

****

Two uneventful days went by with more patrolling, more villages to check and more confrontations with suspected VC. Whalen had his first taste of ambush the evening before when they set up a klick from the platoon’s nightly position. There were four men on ambush that night all nervous and wishing they were back at the camp. Fortunately, it was an uneventful evening that seemed to take forever to end.

Whalen could see that they had arrived at a valley with two very large jungle areas. One was directly in front of them; the other was separated to the north by a narrow valley. Whalen noticed that the other two platoons were concentrated in the same area with a troop of armored cavalry to the south. They had passed the cavalry unit on the way in. They seemed a happy group, with enormous firepower concentrated on their M113 Armored Personnel Carriers and M551 Sheridan tanks.

Captain Murphy sat down in an area of cleared brush with the platoon leaders. Taking out his map, he unfolded it on the ground in front of him and asked that they sit behind him so they could see. Looking at them he explained what was happening.

"Okay, here's the deal. According to S-2, there are two companies of NVA holed up here. One is in this jungle area to the south, the other on the other side of this narrow valley to the north. It's not that often that we find two companies of NVA, especially so close together. We tried to give the VC who scouts for the NVA the impression that we were heading west. Hopefully they bought it. Regardless, what we are going to do is set up some mortars and M-60s along this small ridge. It looks down at the jungle and isn't very far away. We want to push the NVA that are in the southern area to the north thinking that they will cross this valley to join what we believe is the larger company in this jungle area. After we start pouring fire in, we're going to have the FO call in artillery, but it's going to be designed to squeeze them slowly north, forcing them across this valley. At that time, we'll call in the cavalry unit and they along with artillery are going to just beat the shit out of them in this open area here. Cobra gunships are also gonna come in and blast hell out of them. Our job is this. Calhoun, your platoon is to set up here and will move out when the NVA get into the valley. Your job is to provide initial fire to help squeeze the NVA north and to prevent them from retreating back to this area to the south. Hathaway, take your platoon and set up to the north and be ready to stop them from moving west. Bromley, your platoon is to set up back here. I want your three squads positioned so they can act as a reserve in case anyone needs some help. It's a simple plan; and if it works, we should bag at least a company of NVA."

Hathaway looked at Murphy and asked, "What about the company in the area to the north, do we go after them?"

"To do that, we'd have to go in the jungle and rout them out and that would cost us a lot of men and of course we lose our firepower advantage. Right now, we don't want them to think we know about the other company to the north, otherwise the entire plan will be jeopardized. Any other questions?" Seeing none, Murphy stood up and told them to bring their platoon sergeants up to date.

Calhoun sat in the grass and watched Peterson and the squad leaders as he unraveled the plan. After he was finished, he watched their faces. You could tell a lot by that. What he saw was good. Some fear, but not much. Peterson spoke first, "I guess it should work. Hopefully, the artillery will knock hell out of them and they'll react as Brigade says they will. I hope those Rangers that probed this AO knew what they were doing. Do you think the NVA know we're here?"

Calhoun shook his head, "No, I don't think so. We believe that we set them up with all the litter we threw out. A VC scout captured by F Company some time back told us how they track our units with the litter we leave. We left it out deliberately hoping they would think we were trying to set them up. Hell, either way, they have to be confused. Plus, we moved almost all night, so even if they figured out where we were headed, they wouldn't know we covered all this ground so quickly. Get your mortar squad set up and get the rest of the men in position. We're going to fire this up in about 20 minutes."

Peterson nodded to his squad leader who had the mortars. He quickly got up and left. "OK, let's get going. Manrique, make sure the medics are set up. I want the casualties, if we can move 'em, set up down in that clearing to the west. There's some protection there and the dustoffs should be able to come in. Tell the medics not to waste any time on those we can't help. I hope we can do this without any casualties, but we gotta be prepared."

Manrique, nervously twirling his fingers around the rawhide sling on his M-16, answered, "I'm sure they're ready, but I'll check on 'em."

"One other thing, Manrique, check on your new guy, Whalen. I want to make sure he knows what to do."

After talking with the medics, Manrique went to find Whalen. He found him sitting on his helmet finishing a letter he was writing to his parents. As Manrique approached, Whalen folded the letter and put it back in an envelope and placed it in his ruck.

"Whalen, this could be big. What I want you to do is cram all the clips of ammo you got into your pockets and leave your ruck here. You can come back for it, but we're gonna have to move and move quickly. If this thing works, and let's hope to God it does, we're gonna catch Charlie; but if it doesn't, we're in for a long afternoon. The cavalry units set up an ammo dump and a couple of the guys from Bromley's platoon are gonna run it in as we need it. Set up and fire the hell out of that M16. It doesn't matter where. Just concentrate on the tree line. Now the dinks are gonna move forward to the north and hopefully cross that valley. But until they do, we gotta put as much fire as we can in there. We need to move them north, so direct your fire from south to north. You got that?" Whalen nodded that he did.

"Now I suspect that there is another company of NVA in that dense jungle to the north; and I believe they're gonna come out to help 'em. Listen for my voice or Peterson's and do what we say. You stay put unless you hear otherwise. Don't move unless we say so. You got that?"

Whalen nodded his head again, afraid to talk. Manrique smiled and said "You'll be fine Whalen, and maybe after today we'll get you that nickname; but right now get ready, lock and load."

Whalen started removing the clips of ammunition from his ruck. Off to his right he watched as the mortar squad set up their weapons and started inserting the right fuses for the distance to the tree line. Rolling over he crawled to the edge of the tall grass and looked at the tree line before him.

****

Scarcelli sat glumly in the TOC listening to the radio as reports came in from the field. "Shit Scarcelli, you should be happy you ain't out there. Helluva lot better sitting here in the TOC."

"I guess," Scarcelli answered, "I feel kinda funny. Always been there and I'm a little worried about those FNGs. Top had me work with 'em and now I feel responsible. Maybe there's something else I should have told 'em."

"Fuck, Scarcelli, you're starting to sound like a lifer. Why don't you go to Brigade and re-up?"

"Yeah, imagine me a lifer, shit man, they'd have my ass out of this man's army so fuckin' fast. No way, man, I'm going back to Philly and I ain't leavin' again."

“They’re starting to call the artillery in Scarcelli. The shit’s gonna go down now.” Scarcelli subconsciously moved closer to the radio and silently hoped the guys he helped would be okay.

****

The first rounds of artillery pounded the dense woods with such a shudder Whalen could feel the ground shake underneath him. Moments later a barrage of gunfire from his platoon was set in motion. He could hear the thump of mortars, the rapid hissing of the M60 machine guns, and the popping sound of the M16s. With no return fire, Whalen started to feel a little more at ease.

****

Major Nguyen had just started to prepare his daily report when one of his aides came to see him. “Sir, the scouts have not returned. They should have arrived back some time ago. I am afraid they may have fallen prey to an American patrol.”

Nguyen, thinking for a minute on the data he had on American troop movements, didn’t feel there was much chance of that. Perhaps his scouts had wandered off, or were with some of the whores common to the small villages. Replying to his aide, he stopped in mid-sentence as the distinct whine that preceded artillery could be heard. Instinctively he and his aide threw themselves on the ground as the rounds began bursting to the south. Nguyen, recovering his wits, turned to his aide and told him to get the company in position at the northwest edge of the tree line. If the Americans were present, they would be there. Already he could hear orders being shouted as his men set up their mortars, machine guns, and RPGs. Another aide rushed in and informed him that small arms fire, mortars, and machine gun fire were coming from exactly where Nguyen thought it would be. He ordered the aide to commence firing. He must assess where to move, as they surely couldn't remain where they were.

****

With no immediate return fire coming from the tree line, Manrique ordered his squad to stop firing for a moment. Just as he did, a mortar round and several RPG rounds whistled overhead, alerting Manrique to order that firing be continued.

Whalen started firing his M-16 slowly trying to place his rounds in the back of the tree line. Startled, he heard a mortar round thump about 50 yards behind him. At the same time AK-47 rounds started plinking around his position or whining overhead. With so much noise he couldn't tell where the fire was coming from.

****

Colonel Nhuang listened to the artillery pound his company to the south. Shaking his head in disgust, he knew he must move them out. If they could move north, they would be safe. There were tunnels and dense foliage that the Americans would not be able to penetrate. Heavily booby-trapped, they would not dare to enter. Unsure how many Americans were there, he had been informed it appeared to be no more than a company of infantry supported by artillery. He would take one of his platoons and move it south a little and send fire at an oblique angle into their position. That would force them to move south a bit and give Nguyen a chance to move his company thru the valley and into his sector. Instructing an aide to move the mortars a bit south and send fire, he knew that Nguyen would know when to move across the valley.

****

Murphy watched as the artillery and fire from the NVA Company moved forward pushed by their own artillery. "Too easy," thought Murphy, "it's going too easy." The mortar and

RPG rounds had fallen in the back of their line and had not caused any casualties. Within the hour, he knew the NVA would start to move across the valley. That would be his sign to start to move in and trap them in the open. Putting his binoculars away, Murphy heard mortar fire coming from the north and saw several rounds hit where Hathaway's platoon was. Wincing, they seemed to have the range and angle down correctly, and he knew that some casualties were likely.

Sergeant Peterson watched as the mortar rounds struck the platoon to his left. He knew from experience that the rounds would start to move down the line toward his platoon. With no fire being directed on the area to the north, the NVA set up a constant barrage of mortar fire. During a brief lull, he could hear the yells for a medic and hoped that the wounds were not serious. One of the medics assigned to his unit was firing his M-79 into the tree line as fast as he could load the single shot grenade launcher. "Should I move out to help Hathaway's platoon, Sergeant?" he asked, trying to yell over the fire.

"No. Stay put. We're going to need you here in a minute."

Whalen, still firing his M-16, stopped to squirt a liberal amount of LSA into the breech. He could hear the kid they called Moonshine firing next to him. Occasionally he would yell something to him, but with the noise Whalen couldn't understand him. The heat of the rifle seemed to melt the thin grease as soon as it hit. About to load another clip, he heard a mortar round hit to his right with such force that it knocked his helmet off. He felt the sting of debris hitting his legs and bouncing off his flak jacket. For an instant he thought he had been wounded but quickly realized he was okay. Looking to his right to check on Moonshine, he could only see him laying face down. Crawling over, he yelled, "Moonshine, you all right?" Reaching around his shoulders, Whalen saw a pool of blood forming around his legs and right side. Gently rolling him over, he felt for a pulse and found a feeble one. Looking him over, he also saw a wound to the head, most likely from shrapnel. Yelling for a medic, he crawled back to where his ruck was and took out the dressings that Scarcelli has suggested he carry. Crawling back he winced as the fire from the NVA had picked up. When he got back to Moonshine, he cut off the top of his pants and found a wound about 4" long running down his leg and another small wound on his right buttock. Tying the dressings off, he looked at the head wound, which was oozing blood. One of the medics, apparently not worried about getting hit, hurried to Whalen's side and quickly looked Moonshine over. "Shrapnel wounds to his thigh and ass cheek and a head wound from shrapnel. Probably knocked him out. He should be okay. Listen, I want you to drag his ass down the hill. One of the other medics will monitor him and get him out on a dustoff. You did good, now get going." Standing back up, the medic hurried down the line to another casualty.

Whalen, unsure of how to move Moonshine, decided to try and drag him a bit and then carry him once he was out of the range of fire. Fortunately, Moonshine wasn't very heavy and Whalen was easily able to do this. Moving back and down the incline didn't seem to slow the mortar rounds. They continued to fall throughout the area. Whalen set Moonshine down and in seconds a medic looked at him and said he would be on the next dustoff. Looking around, Whalen saw several wounded being attended to. Moving back up the hill, he crawled the last 100 yards or so until he was back to his position. Picking up his M-16, he started firing toward the tree line when Manrique appeared at his side. "How's Moonshine? I saw you moved him down the hill."

"Okay, I guess, at least that's what the medic said."

"Good. We'll be moving down the hill as soon as those gooks start coming out of the jungle. Be ready, we're going to cut their asses off."

Whalen was surprised at how calm he was compared to his first exposure to enemy fire a few days earlier. He continued to fire into the tree line, never seeing a single NVA.

****

Major Nguyen had set a squad near the tree line to continue their fire into the American lines. The rest of his company was ready to move across the valley and into the safety of the jungle less than a klick away. He waited for a signal from a sentry on the other side. It was then that he must hasten his men across as quickly as possible. The company to the north was to fan out from the jungle in order to draw enemy fire and attention from them. It was at that time he was to make his move.

Watching the tree line, he received the signal and his men burst from the dense foliage.

****

Captain Murphy watched as the NVA moved out from the jungle. He quickly gave the signal and the Cavalry unit swung into position. The first Sheridan tank was setting up to fire its cannon when it was struck under the turret by an RPG round. Within seconds, a second Sheridan tank was also hit. Murphy swore under his breath as he saw their plan start to unravel. Apparently the NVA had positioned some men north of their AO armed with RPGs and waited for the Cavalry to move out. Fortunately, other Sheridans maneuvered around several RPGs that were fired at them and managed to fire a number of rounds into the NVA, who were now moving timidly across the valley. Lieutenant Hathaway's men quickly responded and began laying down heavy fire. The NVA quickly hit the ground and began crawling toward the safety of the jungle. Just as it appeared they would make it, Cobra gunships arrived and began raking them with fire. With no choice, the NVA were forced to get up and make a run for the jungle, now less than a few hundred meters away.

Peterson's platoon moved quickly to close any possible escape. They moved forward firing M-16s and M-79 grenade launchers. The mortar squad continued to lay rounds from their position. In minutes it was over.

****

Major Nguyen pulled himself into the jungle dragging his left leg that had been grazed by a bullet or shrapnel. He feared he had lost half his strength, but if he hadn't moved when he did, the entire company would have been sacrificed. He heard the fire die out from the squad he left behind but knew they would hide in one of their tunnels and most likely join them the next day. Not at all discouraged, he knew their day would come. Patience, he reminded himself. They must have patience.

****

Lt. Calhoun caught up with Sergeant Peterson who was writing some notes in a small booklet. "Casualties?" Calhoun asked.

"Not bad," Peterson answered. "We have four wounded, one seriously, and one KIA from our platoon. Hathaway's platoon didn't fare as well. They had two KIA and six wounded. Bromley's platoon had one wounded, but we held them back and really didn't need them."

"Any word on the cav unit?" the L. T. asked.

"Not good; they lost two Sheridans seconds after they were exposed. The drivers and loaders both are KIA. They also lost two others for six KIA and had a bunch wounded. Fucking NVA pulled some of their men out of the tree line to the north and advanced on 'em. I've got some of our men down in the valley getting a body count of the NVA, and I'm sure it will be high. One of the Cobras went down too, sir. Crash-landed a couple of klicks from here. I don't know if the crew got out. They took an RPG round when making a pass over the valley."

"Three KIA from our company. That's a heavy load, I don't give a damn how many NVA we bagged," remarked Calhoun. "Who was our KIA?"

"Whitson. He was here maybe three months. Quiet, didn't say much, I think he was from someplace down south. I don't remember where. Damn near got a direct hit from a mortar. He didn't linger, sir, if it's any consolation. We got the KIA in bags. The medivac is coming back to get them. They wanted to get the wounded out first. The only wounded I'm worried about is Manrique L. T.; Loco got hit when we were moving down the hill. Took a round in his thigh. I think he'll be okay, but I don't think we'll get him back. Moonshine got whacked pretty good too. Shrapnel knocked his helmet off and put him out. He's also got a wound on his leg, but he'll be back in a few weeks. Other wounds are pretty minor."

Hearing a chopper approach, they watched it land and were surprised to see Colonel Hewitt get off. Walking toward them, he bellowed, "Good job men, you smashed the hell out of them. Where's Captain Murphy, Lieutenant?"

"With the third platoon, sir," pointing toward where Murphy was. The Colonel grunted his thanks and started off in that direction. Murphy was listening to one of the platoon sergeants when he saw Hewitt walking toward him.

"Great job, Murphy, great job. Your men have earned that stand down I promised. I understand the body count is close to 100. Hell, that's a damn good body count."

Murphy listened and said in disgust, "We took some casualties, sir, lost some good men. Near as we can figure, we got about 60 NVA, maybe more, we don't know how many we knocked out in the assault on their tree line. All toll, sir, our company and the cav unit had nine KIA. I don't know about the wounded, probably about a dozen men."

Hewitt, realizing that Murphy was sickened over the loss of his men, decided not to talk about the body count but instead told him to move his men out and back to Hawk Hill. Once there, he was to report to his office for a de-briefing. Murphy watched as Hewitt made the rounds of his men, slapping them on the back and praising their work. "He looks like a politician," Murphy thought. Turning to his RTO, Murphy ordered him to get the platoon leaders so he could fill them in.

Bromley, Hathaway, and Calhoun listened as Murphy told them what Hewitt had said. "Let's not tell the men about the stand down just yet. I know they have probably heard rumors, but until we get the final details, let's keep it to ourselves. Calhoun, I understand you lost a squad leader today?"

"I did sir. I lost Manrique, the kid they called Loco. He was good Captain. I guess he'll be gone a while. I'll get a replacement, but hell sir, I don't have a lot to pick from. A bunch of the guys I have that would be good are too damn short to consider. Hell, my best guy is probably Whalen, and he's on his first patrol."

"How did he do today?" Murphy asked.

"Good, Captain, really good. He dragged Moonshine down the hill after he was hit. Carried him part of the way. I'll find a squad leader, but I want Peterson to be involved. He has to deal with whoever we pick."

"Let's get ready to move the hell out of here. We have that company of NVA back there and I don't want them coming after us."

****

Colonel Nhuang, rubbing his eyes, sat down on a small folding wooden chair. He looked sadly at Major Nguyen. "Major, we still have a formidable force and our plans remain to bring the attack to the Americans. We hurt them today. Our rockets took out two of their tanks, and we damaged some of their personnel carriers. We also took out a gunship. The Americans are leaving. We will get strong again and we will get revenge. There were many medical helicopters coming and going, so we must have hurt them."

"Yes, I know Colonel, but we got caught. We had planned for the Americans to send a company through the valley, and as you know, we could have annihilated them."

Standing up, Colonel Nhuang patted Nguyen on the back, "We will fight another day, Major. We are winning the war and before long we will be marching on Saigon."

Chapter 23

Whalen walked into his hootch and lay down on his cot. It took over two days to hoof it back to their LZ. He was tired. He looked at his mail, two letters from his parents, one from his brother, none from Natalie. He closed his eyes and thought of the last few days. He had been moving down the hill with Manrique in front of him. Loco kept turning back to check on him and offering encouragement. He had just turned to say something to him, when a round from an AK-47 hit his thigh, spinning him around. The round was misdirected after leaving his thigh and grazed Whalen on his calf. It was nothing more than a scratch and Whalen said nothing to anyone. Whalen had stopped to render first aid to Manrique, who told him to move down the hill, that medics would be following. Refusing, Whalen started to bandage the wound when a medic arrived and told Whalen he would be of more help if he would help chase the gooks into the jungle.

Whalen heard Manrique was okay, which was good news. He would be gone for a while, but was expected to completely recover. It was a flesh wound, but his days in the field were probably over.

Opening his mail, Whalen read each letter. He smiled as he read the letter from his brother. He wanted to know if he could send him a souvenir from Vietnam.

The war sucked, Whalen thought. Just as he felt in college, there seemed to be little sense to it. The Vietnamese people had been at war for centuries and seemed to care little about the final outcome. The politicians and perhaps some of the people cared, but from what he saw, few took more than a passing interest. The country seemed almost primitive. Highway One, their primary road running the length of the country, was filled with carts, meandering Water Buffalo and double-decker buses. Little employment seemed to be available other than the maze of rice paddies or on one the bases such as Hawk Hill. Whalen had yet to see a school.

Whalen was about to go to sleep when Sergeant Jervis walked in and sat on the corner of his cot. Lighting a cigarette, he blew a cloud of smoke in the air. "Couple of things, Whalen, first I just got back from Chu Lai and talked to Loco. He wanted me to thank you for helping him after he got hit. He's gonna be okay, so is Moonshine. He was knocked out by the shrapnel and sustained a concussion. The wounds to his ass and leg will heel, although they are infected. He said he's gonna kick your ass because you must have used a dirty bandage. Loco also wanted me to tell you that you did good out there for an FNG. Anyway, he has your nickname."

Whalen looked up curiously, "Oh yeah, anything is better than FNG, so what is it?"

"Well, I guess you played some high school football and rumor is you tried out for the Buckeyes at Ohio State." Whalen nodded in agreement as he let out a short laugh.

"My high school coach had some connections and I went to camp in the summer as a walk on, but, those fucking guys they give scholarships to can play. I was a lineman and a little small for college ball, but I stuck until the final camp and was asked back the next year, but I was into other stuff by then and decided not to try again. Hell, I was in bad physical shape after a year of college."

Jervis continued, butting out his cigarette on the plywood floor. "Touchdown," he said, smiling. "That's gonna be you. Doesn't matter if you like it or not, fuck, that's what it's gonna be."

Getting up to leave, Jervis put his boonie hat back on. "Listen, Touchdown, we're gonna have a funeral ceremony for the guys we lost. It's gonna be held in front of the Orderly Room. The cavalry unit is bringing over a track. It's a pretty sobering experience. Keep your chin up. It will be at 0900 tomorrow. Oh, one other thing, I almost forgot, Peterson wants to see you in the NCO hootch. He's waiting for you, so you should get your ass over there."

Whalen stopped him as he was leaving, "Hey Jervis, what was your nickname?"

Smiling, Jervis answered, "Cat, Whalen, it was Cat. Like a cat I had nine lives out in the bush. I got three purples, you know, and that is something you don't want."

Wondering what Peterson wanted, Whalen walked over to his hootch. Not certain what the protocol was, he simply walked in. Sitting on his cot, Peterson was busy opening a large stack of mail from home. Glancing up, Peterson told him to sit down. A little envious of all the mail he had received, Whalen said, "Must be nice, Sergeant, I don't get much mail, I broke up with my girl before I left."

"You're lucky, Whalen, most of these guys lose their girls while here anyway. What's worse is most of 'em continue to write even though they are with someone else. It's a bitch when you get a letter from your buddy telling you that your girl is banging someone else."

Peterson put the letters aside, and taking his time, chose his words carefully. "I understand that when you were in basic you were a squad leader, and a damn good one from what I hear."

Whalen shrugged his shoulders; "I didn't ask for it, the DI gave it to me. I guess I did okay."

"As you know, Manrique will be out for a while, and I don't know if we'll send him back in the bush. Those AK rounds tear you up pretty good, especially when they exit. He's gonna be limping around for a month or so, and he'll be getting short by then. I need a squad leader. I know you're green, but there's not much to choose from in my platoon, and I hate like hell to bring someone over from another platoon."

"Sergeant, I'm only an E-3, I think the guys would resent it. These squad leaders are all Buck Sergeants, and hell, I don't know what the fuck I'm doing."

"We get these Shake and Bake E-5s here all the time; and hell, they take over a squad with no experience. Some of the guys might resent it, Whalen, but no matter who we pick, it will be the same thing. We're gonna be getting a lot of new guys in over the next month or two, and you are a good choice. I've only been here six weeks myself, that means we'll be together for a while. Same thing with Calhoun. He came about the same time as me. Anyway, there's no choice in the matter. I'm not going to announce this until after stand down. It will be a little easier for you then. You did a helluva job out there this week. I'm happy to have you Whalen. I understand you have a nickname."

"I do, it's Touchdown. It's a little embarrassing. I wasn't any star or anything. I played in the trenches, a lineman."

"Well, Touchdown, that's what you're doing here. Back in the trenches. Come see me after stand down in Chu Lai, and we'll talk some more."

Whalen thanked Peterson, shook his hand and walked out of his hootch. In a way, he felt a sense of pride, and in another didn't want the responsibility. "Fucking Army," Whalen thought. Then he thought of Hess and what he said about not letting his men down. Hess knew he would end up an 11 Bush and knew he would be a squad leader. "Fucking Army," Whalen thought again as he walked back to his hootch.

Peterson thought about Whalen, and although he was uneasy about the decision, there seemed to be no other choice. Shaking his head, he thought of the report they had received from Brigade to keep an eye on him because of his anti-war stand in college. Not sure what to make of that, Peterson went back to his letters. Janet wrote a lot about his sons, the car needed a new battery, the weather in Columbia, South Carolina, had been cold and she had made her own short-timers calendar that the boys used every day to color in another day. Finishing the letters, he wrapped them in a rubber band and put them in his locker. Getting up, he walked over to the platoon leader's hootch to tell Calhoun he had talked to Whalen.

Entering the officer's hootch, he saw a bottle of Seagram's 7 Crown on a small table in the center of the room. Hathaway looked up at Peterson and waved the bottle at him saying "Hey Sergeant, have a drink." Peterson looked at the bottle for a second, reached over, and putting the bottle up to his lips took a large gulp, feeling the liquid burn as it traveled to his stomach. Handing the bottle back, he saw Calhoun smiling at him.

"Looks like you needed that, huh Jack?"

"I guess I did L. T." Not wanting to linger in the officer's hootch, Jack got right to the point. " I talked to Whalen. I think he'll be okay. We need to talk to Top and see about his rank. I know we can move him to E-4, but I don't know about E-5. I guess we can make him an acting jack for a bit."

Calhoun nodded in agreement. “I’ll talk to Murphy and Top. You agree with this?”

“I’d be happier with Manrique, but he was getting short, and that’s what this war is about. Guys are coming and going all the time. I’m not gonna announce this until after stand down. Could be some animosity, and Whalen doesn’t need that.”

Chapter 24

Whalen, standing next to Stinson, watched as two armored personnel carriers worked into position in front of the Orderly Room. American flags were draped over the tracks and a pair of boots placed in front of the tracks for each man lost. A Catholic Chaplain stood at a makeshift podium consisting of several ammo boxes stacked up on end.

He started the eulogy and spoke of the sacrifices men have to make in order to be free—free from tyranny, free to choose their own religion, free to choose their own destiny. A bugler, an infantryman from another company, played Taps as both Whalen's infantry unit and the cavalry unit stood in silence. The officers lined up in front were struggling with their emotions, especially Captain Murphy who periodically reached up to wipe tears from his eyes. All had a heavy heart; and as the ceremony finished, the boots were removed, the tracks fired up and all left quietly. The Chaplain walked over and talked to Murphy, handing him the flags, neatly folded, which Murphy accepted before handing them to Top.

Walking into the Orderly Room, Top called the company clerk into Murphy's office. Simmons, an E-4, had spent three months in the field and had an infantry MOS, but when the company clerk they had left to go back to The World, word went out to the field to find someone who could type. Simmons had taken a typing class in high school and had two years of college, so he was given the opportunity to work in the rear as a clerk. Sitting at Murphy's desk, Top said, "Simmons, the men will be going to Chu Lai for stand down and Murphy and I want them to have one helluva time. Now I know you do a lot of shit here, don't think I don't know 'cause I do. I know you're selling black market ration cards and typing up E-5 orders so the men can get into NCO clubs and a bunch of other shit. I don't care about that, but I want you to go to Chu Lai today, I'll get you a chopper. The stand down is going to be at 1st of the 1st Cav's area, which ain't in the best part of Chu Lai. We got a band coming in, a lot of beer and good steaks. I want you to be in charge of making sure they have a good time." Top started fidgeting with a stapler on Murphy's desk, not sure how to continue. "Simmons, I'm sure these boys want to get laid, and I don't want them wandering around Chu Lai looking to get their dicks wet. You figure out some way to get those whores into our stand down, I don't know how the fuck you can do it, but from what I hear, there isn't much you can't do. And get a load of condoms, too. I don't want half our unit coming down with the clap."

"Uh, sure Top, I can do that I guess. I, uh, will probably need some front money."

Top reached into his pocket and took out an envelope stuffed with piasters, the local money. "I can't give you MPCs Simmons. You never know when a changeover is scheduled."

"Sure Top. Uh Top, about the other shit, I…"

"Don't worry about it Simmons, do your work here in the orderly room. We're fighting a war, and I'm worried about our boys, not some goddamn ration cards. Before you go, did you get the letters done that Murphy wants sent to the families of those KIA?"

"I did Top, they're on my desk. I also got letters to the families of the wounded too."

"When we get back from stand down, we need to get some awards going, and you need to put the new kid, Whalen, in for his CIB and also put papers in for E-4 for him too. Simmons nodded and left Murphy's office, sitting down at his desk. "Damn," he thought, "how the fuck did Top know about the ration cards he was having made at home and selling? And the orders he was cutting on the side." Shaking his head he started thinking of ways to get the girls into the stand down area. It wouldn't be easy. The main base of the Americal Division is bordered on one side by the ocean and the other side by Highway One. Heavy wire and guard towers ringed the entire Division. Maybe a chopper was the best bet, but then how would he get them to the stand down area?

Simmons stepped off the chopper at Chu Lai Air Base and hitched a ride on a deuce and a half heading out to the 1st of the 1st Cavalry. Upon arrival, he went directly to the Orderly Room and talked to an acquaintance of his who was working as a Troop Clerk for one of the Cavalry units.

Walking into the Orderly Room, Simmons saw his friend, Glenn Collins, sitting at his desk. "Well," Collins said, "I thought you would show up today. I see you are using our stand down area this week."

"Fuck yeah, we are," smiled Simmons as he gripped Collins in a handshake. "Hey, you gotta help me with some shit though." Looking around to make certain no one was around, Simmons told Collins of his plan to bring some prostitutes in for the stand down. He made certain not to tell him that the order came from his first sergeant.

Shaking his head, Collins said, "I dunno Simmons, it's gonna be tough. A lot of girls work outside the main gate, but fuck, bringin' 'em in, well, that ain't gonna be easy."

"I have a plan that I think will work. If I can get hold of a half-track or deuce and a half, I'll run outside the post and work with some of the pimps out there. I'll dress one of the girls up like a GI, you know, fatigue shirt and boonie hat. Fuck, at night, they'll probably just flag us through. What do ya think Collins? Brilliant, isn't it? Classic fuckin' Simmons at his best."

Smiling, Collins sat down and mused, "Just might work Simmons, but if you get caught, you're fucked, and where the hell you gonna get the truck?"

This time it was Simmons' turn to smile, "Well, I'm gonna use yours. Tomorrow, you let me make your runs and I'll hit the village after dark."

"And what do I get for risking a term in Leavenworth or maybe Long Binh Jail?"

"A cut of the profits. Let's quarter off one of the hoochs with poncho liners. We'll set up a table and put a cot in the back. We'll charge $20, give the girl $10, and we'll split the other $10."

"You'll have to pay the pimp. Where's that money going to come from?"

"I'll take care of that out of my end," answered Simmons, not telling him about the money Top had given him.

The night before Whalen's company went to Chu Lai for stand down was quiet. Most of the men were writing letters, packing some things for Chu Lai, or getting stoned or drunk.

Whalen wrote some letters home and watched a movie outside. Most nights a movie was shown on a screen set up outside the mess hall. That evening the movie was one everyone had seen featuring Dustin Hoffman in *The Graduate*. The scene with Mrs. Robinson, played by Anne Bancroft, jumping in the pool had been re-played so many times the film was worn through much to the disappointment of everyone. Going back to his hootch, one of the men in his squad offered him a cold beer. Accepting it, Whalen asked, "When do you guys get to buy beer?"

"Once a month a pallet comes in, and we buy as much as we can," remarked Bob Winkel.

"Next time, I'll spring for a couple of cases. You guys have given me a few beers and I want to pay you back."

"Hey Touchdown, with Manrique out, who do you think is gonna get our squad?"

"Fuck if I know. Does it matter?" Whalen asked.

"No, I guess not, but we don't want one of those guys from 1st or 3rd Platoons getting it."

"Well, we'll see. I guess it's up to Peterson and Calhoun. They sure as hell ain't gonna listen to us. We'll find out, probably after stand down. You guys been on stand down before?"

"Nitzer has, isn't that right?"

"Fucking 'ay it is," answered Nitzer while lying on his bunk reading a Superman comic book.

Whalen now understood why they called him Krypton. "Hey Krypton, he yelled, "You and my brother should get together. He's got a stack of Superman comics that damn near reaches the ceiling."

Catching his interest, Krypton swung his legs over the side of his cot. "Does he have any of the classics?"

"Fuck if I know, but he's got a lot of 'em. Next letter I write, I'll ask him."

"You know Touchdown, if we had Superman's powers, we'd kick Charlie's ass in a week."

"Ah, you're fuckin' nuts," growled Winkel throwing an empty beer can at him.

At 0800 the next morning, deuce and a halves were lined up near the main gate. The men of Bravo Company filed in, sat down and settled in for the hour or so ride to Chu Lai down Highway One. Escorting the trucks were two armored jeeps, each with a mounted 60-caliber machine gun.

Whalen stared out the window and again was amazed at what he saw of the Vietnamese people and villages. All the activity was within yards of Highway One. Along the road were poorly constructed shacks and people all dressed the same. Sergeant Peterson, sitting next to him, yelled over the noise, "Tam Ky has a large Marine detachment. They have a helluva club there too, very nice, just like back in the states. Cold draft beer, cocktail waitresses, the whole thing." Whalen nodded in surprise.

Pulling into Chu Lai, the trucks rolled down a long road that ran parallel to Highway One, finally arriving in a sandy area with a series of run-down hootchs with simple corrugated steel roofs and screen sides. Moments after getting off the trucks, they pulled away leaving the company standing there wondering what to do. The grumbling started to get out of hand, when they could see a jeep streaming toward them. Pulling up to the company, they watched as Simmons and a young lieutenant got out of the jeep. Simmons had a smirk on his face as the company started complaining, "Aw fuck, if Simmons has anything to do with stand down, we're fucked."

Grinning, Simmons yelled, "Hey, listen up. The L. T. here is your stand down coordinator. He wants to say a few words."

The young L. T. with a CIB sewed on his pocket sleeve and well worn fatigues with an 11th Infantry Brigade pocket patch, had obviously been in-country for a while and was given this assignment to finish out his year. "Men, I know you guys all want to know what's going on, so I'll go over a bit of what's going to happen. You'll be here for the next few days. If you want to go to the main base, the EM or NCO Club, or a movie, phone center, whatever, I'll have a truck leaving here each hour starting at 1300 today. Trucks from the main base back will run on the half hour. Last truck out of here will be at 1800. Last truck back here will be at 2200. Tomorrow night we're going to have a big steak dinner for you, followed by a helluva band in the building to my right. There will be all the beer you want tomorrow. Have some fun while you're here. One last thing, Chu Lai is off limits. Don't go there. I know some of you want to get laid, but that's not the place for it. There are VC running around and a shitload of MPs that will pick you up. If you need anything, see Simmons here. Any questions? Good. On behalf of Colonel Hewitt, Commander of the 196th Light Infantry Brigade, have a good time."

As the L. T. got back in the jeep and drove off, Simmons addressed the company. "One thing, there is beer cooled down in tubs of ice in the building over there. I have a charcoal grill set up too, with real hot dogs and hamburgers. I'll be cookin' 'em all day and night, so anytime you're hungry come and see me. I also have real potato salad and cole slaw too."

"Who did ya steal it from Simmons?" yelled someone from the crowd.

"The Air Force," Simmons yelled back. Walking into the Orderly Room, Simmons told the platoon leaders who had gathered there about his plan to bring in a local prostitute. Bromley and Hathaway were smiling as Calhoun simply listened.

"How did you get the food Simmons?" asked Bromley.

"No kidding sir, I got the food from the Air Force. Fuck, they got flush toilets and real mess halls sir. I went there and bribed one of their fuckin' cooks. Sir, you wouldn't believe how well they eat. Un fuckin believable sir. It's a shame. I ain't seen a flush toilet since I been here, and they got 'em in the mess hall."

****

Whalen took the first truck into the main base and decided to stop at the 98th Evacuation Hospital to check on Moonshine and Manrique. Getting off the deuce and a half, he found out the hospital wasn't that far away, so he started walking. He hadn't walked more than 100 meters when he heard the voice of Lt. Calhoun yelling behind him. "Hey Whalen, wait up."

Whalen stopped as he watched Calhoun running toward him.

"You sound just like a school kid, did you know that L. T.?"

Calhoun smiled and asked, "Where you headed?"

"To the hospital. I want to check on Moonshine and Manrique."

"Me too; let's go together. It isn't far from here.

"L. T., what's with this phone center the L. T. back there mentioned?"

"They have a place set up with real phones. You can call collect back home, but you know the time zones are fucked up. Could be 12 hours difference, and getting a call in the middle of the night will scare the hell out of your folks, so be careful when you call."

"I don't know if I want to. If I called once, they would expect it. I thought about making a MARS call, but you don't know when they will get through."

"Peterson makes MARS calls home every chance he gets. I think he has an in with the Ham Radio Operator that connects him. Anyway, he seems to get through quicker than anyone else."

Walking through the entrance to the hospital, they quickly found the ward Moonshine was in. Walking in, they saw him lying in bed somewhat sedated and pale. Seeing them, he smiled and cheered up considerably. "Hey L. T., Whalen, what are you guys doing here? Jervis said you were still out in the field."

"We're on stand down in Chu Lai Moonshine. The whole company is here," answered Whalen.

"It sure is good to see you guys. I know I don't look good. The wound on my leg got infected."

"Moonshine, if you need anything, you let me know," Calhoun told him. "I want you to get well and get your ass back to our unit. How much time you got left?"

"I'm not that short sir, about five months. I was planning on going on R&R in a month or so, but I don't know. I hope I can make it. I hear Manrique got hit pretty bad. I haven't seen him."

"He'll be okay. The round tore him up a bit, but he'll heal."

"L. T., could you write a letter home for me and tell my folks in Kentucky I'm okay? I know they're worried and I don't know what the Army tells them. Anyway, I'd feel better."

"I will Moonshine, I'll do it when we get back from stand down," Calhoun promised.

"Whalen, I want to thank you for helping me. I woke up in the chopper and the medic said you carried me down the ravine. I don't know what to say. Hell, I could have bled to death there. I understand we kicked Charlie's ass. Big body count."

Getting up, Calhoun smiled and said, "That's right Moonshine, we did get a big body count. Kicked their ass good."

Smiling, Moonshine, now very tired, started to drift off to sleep, "Fuckin' gooks," he said as he closed his eyes.

On the way out, they stopped one of the medics working the floor and asked about Moonshine and Manrique.

"They'll both be OK. Moonshine has a nasty infection, but it's clearing up. The blow to the head will take him a while to recover from. Concussions are tough to figure out. Manrique will recover. I don't know about the field though. He's gonna have a helluva limp for a while. Bullet grazed the bone, but he'll be as good as new in a few weeks."

They walked down the ward through a door and entered another ward where they saw Manrique talking to one of the army nurses.

"Shit Loco," Whalen said, "Here we come in here from stand down to give you a little support, and you're talking to some pretty nurse."

Manrique, happy to see them, thrust out his hand, "About time you guys showed up. Jervis came in, but I was so out of it, I hardly remember seeing him. He's all right that guy. Three purples and he still has a good attitude."

Whalen and Calhoun filled Loco in on what happened, and got up to leave when an orderly came in and told them that he needed to rest.

"Hey L. T., I'm going to be out for a while with this wound. Who's going to get my squad, do you know yet?"

"Not 100% yet, but we'll know by the time we get back to the LZ. We'll stop in before we go. Do you need anything?"

"Naw, but next time you come in here and I'm talking to that pretty nurse, you guys just wait until I'm done."

"Hell no, we won't wait," laughed Calhoun. "Why should you be making out with a round eye while we're sitting over on the Hill or out in the bush?"

One of the orderlies started giving them a nasty look and told them it was time to leave. As they walked out, Whalen said, "He looks good, better than Moonshine."

"What are you going to do today Whalen?" asked Calhoun.

"Ah, I don't know. I want to hit the PX; I haven't been there yet. I understand it's pretty good size. Maybe have a beer or two at the EM Club. How about you?"

"Same thing. But before I do that, I'm going to go to the phone center. It's maintained by the Red Cross."

****

Lieutenant Calhoun sat at the phone staring at it wondering what he would say to his parents. He hoped his father wouldn't be home. It would be easier. Taking a deep breath, he placed the call. Looking at his watch, he realized it was after 11:00 PM at home, but his parents rarely went to bed before midnight. Maybe his sister would be using the phone and the line would be busy. After what seemed like an eternity, the phone rang and his mother answered. "Hello Mom, it's Brian."

After a short period of silence, his mother came back, "Brian are you home, where are you calling from?"

"I'm in Vietnam Mom, in Chu Lai. We have a stand down. I can't talk long, but I wanted you to know that I'm doing well and that everything is going good. Is everything okay at home?"

"Yes Brian, everything is fine. Your father is in Carlisle, Pennsylvania, at the War College. I wish your sister was here, but she is on a date tonight."

"Tell them I'm fine and I love them all. I'll call again, I just don't know when."

Brian's mother was having a hard time holding back the tears. Her only son was far away, fighting a war that seemed to never end. She had a strange premonition that something was going to happen. Something only a mother could feel, but she could not let her son know. "Brian, you be careful. I'll tell your sister and your father you called. I'm going to send a care package to you this week. Let me know if you like what's in it."

"Sure Mom, I will. I love you and please don't worry. Goodbye."

Walking out of the building, Brian sat down next to Whalen on a small bench. Using Whalen's given name for the first time, he shook his head, "John, it's hard calling home. It's times like that when you realize that the ones that love you have to worry about you 24 hours a day. They never know what danger you face."

Whalen, not knowing what to say, took a safe approach, "Ah, you West Point families are tough, nothing phases you. I'll bet your Mom is a lot tougher than you realize. I'll bet she can beat hell out of you, can't she?"

"She never did, but she probably could."

Suddenly Calhoun's eyes lit up, "Hey, you know what? Let's get drunk."

"That's going to be tough. I can't go in the Officer's Club and you ain't gonna be welcome in the EM Club."

"Ah hell, I'll go in your Club. All I gotta do is find another shirt and they sell fatigue shirts in the PX, so let's go."

An hour later Whalen and Calhoun were sitting at a crude bar at the Enlisted Man's Club drinking canned beer. No other alcohol was served there, only beer.

"Now I know why I went to West Point," complained Calhoun. Fuck, why don't they have liquor here?"

"I guess they don't trust us with it L. T."

"Whalen, while we're at the bar in your Club, just call me Brian. I'm sure there's some stiff penalty for an officer to be in your Club. Next stand down, you're coming to the Officer's Club OK?"

"Yeah, and how the hell am I gonna get in? Go back to The World, go to OCS and then look you up so I can get some hard liquor?"

"That's not a bad idea, John, you'd make a good officer, but there is an easier way. All you have to do is go see Simmons."

"Simmons? The company clerk?"

"Yeah. He can do anything. He has black market ration cards and a Gestetner printing press. He runs off his own orders promoting dudes like you all the time. Not officially, but to get into the different clubs. We'll have him print you some orders.

"I don't know, we'll see, but I sure as hell could use another ration card. That one I have is already getting full, at least for cigarettes."

After several beers, neither Whalen nor Calhoun felt very drunk. Whalen told Brian about Natalie and also about the demonstrations he participated in during college. "You probably know about that anyway. Murphy did. Called me on it you know. Said he was going to keep an eye on me. I guess he thought I was a commie."

"Yeah, we knew. But to be honest no one gave a damn. I told Murphy I thought you were all right."

"You have to stay in the Army for what 20 years?"

"I don't know, John, I really don't. I wasn't kidding when I said I wanted to be a lawyer. I'll be in the Army for a while I guess. Even if I stay in 20 years, I'll only be in my 30s. I'm thinking about taking classes at some college near where I'm stationed when I get back to The World. You know, work on my law degree so I have it when I retire from the Army. Hell, there would still be time for a second career, but I gotta get this tour over with first. It wears on me. It's a lot of responsibility. Seeing the men, kids really, get wounded or KIA. It's tough. I don't think it ever leaves you."

"I know," said John. "I wish this war would come to an end, but from what I have seen, it's not going to anytime soon."

"What are you going to do when you get home, John?"

"I don't know. I have a liberal arts degree, which doesn't mean shit. I would like to teach, maybe coach football, I don't know. Who knows, maybe I'll go to law school," he joked.

Laughing, Brian said, "Let's get the hell out of here and go back to the stand down and see what everyone is doing."

Chapter 25

Simmons drove the deuce and a half all day with a helper from the 1st of the 1st Cavalry. Pushing his helper all day, they managed to complete their work by late afternoon. They headed back down Highway One toward Chu Lai, passing the main gate when Simmons' helper noticed that they were heading south past the entrance. "Hey, where the fuck you going?" he said clutching his M-16 even tighter.

"Oh just a little detour is all; just one more stop; you just sit tight."

"Fuck, Simmons, this better be on the up-and-up. I only got six weeks left, and I don't want to spend it in Long Binh jail."

"Don't you worry. I want to get laid is all," Simmons said.

Seeing some local girls dressed in American mini skirts with heavy makeup, Simmons pulled over to the side of the road and got out. "Watch the truck, Collier. If anyone gets close, you blow their shit away, OK?"

With a cigarette dangling from his lips, Simmons approached the first girl he saw. No sooner had he got within talking distance when a Vietnamese man of about 30 showed up and smiled. "You like?" he asked with a wide smile that showed several gold teeth.

"How much?" Simmons asked flatly.

"Twenty dollars MPC," the Vietnamese said.

"How much overnight?" Simmons asked

"Overnight? $100," the Vietnamese man stated.

"Fifty dollars," Simmons countered.

"$100," the Vietnamese man offered again.

Simmons, removing his boonie hat, threw his cigarette on the ground. "Okay, Pap San, I'll give you $100, but I want to take her inside," he said pointing to the base.

"Inside? You crazy? MP arrest. No Way. You get caught."

Simmons pulled out the $100 and handed it to the man. "I'll have her back tomorrow and will give you another $100, OK?"

The Papa San looked at the money in his hand and said, "OK, $100 tomorrow."

"Is she any good Pap San?"

The Papa San smiled and laughed, "She number one, you see."

The Papa San walked over to the girl and spoke in Vietnamese. She looked at Simmons and then looked at the base. Speaking rapidly in Vietnamese, Simmons could clearly see she had some reservations about going inside the base. After several minutes of heated exchange, she turned to Simmons and asked, "Where I hide?"

"No hide," Simmons said, "here put these on." Simmons handed her a fatigue shirt and a boonie hat. Taking off her silk top, she put the fatigue shirt on and tucked it into the top of her mini shirt. Simmons motioned for her to put her hair under the boonie hat, and with Simmons' help managed to get the hat on. He put her in the truck between his helper and him and kept his fingers crossed as they turned around and headed for the main gate.

"Ah hell," Simmons muttered as he saw the MPs checking the trucks in front of him. Pulling up to the main gate, Simmons held out his ID card and showed it to the MP while saying, "Sergeant, I delivered some crap to LZ Baldy today and I'm coming back empty." After looking at his ID, the Sergeant looked in the back of the truck and waved him on.

Breathing a sigh of relief, Simmons looked over at his helper who said, "Fuck Simmons, you're crazy."

Simmons slammed on the brakes as it skidded on the sand in front of the stand down building. Getting out, he grabbed the girl by the arm and escorted her to the hootch farthest away from the orderly room. Walking through the door, he saw Collins as he was stretching a poncho liner between two cots. "God damn Simmons, you did it."

"Damn right Collins, piece of cake. I want her to be kept out of sight until tonight. You stay with her until then. If you gotta leave, have someone get me and I'll give you relief, okay?"

Collins nodded his head. "Still the same deal, $20?"

"Yeah $20," Simmons answered. Turning to the girl, he said, "We're going to have beaucoup business for you tonight. Beaucoup. I'll give you $10 for each GI, okay?"

Shaking her head, she said, "No, $15 MPC."

Simmons opened his wallet and pulled out the money Top had given him. Counting it out, he showed it to her. "I give you all this and $10 per GI." She looked at the money and nodded her head. "Wait, $15 for black, they too beaucoup."

Simmons, walking to the door, laughed, "No matter, $10, no matter."

****

Debbie Fisher was tired. It seemed that there were more and more papers to type each week. She looked down at the longhaired young man sitting in front of her. He had been issued a draft notice but had failed the Armed Forces Qualification Test and his physical. She looked at him skeptically, "You went to Ohio State, yet you failed the AFQT?"

"I guess I don't feel very bright today. My blood pressure has been high."

Debbie suspected he had taken some sort of drug to increase his blood pressure.

"You'll have to see the Army Psychologist. Wait over there," she said, while handing him a slip of paper. "Someone will call you shortly."

He slowly got up and smiled at her, "My name is Benjamin, and I think you're cute. If you would like to go out, maybe get something to eat, blow some weed, I would love to take you."

"I don't think so. I have a boyfriend," she lied.

"My friend came through here a few months ago," Benjamin said. "Poor guy is in 'Nam. I feel bad for him, man, he's not a killer."

"What was his name?" Debbie found herself asking for no reason.

"Whalen, John Whalen," answered Benjamin as he shuffled off and sat in one of the metal chairs to await the psychologist.

Debbie thought for a moment, remembering the guy he had mentioned. He had promised to call her when he got back. For some reason, she often thought of him and wondered how he had made out. Trying to put him out of her mind, she went back to another file and began typing.

****

Simmons was busy checking on the steaks, beer, and other food when Bromley approached him. "Hey Simmons, the officers would like first crack at that girl you brought in. We don't think it would look good, us standing in line with the men and all."

"Sir, I don't know, she's gonna be awfully busy tonight. I'd like to keep her as fresh as possible. She's resting now; I got Collins in there with her. Right now I don't want anyone to know she's here. I'm going to set her up after the band has been playing an hour or so. Let the guys get blown away a little bit."

"You got any security?" asked Bromley.

"Sure do. I got Findley. I'm giving him a free lay for watching her. She's in good hands."

Bromley knew Findley and nodded his head in agreement. He was a big kid from California, so big that he presented a huge target to the VC and NVA, and therefore was given a job in the rear after getting wounded the first week he was in the field. "Simmons, I'll tell you what. We'll wait, but I want you to get me before you open for business. Hathaway and I both want to get our licks in."

"Okay, I guess. I'll come and get you when it's time." "Fucking officers," Simmons muttered under his breath. "This stand down is for the men, not the officers." Simmons vowed not to tell the officers shit. "Let 'em go to Chu Lai if they want to get laid."

By the time the steaks were served, most of the men of B Company had already drank too much and were starting to get a little out of control. The band, a group from the Philippines, featured two women and three men. They played well and focused on current and old rock hits.

After one of their early breaks, one of the women came out and started to strip.

Whalen, standing near the back of the building, watched as the entire room erupted in a chorus of calls encouraging the woman to continue to take her clothes off.

John watched curiously as she called one of the men from B Company to the stage and invited him to feel her crotch, which he did to the delight of the 150 men present. Turning to Calhoun standing next to him, he said, "I don't know, something is wrong. I think that girl is a guy dressed up like a girl. What do ya think?"

"You're nuts Whalen, that is 100% woman up there and in a minute we're gonna see what she has."

Turning her back to the company, she removed her bra and panties throwing them into the crowd. A fight almost broke out as the men thrashed around trying to recover these cherished items but finally the biggest man in the group emerged from the skirmish proudly holding the clothes high overhead. At the same time, the girl, finally giving in to the calls of the men, turned around. Almost immediately the noise and clamor stopped and the room echoed in groans.

Whalen slapped Calhoun on the back, "Hey, what did I tell ya, it's a fuckin' guy."

Calhoun stared in disbelief. The man who went on stage to feel the girl was shunned from the room in good-natured ribbing.

Right after the stripper finished his routine Simmons went around the room whispering to the men that he had a Vietnamese girl in the hootch and that for $20 they could get laid. Within minutes the word was out and men started lining up at the door. Collins was ready, skillfully taking the money and dropping it in an old cigar box.

After an hour, Simmons halted the procession and went back to talk to the girl.

"Are you doing okay?"

"I do okay. Lots of small dicks. Cum fast. Everybody done?"

"No, I just wanted to check on you that's all." He handed her a can of coca cola and left, stopping to talk to Findley as he left. "Any trouble?"

"Yeah, I had to throw Kaminski out. Fucking guy was biting her tits. Hauled his ass off of her and threw him out the door. You know Simmons, the fucker had the balls to get back in line."

"No shit, he must have been drunk," laughed Simmons.

"Naw, no fucking way, he was stoned man. Hey Simmons, thanks for letting me do this. I like it. I hope a couple other fucks start some shit. It's fun throwing their asses out."

Two hours later Simmons shut the hootch down. No one was in line except a couple of men who had already been through once. Collins silently counted the money and whistled softly, "Holy shit Simmons, fuck if we don't have over $500 here. Fucking girl must be sore."

"Ah, they're used to it, I guess. Give me $250 for the girl and another $100 for the pimp. That leaves $150, so we'll take $75 each."

"I wish we had stand down every week. How you gonna get the girl back?"

"I'll take her out in the morning the same way as I got her in. You got another run to LZ Baldy, right? Well, I'll get her out then."

The next morning Simmons drove the girl out with his luck continuing. The MP simply waved him through. Stopping at the same spot he picked her up, the Papa San materialized from nowhere.

"You have money?" he asked.

Simmons handed him his $100. Smiling, he asked how much the girl got. Lying, Simmons said $100, knowing he would take half of it.

"Good," Papa San said, "we do business again." Grabbing the girl's arm, he quickly led her away.

Getting back in the truck, Simmons breathed deeply, started the truck and nervously headed back to the main gate. The MPs again simply waved him through. Arriving at the 1st of 1st stand down area, he stopped the truck in the sand and got out, coming face to face with Bromley and Hathaway.

"Did you forget about us last night Simmons? We went by the hootch where you had your little business going. Why didn't you call us first?" Hathaway said angrily.

"Sir, everything happened so fast. Fuck, I'm sorry, but word got out and the guys started lining up early."

Hathaway, hung over and still stoned, grabbed Simmons by the fatigue shirt and glared at him, "Listen you little puke, when we get back to the Hill, you better pack your shit, because you're coming to the field in my platoon. So I hope you remember how to pack your ruck and fire your M-16, because that is what you are going to be doing."

Simmons winced at the smell of Hathaway's breath and glared back at him saying nothing. After a few seconds Hathaway let him go. "I'm not done with you, you fucking asshole. Remember, report to me on the Hill."

"Fuck him," thought Simmons. "Fucking officers think they own the world."

****

Bromley and Hathaway took a chopper back to Hawk Hill arriving ahead of the deuce and a halves that carried the tired and hung over men of B Company. Still hung over, but thinking a little more clearly, they walked into the Orderly Room just as the First Sergeant was sitting down at his desk.

"Top," Hathaway said as he entered," I want Simmons transferred to my platoon when we go back out in a few days. You can have him after the patrol is over, but I want him out there with me for this next patrol."

Top looked down at his coffee, and taking a spoon from his drawer added a little more sugar. "What's this all about?" he asked casually.

"The fucker had a whore in the hootch down in Chu Lai and was selling pieces of ass for $20 MPC. How the fuck he got the whore in, I don't know, but he did. Anyway, I want his ass out in the bush. Make it happen Top." Bromley and Hathaway started to leave when the first sergeant stood up and yelled, "Where the fuck are you two going?"

Stopping, the two lieutenants turned and watched as the first sergeant, red in the face, walked to the counter that ran the width of the room. Glaring at them he said. "You don't come in here telling me what the fuck to do. Secondly, I told Simmons to get the girl and gave him the money to do it. I did it for the men, those 18 year old kids out there, some of whom won't live long enough to get home or get laid again. Most got drafted. They didn't ask for this, so I gave them a little something. If you have a bitch with that, you better address it with me." Top placed his beefy arms on the counter and waited for the officers to say something. Surprised, they stared in disbelief at what they heard.

"You authorized it?" Hathaway asked heatedly.

"God damn right I did."

Not sure what to do next, the lieutenants walked outside without saying another word. "We should write the son-of-a-bitch up. We're officers," Hathaway said.

Shaking his head, Bromley said, "I think we better just forget it. Top will just go to Murphy and we'll get fucked. What the hell, she was ugly anyway and I'll bet half the guys come down with the clap."

Chapter 26

The morning before the company was to go on patrol, Whalen found himself sitting in Captain Murphy's office with Calhoun and Peterson. Murphy looked at Whalen for a long moment and said, "Whalen, you have made only one patrol, and as you know, we lost Manrique. You have been recommended to take his place, and frankly, I'm concerned. Your squad is down to 12 men and most, if not all, have been here for some time. I don't know how they are going to react to you. On the other hand, I can't say any of the twelve would be good squad leaders and most are too short to make it worthwhile. So, we're going to give you a shot. I want Sergeant Peterson to get the squad together this afternoon and let them know. In the meantime, I have processed orders for you to go to E-4. For now, we'll run with that. If everything goes okay, I'll see what I can do to get you sergeant stripes. Now, this afternoon I want Peterson to sit down with you and tell you what it takes to be an effective squad leader, but first I want to ask you point blank, do you want this?"

Whalen wasn't certain what to say, but he was always a team player and leader. Looking over at Calhoun, he said, "Well Captain, the way I see it, someone needs to keep the L. T. here in line and I can do that." Chuckling a little, Whalen turned his head and looked directly at Murphy, "Seriously, sir, if you think I can help get these guys through safely, then I'll do my best."

"That's all I needed to hear Whalen." Standing up, Murphy reached across his desk and shook Whalen's outstretched hand. "Peterson, go ahead and tell the boys in his squad this afternoon."

****

Three months went by and during that time B Company went on four extended patrols. Whalen was surprised at how easy the transition to squad leader was. After Peterson announced the change, the twelve men in his platoon barely said anything about it. For a week they said nothing to Whalen at all. During their first patrol, Whalen picked three men for ambush.

"Whalen, that's only three, we need four for ambush," one of his men reminded him.

"I'll be the fourth," Whalen answered.

After dark, they set out for ambush setting up their perimeter and laying out the claymore mines, each with 700 BBs packed in with C-4 explosive. Running the klackers back to their position, they hoped Charlie wouldn't appear. Wayne Mulligan from Colorado looked curiously at Whalen after the ambush was set. "Whalen, what the hell are you doing out here? Shit man, if I was squad leader, no fucking way I'd be on ambush. Bad enough to be out in the bush, but it sucks to be out here at night. If Charlie decides to come through here with more than a couple of men, we're fucked."

"I'd rather be back there too Mulligan, but this is what we have to do. Our job is to keep the gooks out of the perimeter back there. We should be getting some new men in soon, and hopefully, they'll do the bulk of this. Anyway, let's keep quiet and hope the night passes quickly and without Charlie fucking it up."

Returning from the latest patrol, Whalen laid on his cot in the back of the hootch. He took over Manrique's spot, since he was now working in Chu Lai at the reception center helping FNGs get ready for their unit. Whalen was happy for him. It was a good job. Virtually on the beach, it was a beautiful area. It was hard to believe looking out at the ocean in one of the most picturesque areas of the world that Vietnam had known almost nothing but war for centuries. Picking up his mail, he stared dumbly at one envelope that was from the Armed Forces Examining and Entrance Station in Cleveland. Opening it, a picture fell out that showed the lower half of a woman sitting on a chair with legs crossed. Dressed in a very short mini skirt, there was no face to go along with the photograph. Unfolding a note written on a memo pad, Whalen read the neatly printed letter.

****

Hey Whalen,

I thought about sending you a picture of my face, but when you were here, all you looked at was my legs, so I thought you would have a better chance of recognizing me if I sent you a picture of them. Hope everything is going well. Stay safe.
Fisher

P.S. By the way, someone you knew, I believe his name was Benjamin, came through. He failed his physical, so he is classified as IV-F.

****

Whalen laughed to himself thinking of that day when he went for his physical. It was the only letter he had received from a girl back home since he had been in Vietnam, unless you count Pauline Miller. Pauline was the neighborhood tomboy and had grown up with John. Always friends, they drifted apart after they went to college. She had written him several times and he graciously answered each letter. Thinking of Debbie, he wrote a short note back commenting on her legs and telling her that he had not forgotten his promise to call when his time was up. Thinking about Benjamin, Whalen shook his head, thinking what he must have done to fail the physical. But Benjamin was Benjamin, and he certainly would have gone to Canada if he were drafted. About to write another letter, Brian Calhoun walked into his hootch. "What the fuck, didn't you get enough rest in the bush?"

"Hell no," Whalen retorted. "Being a squad leader is a lot of work."

"Hell, try being a platoon leader sometime." Seeing the photo of Debbie Fisher, he picked it up, smiled and said, "You been holding out on me boy? Who's the girl with the great legs?"

"You wouldn't believe it, but she works at the Induction Center in Cleveland. When she was typing my papers, we started talking. Something about her, I don't know. You ever get that feeling about a girl?"

"Yeah, when I was in 8th Grade, a girl named Diane. Sat next to her in class, and boy did I have a case of the hots for her? But 8th Grade is 8th Grade and what the hell do you know about girls at that age?"

"Are you going to write her?" Brian asked.

"Yeah, I already did. I don't want to say too much, but I'll call her when I get home." Thinking about home, he really was starting to miss it. "I wish I was there now."

"That's actually one of the reasons I came to see you. You know, Simmons, the company clerk? He has his nose up everybody's shorts at HQ in Chu Lai. He told me that the rumor down there is, starting this September, they are gonna start downsizing the forces here, which means our tour may be reduced to ten months."

Swinging his legs over the cot, John looked at Brian in disbelief. Grabbing his fatigue shirt by the front he pulled him toward him and threatened, "Calhoun, I swear if you're fucking lying, I'll kick your ass all the way back to those 100 cities you lived in back in The World."

"Hey, I'm telling you what Simmons said. I got other news too. Miraball, our Executive Officer, is going back to The World, and they put Bromley in as XO. That means we'll be getting a new platoon leader."

Rubbing his chin, Whalen thought of the riff between Bromley and Simmons a couple months ago. "How's that gonna work Brian? Bromley wanted Simmons out in the bush for not getting him laid during that stand down a couple months back."

"I guess they patched things up. Besides, Top has time left and he watches out for Simmons. Murphy ain't gonna be here long. He's getting short, maybe another month or two, so other changes will be coming." Shaking his head, Brian looked at John and scowled, "Fuckin' Hathaway will probably go to Captain. He's been gunning for it, and I know he's been kissing Hewitt's ass during debriefing. I found out he applied to all the service academies out of high school and couldn't get in. That's why he settled for ROTC. I think he figures he has something to prove. Look, they got the Doughnut Dollies coming to the mess hall in about ten minutes. Let's go over and see what's going on. At least we'll get to look at some round eyes."

"Ah hell," Whalen complained, "those girls are all fat, dirty, and bored, but fuck, I'll go with you."

Getting a seat up front, the men of B Company waited impatiently for the arrival of the women who represented the American Red Cross. Called "Doughnut Dollies," they would come around every month or so to lift the morale of the men by playing games and handing out short timer calendars.

As they walked in accompanied by a captain and an MP, the entire company stood up, whistled, made numerous cat calls, and shouted out that they wanted to get married but just for the night. The women, both maybe 24 years old at most, smiled and told them to sit down and behave. Dressed in flowing blue skirts that were unattractive and wearing no make-up, the men still appreciated their presence. Playing a number of foolish games, with equally foolish prizes, they stayed about an hour, finishing by handing out short timer calendars.

Much to John's and Brian's amazement, one of the men from the company started talking to one of the Doughnut Dollies, receiving a big hug and kiss on the cheek before he turned away with a big smile. Walking over to him, John spouted, "What the hell did you do to get a kiss like that?"

"Take it easy Touchdown. I know her. We're both from Chattanooga. She lives on the next street. She dated my older brother for a while. I didn't think she would remember me, but she did. Small world isn't it? She was a lot cuter back then, thinner too. She used to make out with my brother in the garage. I walked in on them once, and did he kick my ass. He had her bra off and I saw her tits. Wish I could see them now. Shit that was maybe eight years ago. I was only ten at the time. Tits don't mean much when you're ten."

About to say something, Whalen and Calhoun were interrupted by the sound of an M-16 popping off, obviously in the company area. "What the fuck is that?" Calhoun yelled, not sure what to do. Running to the door, they saw a commotion in the area where the Vietnamese civilians who worked on the base were busy washing dishes in crude kerosene-fired tubs. Lying on the ground was a young Vietnamese boy of about twelve with a life-threatening M-16 wound to the chest. "What the hell happened?" Calhoun yelled, as he kneeled down by the boy.

"Newkirk here shot him, L. T.," answered one of the men.

Whalen looked over at Newkirk, "Is that true?"

"Yeah, I shot him. The fucker wouldn't do what I asked him. I wanted him to bring me some shit from the ville and he refused. Fuck, I offered to pay him."

Calhoun and Whalen knew that Newkirk wanted the boy to bring in some Heroin, or what the men called "H."

One of the company medics came running up and kneeled down by the boy. Removing his black shirt, he looked at the wound and shook his head. "No way is he gonna make it."

Jervis came roaring over with the jeep, slamming on the brakes and skidding to a stop, almost running down a couple of men who quickly leaped out of the way.

"Holy shit, Jervis, what the fuck you doing?"

Together Jervis and the medic gently placed the boy in the jeep and sped off to the medical detachment on the Hill.

Newkirk was still standing there when the First Sergeant came puffing up. "What the hell is going on?" he said to Calhoun as the only officer present.

"Top, why don't you let Newkirk tell you what happened."

"Not much to say. I asked the kid to bring me some shit from the ville tomorrow and he said 'No bic.' Fuck Top, I know he speaks English. Kept speaking Vietnamese, then he and this other gook," he said, pointing his M-16 at another boy about the same age, "started laughing. I warned them Top. I told them to stop laughing or I would shoot their asses. They kept on laughing, so I shot him."

"Newkirk," Top ordered, "get your ass over to the orderly room and gimmee your goddamn weapon. Anyone know where Simmons is?" Everyone shook their heads. "Well, one of you better find his ass in the next five minutes and tell him to get to the orderly room." Grabbing Newkirk by the arm, he led him off to the orderly room.

One of the men looked at Calhoun, "What are they gonna do to him L. T.?"

"I don't know, we'll have to wait and see."

Simmons was walking out of the mail shack when Whalen walked up to him and told him what happened. Scurrying off to the orderly room, he hustled in and found Top red faced and impatient. "God damn it Simmons, every fucking time I need you you're never here."

"I was getting the mail Top," he answered, handing some letters from home to the First Sergeant.

"Get your ass over to that typewriter and type up an Article 15 for Newkirk here. He unlawfully discharged his firearm in the company area."

Simmons took out the long form from his desk and busily typed the information in the appropriate spaces. Wondering what the hurry was, he dared not ask, as Top, still fuming, stood over him as he typed. As he finished, he glanced at Newkirk who fidgeted in his seat as he waited to see what was happening. Ripping the Article 15 from the typewriter, Top hustled off to the officer's hootch, returning minutes later with Captain Murphy's signature scrawled on the form. Just as he entered, a jeep pulled up with two MPs who got out of the jeep and strode into the orderly room. Top told Newkirk to go to Captain Murphy's office and shut the door behind him.

"Top, we need to talk to one of your men about the shooting that occurred here a bit ago. We got a young boy in critical condition down at the med station."

"I already took care of it boys. I wrote the man up for unlawful discharge of a firearm in a company area. He'll be fined a week's pay and we'll impose some other restrictions on him too."

One of the MPs took off his helmet and stared at Top in disbelief. "You have a man here who shot and possibly killed a 12 year old boy and you're giving him an Article 15, fining him, what $60?"

"That's right. It was an accident."

"We need to see him," the MP ordered.

"I'll round him up Sergeant, but right now he's pretty upset, as could be expected. I'll have my driver take him to you in an hour or so. Let's give him some time to settle down."

The two MPs looked at each other and told Top that they expected to see the man within the hour.

After they left, Top went in Murphy's office. "Newkirk, just what the hell were you thinking? You could spend ten years in military prison for that. This ain't the field here."

"I know Top," Newkirk answered, his voice shaking as the reality of what he did set in. "What's going to happen?"

"I don't know for sure. There's a double jeopardy rule that says you can't be charged with the same crime twice, so hopefully I saved your ass with that Article 15. We'll have to wait and see. In the meantime, you're restricted to your hootch. You leave to shit, piss and eat only. And no fucking drugs. I'm gonna assign some men to watch you. You got that Newkirk?"

"I do Top."

"Simmons, get him over to his hootch. Have someone stay with him until I get this sorted out and then get your ass back here."

****

Janet lay down for a moment, her hand resting on her stomach. Her morning sickness had passed but she didn't feel well. It was nerves, she was sure of that. She worried constantly about Jack. Although she received daily letters, the news coming from Vietnam was never good. Several hundred KIAs were reported each week, with many more wounded. Last week she overheard some other wives talking about how their husbands had mentioned in letters home how lucky they were in not being assigned to the Americal Division. Janet had still not told Jack about the baby and decided to wait until she saw him on R&R in Hawaii. That could be as soon as two more months. She suddenly felt the baby kick. It was a good feeling. Closing her eyes, she drifted off to sleep. She sorely needed a nap before her boys came home from school.

Chapter 27

The squad moved slowly through the light underbrush. It was their tenth day on patrol and so far everything was working well. Whalen took the number four spot in the squad as they moved through an area that was reputed to have some local VC holed up. Since Whalen had been made a squad leader, his platoon had not suffered any major casualties. During that time they patrolled, chased some Viet Cong, burned rice found in villages and occasionally got into short firefights with small elements of the NVA or Viet Cong. The nightly ambushes had gone well, but on this day Whalen had an uneasy feeling that their luck would eventually run out.

Moments later, their point man, Box Car, held his arm out, indicating for everyone to stop. With a deft motion, he called Whalen forward. Hunched over, Whalen moved the few yards to where the point man was crouching. Looking out over a rice paddy, Whalen could see a squad of six VC talking to a Vietnamese farmer. They had their AK-47s slung over their shoulders or held loosely in their arms. It was clear they weren't expecting any American patrols. The farmer was frantically pointing to the south. Exactly what his concern was, Whalen couldn't tell. To his knowledge, no other American troops were operating in this area. From the argument, it appeared the farmer was upset with the Viet Cong for plundering his property, something that happened often.

Whispering, Box Car asked if they should take them out. It was times like this that Whalen didn't like being a squad leader. He thought of Natalie and how she had told him that war was nothing more than government-authorized murder. Whalen contemplated using the radio to call Calhoun, but ultimately knew it was his decision.

Looking at a distant tree line, John knew there could be more VC nearby. His squad was down to ten men, certainly not enough to engage any large group of VC. He also knew that the other platoons weren't far away and that air and artillery support was just seconds away in case things did get out of hand. John reached for his map and marked the coordinates down in a small notebook. If he needed air support, that information would be needed.

Box Car, getting impatient, asked again, "These fuckers hit us all the time from tree lines and catch us cold. Let's get these bastards, or otherwise they could be shooting at us later today from some fucking hole they climbed into."

"Okay, but let's not be bunched up, and I don't want to hit the Papa San." Waving back, he called for the M-60 machine gun and spread the other men out as best he could.

"This is what we are going to do," explained Whalen, "I want Stoner here to let loose his M-60 with some rounds over their heads. Got that Stoner, over their heads? That should get Papa San the hell out of the way. As soon as he runs, start firing with everything we have. There isn't much cover down there, so we should have 'em cold. I suspect that tree line back there has more VC and they'll be flying out after us. After we knock 'em down, I want the RTO to get off a report to Calhoun. We may have to meet up with them if we run into the rest of their platoon. After we get done with those VC, we'll wait a bit to see if any more come out of that tree line. Everybody got that?" They all nodded in agreement and moved off to their positions. When Whalen gave the sign, Specialist Stoner fired a short burst just over the heads of the unsuspecting Viet Cong. Just as planned, the farmer headed for cover at a dead run to the left of the VC. The VC hit the ground and with only AK-47s to fight back, were at a disadvantage. The ten men in Whalen's Squad laid down a deadly fire and the M-60 roared and belched over 200 rounds per minute. Satisfied that they could do no more, Whalen ordered the firing to stop. The return fire had ceased and it appeared that the VC were either dead or badly wounded.

Stoner motioned to Whalen, "Should we go down to check it out?"

"No, too risky and no real advantage." Signaling to his radio operator, he told him to get the report off.

"Romeo Tango 22, this is Romeo Tango 24," he heard him say. Completing the transmission, the RTO said, "Whalen, the other squads are engaged, too. It appears that Charlie is spread out all over the place. We seem to be in the middle of it."

John thought of his premonition earlier that day. “Let’s get the hell out of here. We’ll leave the same way we came in. Keep your goddamn eyes peeled.” Whalen glanced back at the tree line and saw nothing. Looking to where the VC had been, he watched as the Papa San cautiously returned and went from VC to VC. Whalen was sure his fire had killed them all, but he was worried as to what lay ahead. Just as he started to move out, he heard Box Car load a clip into his M-16. Turning, he watched as he took aim on the Papa San below. Moving quickly Whalen pressed the muzzle of his M-16 into Box Car’s neck, just below his right ear. “You pull that trigger and I’m going to pull mine,” Whalen said acidly.

Box Car lowered his M-16 and stared back at John. “Papa San is picking up those AK-47s. In an hour he’ll sell them to other VC and they’ll be shooting our men with ‘em by tomorrow.”

“That may be, but even if you killed him, the VC will end up with ‘em anyway. There’s no fucking way I’m sending men down there to recover a handful of AK-47s. Now let’s move out,” Whalen ordered. Muttering to himself, Box Car let the issue pass and took up the point once again.

Moving through the underbrush and then a rice paddy, they joined up with one of the other squads. Sergeant Peterson was with them and listened as John explained what happened. “Charlie is spread out. We’re running into pockets of them. We just chased down about a dozen of them. I think we got about half of them. The others simply vanished as they sometimes do.”

Peterson looked off to the west, “I talked to Calhoun and he wants us to continue patrolling this AO here,” he said pointing to an area marked on his map. “Your squad may as well stay with us. We have only a couple more hours of daylight, and we’ll need to go into our night perimeter. We’ll have to set up additional ambush points tonight. I don’t want to take any chances.”

After an uneventful hour, Peterson signaled for the two squads to stop. They began setting up their perimeter and rested as much as they could. Peterson, sitting on his helmet, motioned for Whalen to come over. Sitting down next to him, he listened to Peterson. "Remember a few months back we destroyed part of that NVA company as they crossed that valley?" Whalen nodded that he did. How could he ever forget his first major fire fight? "Well, I think the other company of NVA holed up in that jungle on the other side of the valley has the VC creating a lot of shit right now. I think they are purposely staging these little skirmishes. For what reason I don't know. I'm sure that other company of NVA is back there waiting for something. Maybe they want to overrun an LZ or try to destroy one of our platoons, I don't know. I do know that we haven't seen any NVA, just VC."

"What are we going to do?" Whalen asked.

"Just what we been doing. Patrolling. Search and destroy. We got some good body count today. They should be happy back at Brigade."

Chapter 28

Colonel Hewitt sat at his desk reading the brief reports that had been coming in from the field. Numerous pockets of VC had been destroyed throughout the AO. Putting down the reports, he called on his intercom. Poking his head in the door, the clerk asked him what he needed. “Get Lt. Saban in here from S-2.”

In less than five minutes Lt. Saban arrived with a brief case full of maps and reports. “What do you make of the increase in activity Saban?”

“We don’t know for sure sir,” Saban answered while spreading out a map on Hewitt’s desk. “I have marked in red where our units have found pockets of VC. They all seem to be concentrated in this sector here, which is to the northwest of Hawk Hill. They are well supplied and operating in small squads. We think the NVA pulled some VC units up from the south. Activity to the south of us in II Corps has diminished. Sir, I think they are trying to build up some forces in one area so they can mount some sort of offensive against us. Some of the platoons out there have taken some heavy casualties, others haven’t; and it just depends whether we catch them or they catch us.”

Hewitt stared at the map for a minute like a chess master looks at his board. He was desperately looking for an answer to the puzzle. He had great respect for the VC and NVA and knew that everything they did had a motive. “Do we know what happened to that NVA company that was holed up in this jungle area here a couple months back?” Hewitt asked pointing to the dense area of foliage just to the north of the valley where they had wiped out the major portion of an NVA company.

“Not really sir. As far as we can tell, they’re still there.”

Dismissing Lt. Saban, Hewitt wondered what the NVA and VC were up to.

****

Colonel Nhung in the cover of darkness had removed half of his remaining men from the jungle and into the base of a mountainous area to the extreme west of his AO. From there he directed two companies of VC regulars broken down into small squads to harass the American patrols. He had purposely not engaged the Americans very often over the last few weeks, wanting them to feel complacent; but now he was asking his men to be more active, cause confusion and spread the American patrols out. He had reinforcements coming from the North soon, and he longed for a major battle in which he could eliminate an American platoon or company. It would be retribution for what they had done to his men back at the valley. For now, he knew the Americans were confused and worried. Smugly, he sat down, satisfied that his men would be victorious.

****

"I want three ambush patrols tonight and I want to set up an M-60 at these points within the perimeter. If Charlie starts some shit, I want to be ready. Got that?" Peterson asked his squad leaders. A look of worry crossed Whalen's face. Peterson, catching the look, asked, "What's wrong Whalen?"

"Setting up three ambush points leaves us with only about 16 men in the perimeter. Almost half our men will be on ambush."

"It will have to do John. Here in the 'Nam, if we can survive the first ten minutes of a firefight, we should be okay. We have air and artillery support only moments away, but we can't use 'em if Charlie gets too close. It's our only choice. Charlie is all over the AO, but they're spread out too."

Those going on ambush left after dark heavily laden with extra claymore mines, starlight scopes and rifles mounted with night scopes. The perimeter was quiet. Whalen walked around and saw few men doing much. Empty C-ration cans and boxes were strewn around and slit trenches had been hastily dug that afternoon.

Laying in his slit trench, Sergeant Peterson thought of his wife Janet. He had an uneasy feeling about her, as if she was not telling him something. Although he wasn't sure what it was, he was worried. Maybe her health wasn't good, or perhaps one of their boys was in some sort of trouble. Jack knows his wife and knew that she wouldn't burden him while he was in Vietnam. He was eligible for R&R and made a mental note to see if there were any allocations for Honolulu when they returned to Hawk Hill.

Rolling over, Whalen tried to get comfortable in his slit trench when he heard the thump, thump of 40 mm rounds fired from an M-79 grenade launcher hit around the perimeter. Instantly he was up, grabbing his M-16. Peterson was up too ordering everyone to fire white star shells to illuminate the area. Calling his RTO, he ordered the artillery back on Hawk Hill to send up illumination to his AO. Within seconds the area was lit as bright as day. Cursing as his eyes adjusted to the light, Peterson looked out beyond the perimeter and could see nothing. "Any word from the men on ambush?" he asked the RTO. "Negative Sergeant, nothing."

Several more 40 mm rounds plunked around them with none hitting the perimeter. "Keep the star shells going," he ordered again. Straining to see beyond the perimeter, Peterson couldn't detect anything. The range of the grenade launchers was only about 400 meters, so Charlie couldn't be too far away.

Just as Peterson was about to crawl off to his left, he heard the M-60 roar to the right of him. Almost at the same time, he heard the frantic shouting of "Gooks coming at a dead run." Standing up momentarily, Peterson saw about a dozen VC running full speed toward their position. He could clearly make out their AK-47s and satchel charges slung around their shoulders. They were firing sporadically into their perimeter. Peterson yelled for his men to hold their position around the perimeter. He was certain other VC would be pushing ahead at other points hoping he would re-position his fire to take care of the charging VC. Peterson swore under his breath as someone fired off a claymore mine way too soon to have any affect. The M-60 cut down the charging VC, with some crawling off in the direction they came from, most likely wounded. One VC got close enough to weakly fling a satchel charge, but it went off too early, harmlessly out of range.

Whalen crawled over and reported that they had no casualties. "I think we should bring in some air support, maybe get a gunship out here Sergeant. They're just probing, but they'll be back."

"I know John, but the gunship can't stay all night. I've got the illumination continuing. Any word from the men on ambush?"

"They're fine. Should we bring them in?"

"Negative," Jack said shaking his head. "We may need them out there. Charlie must not know where they are, so let's keep things the same. It's going to be a long night."

An hour later, the VC moved in again, this time from two positions, with about eight men in each squad. Their attack was preceded by mortar fire, which Peterson answered with artillery rounds directed from Hawk Hill. Once again, after unleashing all his firepower, Peterson's two squads succeeded in turning the VC back.

Unfortunately, two men were wounded, neither seriously. Peterson had the RTO call in for more illumination and artillery to continue to pound the area in the direction that the VC came from.

The third attack was staged differently. Four small squads began a slow movement toward their perimeter, this time concentrating fire on the sandbagged M-60s. Within minutes one of their M-60s went silent. Crawling over in the hail of AK-47 rounds whizzing through the air and the plunk of mortar fire, Peterson saw that his M-60 gunner had a serious wound. One of the other men had taken over the M-60 and it continued to pound out rounds.

"Sergeant," the gunner gasped, "they hit the sandbags with a 40 mm round. I caught some shrapnel." Peering down, Peterson could make out the blood soaked right side of his gunner. Calling for a medic, Peterson fired his M-16 at the VC as best he could until the medic arrived. "Hard to do anything here Sarge with all this shit going on," he snarled.

"I know, I know," Peterson retorted. Despite the barrage of fire, the VC seemed to be gaining. The VC slowly crawled forward, putting out enough fire to keep Peterson's platoon pinned down and unable to return a high rate of fire.

Off to the north, Specialist Tennison heard the firefight from his position on ambush. "Holy fuck, look at that, those guys are getting hit hard. We gotta go in there and help 'em out. Let's get going." One of the men, an FNG, started shaking, "Tennison, if we go in there, we'll get killed. The VC are all over the place." Tennison swung around and placed the muzzle of his M-16 under the chin of the FNG. "Listen you puke little fucker, if we don't get down there, our guys will all be killed and then they'll come for us. Now you get your ass up and help us out, or I swear to God I'll kill you myself."

Tennison and his three other men quickly ran through a section of underbrush and tall grass. They could clearly make out the VC under the illumination being sent out by artillery from Hawk Hill. Just at the edge of the tall grass, the four men threw themselves down, trying to catch their breath. "Let's start firing," said Tennison. Give it all you got." Their four M-16s started cracking out engulfing fire. Now the VC had fire coming from the perimeter and from the side as well. Unable to sustain, the one squad quickly fell back.

"We got Charlie on the run, now lets move around and help out on the other side," Tennison ordered.

Just as they were to start their move, the VC began firing into their position. Tennison started to say something when an AK round caught him in the thigh. Yelling in pain he fell down clutching his leg. The pain burned through him and for a moment he lost consciousness. Shaking his head, he told the other three men to move out to the east and lend some support to the perimeter still under heavy fire. "What about you Tennison?" one of the men asked.

"I'll be fine, now get your asses out of here." As the men left, Tennison threw another clip in his M-16 and looked out from the tall grass to see if he could find out where the fire had come from. Not seeing anything, he tried straightening his leg, which wasn't responding. In incredible pain he thought he was going to pass out again, when he heard the sweet sound of a Cobra gunship arriving with its multitude of machine guns. They quickly swept the area in one pass with another gunship following to add more fire support. The VC, realizing that any further attempts were futile, moved back into a heavy tree line to the west. Minutes after they left, Tennison could hear someone approaching.

"Tennison, if you shoot my ass, you'll never get out of here." Lowering his M-16, he saw Whalen emerge from the grass.

"Fuck Touchdown, am I glad to see you." Whalen picked Tennison up and carried him back to the perimeter. Setting him down, he saw that the other squad had arrived. Lt. Calhoun came over and helped Whalen with Tennison.

"What the fuck Tennison, did you shoot yourself to get out of the field?" joked Calhoun.

"Fuck you L. T.," moaned Tennison. That's the last time I go on ambush. In fact, I'm hoping not to see any of you again."

Standing up, they watched as the dustoff chopper came in and landed. "Well, let's get you over there," said Whalen.

After the chopper left, Peterson, Whalen and Calhoun sat down. Calhoun looked at Jack and asked, "That was it, three wounded?" Shaking his head, Peterson said, "No, Uminksi, my M-60 gunner got it. I thought he would be okay. Took some shrapnel on his left side, but some pieces cut his inside up. Nothing we could do. Bled to death. We got him in a body bag. One of the gunships is going to take him in. The dustoff didn't want to deal with it."

Calhoun nodded his head thinking of Uminski. Good man. Quiet. Did his job. "We're going back to the Hill tomorrow. We'll move out at sunup. This patrol is over. Brigade wants us to get a body count in the morning."

"Those VC kept coming, and we must have knocked down a bunch of them. Doesn't hardly seem worth it though," a dejected Peterson said. "You shouldn't have come through the dark to help L. T. You could have risked our other squad," Peterson said.

"I didn't have any choice Jack. I knew you were catching hell. I was only a couple of klicks from here."

In the morning, Whalen and Calhoun were shocked to see the devastation to their perimeter. Sandbags were chewed to pieces. AK rounds had pockmarked rucksacks and two M-16 stocks were found shattered. Peterson looked around and laughed, “I think I must have had some of these VC at Fort Jackson. The last group I had couldn’t shoot any better than these guys.”

Walking over to Calhoun, the RTO, smiling, said, “Hey L. T., good news, we don’t have to hoof it back. Brigade is sending some choppers out to get us.”

Smiling, Calhoun said, “Well it’s about time we caught a break.”

****

Whalen walked into his hootch and sat his ruck on the floor by his cot. Once again, he looked at the mail he had in front of him. He had letters from his parents and Pauline, but none from Debbie or Natalie. Although she had yet to write, John still hoped for the day he might get a letter from her. One letter caught his eye and looking at the return address he quickly opened it. The letter was from Scarcelli, who was now back in The World and finishing his time with a basic training unit at Fort Dix, New Jersey. Whalen laughed as he thought of the shit Scarcelli must be telling those scared recruits. He was happy to hear from him though. He had been a help and was a good soldier. Those that had been in the bush with him had nothing but good things to say about him. Getting up, Whalen walked over to the orderly room. Just as he got there, the company clerk, Simmons, started walking out. “Hey Simmons, what do you have for R&R allocations?”

“I got two for Bangkok and one for Hawaii. That’s it. If you want one of the Bangkok, you can have it. Calhoun wants the one for Hawaii.”

“Yeah, I do. I need to get the fuck out of here. When does it leave?”

“In two weeks. You got to hitch a ride to Da Nang. I’ll put it aside for you.”

Whalen walked over to the officer’s hootch and went inside. Their hootch was mostly underground and seemed a lot cooler than the enlisted men’s hoochs. Sitting on the cots bullshitting about the last patrol were Calhoun and Bromley. Looking up, Bromley threw a Frisbee at Whalen. "Get the fuck out of here Touchdown; you ain't no officer."

"Neither are you," sneered Whalen as he threw the Frisbee at Bromley. Sitting down on the cot, Bromley reached down beside his cot and pulled out a bag of potato chips and a cold beer. "Care package," he said holding up the bag of chips.

"I signed up for R&R in Bangkok, Brian. I guess it runs the same week as yours to Hawaii. Maybe we can hitch a ride to DaNang together."

"I guess we can." Turning to Bromley, Calhoun asked him what the best way to get to DaNang was.

"I hung out at the chopper pad the day before I was to fly out and caught a ride on a LOACH. If you can't catch a ride from here, you gotta go to Chu Lai and that is a pain in the ass. Hell, they got trucks running to Da Nang every day, you should be able to get up there easily enough."

Just as they were starting to unwind from the patrol, they heard a shot ring out. "Holy fuck, not again," Whalen yelled.

The three of them bound up the short set of stairs and went outside. Seeing everyone clustering around the TOC, Calhoun, Whalen and Bromley pushed their way through the gathering crowd. Standing there was one of their platoon sergeants, Sergeant Lunsford from the 1st platoon. Dangling from his hand was his .45 pistol. Sprawled out in front of him was Specialist Fetter. Blood was pouring out of a gaping chest wound as two men tried to stop the bleeding. One of the medics arrived, pushing everyone aside. Seeing the wound, he shouted, "We better get this guy to the aid station fast or he ain't gonna make it. Where the fuck is our jeep?"

"I'll get it," Whalen said as he sprinted to the orderly room. Bursting in the door, Whalen yelled to Top, "Lunsford shot Fetter. It's bad, Top. I'm taking the jeep." Top and Whalen climbed into the jeep and drove the 200' to the TOC. There they loaded Fetter in the back seat as best they could and sped off to the aid station leaving Top to deal with Sergeant Lunsford.

Top looked at Lunsford, "What the fuck happened Lunsford?"

"It's our turn for guard duty. I told Fetter he was on tonight and he gave me shit. Refused to go. We argued, so I shot his ass, Top." Top grabbed the .45 still dangling from his arm and looked at the crowd of men still gathered around. Seeing B Company's man of steel, Findley, he told him to escort Lunsford to the orderly room and watch him. "Findley, don't let him out of your sight, not even to piss. You got that?"

Smiling, Findley moved over, grabbed Lunsford's arm and roughly started moving him in the direction of the orderly room. "Sergeant, it will be my pleasure."

Top quickly ordered one of the other men to go in the TOC and call the MPs.

Walking back to the orderly room, Top walked in and saw Findley standing over Lunsford. "You can leave now Findley. Thanks for your help."

"Sure thing Top, glad to help."

Top pulled a chair over to where Lunsford was sitting. "What the fuck got into you Lunsford? First of all, you never ask men to go on Guard Duty after they just got back from patrol. Fuck, there are a million REMFs that can do that. You goddamn better hope Fetter lives, but chest wounds are a bitch." Hearing a jeep pull up to the orderly room, two MPs got out, the same ones who had been there when the Vietnamese boy was shot.

"We got another Article 15 for discharge of a firearm in a company area Top?" Shaking his head, Top said, "No, not this time. If you want to know what happened, you better catch some of the men outside who saw it. They just got back from patrol, so you better catch them quick before they get drunk or stoned."

Looking at the MPs, Lunsford kept saying, "Shit, the fucker said he was going to frag me when we got back Top. He was pissed because I put him on ambush two nights in a row, but he was the only good guy I got. Fucker was going to frag my ass. I thought guard duty would be the best Top. Fuck, you understand don't you?" Lunsford said as the MPs cuffed him and pulled him outside, sitting him down in the jeep.

Just as the jeep drove off, Captain Murphy walked in. "What now Top?"

"Sir, Lunsford shot Fetter for not going on guard duty."

"How bad?"

"I don't know, maybe we better get over to the aid station to see."

Walking into the aid station, Top and Murphy saw Fetter on one of the gurneys being tended to by a doctor and two medics. Walking over, the doctor looked up and shook his head. "I don't know yet, we'll see. He has a chance. We'll know more in an hour." Nodding their heads, Murphy asked Top to stay, and he would go back to the Company area. Murphy left just as Colonel Hewitt arrived at the door. "What's this I hear that one of your platoon sergeants shot one of his own men?"

"You heard right sir. The MPs have him. I don't know anymore sir."

"Goddamn it Murphy; it wasn't long ago one of your men shot a Vietnamese boy back at your AO, now one of your sergeants shoots his own man. Aren't you shooting enough gooks outside the wire?"

"We are sir, I don't know what happened. We'll find out sir."

"How's the man who got shot?"

"The doc is working on him. Won't know for a while. I got Top in there. He's gonna report back to me when he finds something out."

"Let me know as soon as you do." Hewitt spun around and headed back to Brigade Headquarters. Murphy walked back to his company area wondering what could go wrong next.

Returning to his hootch, Whalen sat down on his cot and again looked at his mail. Stuffed in his shirt was the letter from Scarcelli. John had meant to tell Brian about hearing from him, but he forgot. Walking out to the front of the hootch, he watched as some of the men were loading cases of beer behind a makeshift bar they had built.

"We're gonna have a helluva party tonight Touchdown. You should be here for it."

Whalen looked on as an eight-track tape player was set up and plugged in. Whalen winced as someone inserted a Tammy Wynette tape and the sounds of her singing *D-I-V-O-R-C-E* filled the hootch. "Haven't you guys ever heard of the Doors, the Beatles, the Stones, the Who? That broad sucks."

"Ah, fuck you Whalen, that's good old country music you're listening too."

Sitting down on a bar stool, Whalen said out loud to no one in particular. "You fucks are gonna have to get by without me for a while. I put in for R&R in Bangkok today."

An FNG with only the last patrol to his credit looked at Whalen enviously. "I wish I was that short. I got more time than Grandma Moses," he joked.

"It'll go fast," Whalen promised.

****

Debbie Fisher opened the door to her mother's house and walked into the kitchen. Setting her purse down on the counter, she bent over to greet her dog, Maggie. Petting her, she could hear her Mom call her from the living room. "I have a meeting tonight honey, but there is a casserole heating in the oven for you." Her mom briefly poked her head into the kitchen, bid her goodbye and started to leave. "I almost forgot, a letter came for you today. It's strange because there is no stamp on it. Just the letters FREE printed in the upper right hand corner."

"Thanks Mom."

Walking into the living room, she looked at the letter. Her name was written neatly on the envelope and in the upper left hand corner an APO address from San Francisco but no name. Opening the letter she unfolded a half sheet of paper and read the simple note.

Fisher,

I would remember those legs anywhere. But what I want to know is who took the picture? I have no idea how you found me here in Vietnam, but I am glad you did. Thanks for the picture, I carry it with me and I will call you when I get back to The World.

Whalen

Debbie sat down and wondered why her heart felt so funny when she thought of John. She was with him for maybe fifteen minutes. Dumbfounded, she folded the letter and put it back inside the envelope.

Chapter 29

Whalen and Calhoun sat near the end of the chopper pad waiting for a chopper to land that was heading to Da Nang. Both men had bags with them, packed with as many civilian clothes as they could find. After an hour, Whalen started to get impatient. "Hell, we could be here all day."

"Don't worry, here comes another chopper now." Both Whalen and Calhoun groaned as they saw the chopper's insignia was from the Iron Horse, or 1st Cavalry Division. About to sit back down, Calhoun stood up rapidly as the chopper landed, "Hey, I think we're in luck." Running toward the chopper, he started yelling, "Hey Swanson." The pilot, about to take off, saw Calhoun running toward him and shut the motor down as he got out of the pilot's seat.

"You son-of-a-bitch," Swanson said, giving Calhoun a big bear hug. Walking over, Whalen wondered what was going on.

Calhoun introduced Whalen to Swanson and told John about Swanson being a classmate of his at West Point. "Look Swanson, we need to get to DaNang. We're both going on R&R and we've been here all morning trying to hitch a ride, but fuck, no one has been able to take us."

Swanson with a gleam in his eyes said, "Well, you are in luck, because that is where we're headed. We got some crap to deliver."

"I thought only warrant officers flew these things not regular officers," Calhoun asked.

Swanson pulled out a cigarette and lit it blowing a big cloud of smoke in the air. "After I completed infantry training, I went to jump school and ranger school. I was wounded twice in the first two months here. Once by a booby trap, and once by an AK round. We're losing a lot of officers, so after another month in the field, they pulled me out. They got me delivering confidential materials to the different brigades for S-2. I talked the pilot into teaching me to fly the thing. Not supposed to, but goddamn it's fun."

“You always were up to something Swanson. I guess you haven’t changed. Have you heard about any of the other guys we graduated with?”

“Nothing you’ll be happy about. Seymour is KIA, so is Butterby. A bunch wounded, a few missing, maybe POWs, I don’t know. It’s a lot tougher than I thought it would be, a lot tougher. Fucking gooks; they can fight. Not the way we want, but they can fight. Putting out his cigarette, Swanson motioned for them to get in the chopper. It didn’t take long to get to Da Nang, and after arriving they quickly went to the area where the R&R flights left. There was separate billeting for officers and enlisted men, so Whalen and Calhoun bid each other goodbye and promised to meet in Da Nang when they returned.

Whalen found a bunk, chained and locked his small bag and went to find the mess hall. It was where he thought it would be. He had heard the Air Force had much better food, but was skeptical of that, thinking all the services would be the same. He walked in and signed a register as a guest. Astounded, he went through the chow line where a selection of meals was available. Real mashed potatoes, steaks, desserts, soft drinks, a selection of vegetables, he couldn’t believe it. Sitting down, an air force sergeant smiled at him. “A bit different than what you are used to, isn’t it?”

Whalen tried to answer, but his mouth was full of food and could only nod.

“If you have time, make sure you get here for breakfast. It’s even better,” the sergeant suggested before he got up to leave.

Stuffed, Whalen walked outside and lit a cigarette. The quiet of Da Nang surprised him. Although he could hear occasional outgoing artillery rounds, it was nothing like Hawk Hill where the artillery was constantly in motion. John noticed that over the last month or so his ears had started to ring and wouldn’t stop. Others had the same complaint. Sitting on his bunk, he was wondering what to do when he glanced over and saw someone on the next bunk rummaging through his bag who looked very familiar. Whalen tried to place him but wasn’t sure where he had seen him. Giving up, Whalen walked over and asked him, “Hey, my name is Whalen, John Whalen. You look damn familiar, but I can't place you. Am I going nuts, or have we met?"

Staring at John for a minute, he smiled, stood up and said "If you could remember back to 8th Grade, you would remember that we sat next to each other in English and terrorized the hell out of Mrs. Backus the whole year."

"Now I remember. Your name is Keith, Keith Verby." Standing up they hugged and shook hands.

"It's sure been a long time. Last time I saw you was high school graduation at that party we all crashed."

Laughing, Verby remembered. "Yeah and the cops came too. Who knew that the kid's old man was a cop? I thought you went to Ohio State. Didn't you get a deferment?"

"Yeah, I did, but they don't last forever. I graduated and got drafted. I'm in the 196th down on Hawk Hill. 11 Bush. They made me a squad leader, can you believe it?"

"I'm not surprised. You were always a leader."

"What about you?"

"I went to Ashland College for a couple of years, dropped out, which was a mistake. Girl problems. Fell in love, lost her, and couldn't stand being in school with her. Ashland is small. She started going out with an asshole. So I quit. Next thing I know, I get drafted and here I am. Lucked out though. I was majoring in accounting in college and they sent me to Clerks School at Fort Leonard Wood in Missouri and then to finance school at Fort Lee, Virginia. I guess I'm a REMF. I hope you don't resent it."

"Naw, no way, the real REMFs are sitting back in The World. Everyone here is doing their job."

"Part of my job is visiting the LZs and fire bases to go over the finance records of the men. Right after I got here, I went out to an LZ west of here for the night. At about 0200 we had a bunch of gooks try to break through the wire. I left the hootch with my M-16 and son-of-a-bitch if I didn't get wounded. Caught some shrapnel in my leg from a mortar round. They had to medivac me out. Keith rolled up his pant leg and revealed an ugly scar that ran down his calf. I wouldn't let them put me in for a purple heart. My parents, if you remember, are a lot older than most. They're worried sick as it is."

John remembered how the kids used to talk about Keith's parents. They were in their early 50s when they were in 8th Grade. Most thought Keith, an only child, was adopted.

"You heading on R&R?"

"I am, Bangkok. What about you?"

"Same thing. You want to stick together?"

"Hell yes. We'll tear the place apart."

The next day, John and Keith exited the plane at a military base in Bangkok. They were immediately escorted to a secure area where they changed their Military Payment Certificates into U. S. Currency. Escorted by Military Police, they then quickly turned it into Thai Bahts. John was amazed at the size of the stack of bills. Turning to Keith, he said, "Well I hope you know what the conversion rate is because it sure looks like I got a lot more money than I should have."

Keith laughed, and said, "The exchange rate is good. Where our money is based on a dollar, theirs is based on a Baht. You get twenty Baht for one of our dollars."

Boarding a military bus, they were just sitting down when a burley sergeant stepped onto the bus. "Listen up men, this bus ride is only about 15 minutes and I have a lot to say. So keep quiet until I am done. We're going to take you to a terminal where you can select a hotel and get transportation to wherever you want to stay. The only hotels represented are ones we feel are safe. Now, all of you know about the girls here. Most likely you will hire a driver for the week. Should cost you no more than $30 or so. He'll take you to the bars. The girls are $20 for twenty-four hours. Most have cards issued by the U. S. Government stating that they have been checked and are disease free. Ask to see their card; don't be embarrassed to do so. You won't deal directly with any of the girls. All the bars will have men that will contract the girls to you. Make sure you bring them back on time, or you will be charged another 24 hours. Very few of these girls speak English. Another thing, prostitution is not looked down upon here. These girls may ask you to meet their parents; you can do so if you want. The main PX is a good one here. Spend some time there. The food is generally okay to eat, but it's damn spicy. Last thing is don't do this alone. Find someone and stick together. This is no place to be running around alone. Buddy up, be smart, and have some fun."

Whalen looked at Keith and smiled, "This is going to be a helluva week."

Chapter 30

Brian Calhoun got off the plane in Honolulu and saw his mother and father waiting for him. Brian was dressed in casual civilian clothes, his father impeccably dressed in his uniform. Giving his mother a big hug, Brian let out a huge sigh. All the pressure and tension of the last few months seemed to flow from his body. Pushing him away, his mother looked at her son, "Brian, you've lost weight and you look so old." Examining his face, she could see that the stress of combat had taken it toll. Only 23, he looked much older.

His father, ever the stoic figure, took Brian's hand and shook it vigorously. "We have a lot to talk about, Brian, but there is plenty of time for that. Let's go to the hotel and you can get some rest."

On the way to the hotel, Brian was brought up to date on his sister, her many boyfriends, her sliding grades at college, his grandparents, and how the country was not supporting the war effort.

Arriving at their hotel, Brian took a hot shower, the first since he had left for Vietnam. Lying down on his bed, he drifted off to sleep, waking almost eight hours later. Looking at the clock, he was surprised to see it was after 10:00 PM. Getting dressed, he went to the lobby and walked into the bar. Sitting down he asked for a menu and was happy to see that he could still order food. Wasting no time, he ordered two cheeseburgers and French fries. After eating them, he felt better than he had in days and decided to walk down Waikiki Boulevard. Swarmed with military, he walked for about an hour, finally turning around and beginning the walk back. By then the streets were less crowded and Brian could smell and feel the ocean air. Breathing deeply, he felt alive.

Passing a corner, he heard a commotion going on near the door to a bar around the corner. Looking, he watched as an army soldier was arguing with a young Hawaiian girl about 20 years old dressed in a pretty skirt. She had long flowing dark hair and very pretty eyes. The soldier, obviously drunk, was attempting to pull her into his car. Brian walked over and politely asked the girl, "Miss, is there a problem here?"

The soldier, cigarette dangling from his mouth and his uniform in a state of disarray sneered at Brian, "Hey fucker, butt out." Looking at the uniform insignia, Brian noticed the Americal Division patch on his right shoulder and a CIB pinned over his breast pocket.

"I see you were in the Americal. That's my unit too. I'm an infantry officer in the 196th.

The soldier, removing the cigarette from his mouth, stared at him for a second. "No shit? I was in the 11th brigade, south of where you are. Just got back a few months ago. I'm stationed here now."

Softly, John took the girl's hand and said, "Look soldier, you had a lot to drink and it's obvious this girl doesn't want to go with you. Why not head back to your unit? Tomorrow is another day."

"Sure, but you ain't gonna get anywhere with her, she's just a tease." Jumping into the car, the soldier sped off, almost hitting a parked car at the end of the block.

Thrusting her hand out, the girl said her name was Amy and that she worked as a waitress in the bar owned by her Uncle and went to the University of Hawaii during the day.

"I don't like the job that much, but it pays well and I need the money for school. The military can be hard to deal with. If you are not friendly, you don't get any tips. If you are friendly, you get the tips and then they expect you to go to bed with them."

Brian smiled at her and said, "Well, you are very pretty, so I can't say I blame them. Are you okay to go home?"

"I'll be fine. I take the bus. I only live about ten minutes from here. Three of us from school share an apartment. I would like to pay you back for helping me. The bar I work in has excellent food. Come by tomorrow night and I will give you a meal you'll be telling everyone about back in Vietnam."

"Thanks," Brian said, "that's a deal." Walking back to the hotel, Brian lay down and had trouble going to sleep. His mind was going a mile a minute. Finally, he drifted off to sleep.

****

Keith and John selected a hotel and located the courtesy van that dropped the soldiers off at the various hotels. When they arrived, they checked in and were immediately taken to their rooms. John had no sooner tossed his bag on the bed when he heard a small knock on the door. Opening the door, he saw a young Thai girl about 20 years old standing there with a rose in her hand. Inviting her in, she sat down on the bed. "I give you #1 massage?"

Smiling, John said, "Yes, I would like that." Picking up the phone, she spoke to someone in the lobby. Moments later, a young man came up and asked John if he would like the girl to stay for the night. "Twenty Dollars or 100 Baht for night," he said. Paying him, John closed the door and sat down next to the girl. Getting up, she went into the bathroom, filling the tub with water. Calling John, he took off his clothes and climbed in. He watched as she methodically washed him from head to foot, dried him off and escorted him to the bed. She then gave him an expert massage. Finishing, she murmured in his ear, "You like pussy?" Rolling over, John took her in his arms and made love to her like he had known her for years.

Chapter 31

Waking up in the morning, Brian showered and went down to the lobby. His mother had left a note for him that she would be back at the hotel by 10:00 AM and to meet her at that time by the pool. Since it was only 9:00 AM, John walked over to the restaurant and ate a meal of six scrambled eggs, fresh coffee and a stack of pancakes. The waitress laughed as he finished with an order of sausage. “Here from Vietnam, aren’t you?” she smiled. Finishing his breakfast, Brian walked out to the pool area. Seeing his mother, Brian walked over and sat down next to her.

“You look so much better today Brian. Did you sleep well?”

“I did Mom. Where’s Dad?”

“He is combining business with pleasure as usual. He had a meeting with someone, but my guess is he’s playing golf.”

“Mom, I don’t know if you had plans for dinner, but I met some people here I know and they invited me to dinner. I’d like to go with them if that is okay?”

Smiling, she nodded, “Of course Brian. This is your time. I know your father wants to talk to you, but there is plenty of time for that. He said he would be back by three, why don’t we meet in the lounge at 5:00 PM and then you can go to your dinner after we talk a bit.”

“That would be great Mom, thanks.” Laying on the lounge next to his mother, Brian closed his eyes and once again tried to relax. The jitters from the time in Vietnam had started to wear on him, and relaxing without having to worry about his men, the VC, booby traps, mines, or any other part of the war felt so good. After an hour or so, Brian excused himself and walked to the beach. He hadn’t swam in the ocean in quite some time and found the waves exhilarating. For some reason he tired quickly and decided to walk back to the hotel. Stopping at a small restaurant, he ate lunch before going inside and lying down. He slept for a couple of hours and felt refreshed. He got up, changed, and got ready for the evening.

Walking into the lounge, Brian saw his parents sitting at a small cocktail table sipping on drinks served in pineapples. Sitting down, Brian leaned over and kissed his mother. His father smiled, something he seemed to rarely do, and said, "I understand you are doing very well son. We're proud of you. I know that I Corps is a tough spot to be in right now, but your brigade commander, Colonel Hewitt, is one of the best. I served with him and I'm happy that he has command. How are the other platoon leaders? Are any others from the Point?"

"No Dad, one's from OCS, the other is an ROTC officer. They're good officers. It's a tough war Dad. I don't know if we're wining or losing. A lot of good men are dying over there and a lot more getting wounded everyday. It's hard to see much progress. We're fighting in the same spots, taking them over from the VC only to see them fall into their hands again a few days later."

Brian's father sipped slowly on his drink. Setting the drink down, he turned to the waitress and said, "Miss, this is a little sweet for me. I would like a bourbon on the rocks with a twist please." Looking at John, he simply shook his head. "I know how you feel son, but our country doesn't make mistakes on issues like this. Communism, if not stopped, will eat its way into every free country in the world. We have to stop them somewhere and Vietnam is where we have to do it. Give them Vietnam and most of Asia will fall. We have to stand tall son. We're what keep our country free. Not just today but for tomorrow as well."

Brian stared at his father. He felt a slow anger build up inside. Controlling it, he decided the best thing to do was to get up and leave. "Dad, I have some friends I want to meet for dinner. I ran into some guys I know. I really don't want to think about the war this week. I'll have enough of that when I get back to my unit. For now, I just want to try and unwind." Excusing himself, he left and walked outside.

He easily found the restaurant that he had met Amy at last night. Going inside, there was already a modest crowd on hand. A hostess asked him if he wanted to sit at the bar or at a table. Looking around, he didn't see Amy. Disappointed, he decided to leave and come back later. Heading for the door, he heard Amy's voice behind him.

"There you are. I didn't think you would come back." Grabbing his arm, she led him to a small table at the back of the bar area. Sitting down she handed him a menu and told him the seafood was outstanding. Taking her advice, he ordered the Seafood Platter and a bottle of beer. The food turned out to be delicious. As Brian ate, the restaurant became crowded. A popular spot, every table was taken by the time Brian finished. Amy seemed to be everywhere at once and knew many of the clients who came there to eat. About to wave at her to bring his check, a large Hawaiian man emerged from the kitchen and sat down at Brian's table. Holding out his hand, he said, "My name is Robert and I own the restaurant. Amy is my niece. She told me what you did last night." Shaking his head, he continued, "I was born here, so I have grown up with the military; but for young women, it can be a problem. Anyway, the dinner is on me. I hope you liked it."

After thanking him, Brian left a tip on the table and started to leave. Disappointed he didn't get to talk to Amy; he was almost at the door when she came rushing over. You weren't going to leave without saying goodbye, were you?"

"No, I just didn't want to bother you. I can see you are very busy. Thanks for the dinner. Your Uncle is very nice."

"He is. He's like my guardian angel."

"I don't want to seem too bold, but would you like to go out with me after you get off tonight, maybe have a drink somewhere?"

"Well, I don't know, can I trust you? After all, you are a soldier, right?"

"I am, but I'm not drunk and I really would like to talk to you."

Blushing, Amy said, "Of course, I'll go out with you for a drink. Meet me outside at 11."

With four hours to kill, Brian wasn't sure what to do. Walking around Waikiki Boulevard, he came to a store that sold beautiful coral jewelry. On impulse, he bought a bracelet and had it gift-wrapped. The bracelet had coral stones alternating with black opal. The price seemed reasonable, but as Brian walked out of the store, he wondered what he would do with it.

At 11 PM he returned to the restaurant and waited only a few minutes before Amy appeared. Taking her arm, he walked down the street, letting her direct the way. After a few minutes they arrived at a small, quiet bar. Sitting down, she ordered a mixed drink while he ordered a local beer.

"Thanks for coming with me. I really just wanted some quiet time with you. You are very pretty and it's been so long since I have talked to a girl." He told her about West Point, his father and how he wasn't sure a military career was for him.

Taking his hand in hers, Amy said, "You always follow the heart. It is seldom wrong. I wish you well and I know you will return safely."

"I don't know about that. Old Charlie tries very hard to make sure I don't come back, at least not in one piece." Changing the subject, Brian asked, "I have to leave to go back on Thursday. I would like to see some of the Island, maybe take in a sight or two. I don't know if you have any time, but I can't think of a better way to spend a day than with you."

"You are really very direct, aren't you? Is that something they teach you at West Point?"

"No, they don't. I guess it's just the way I am."

"I have tomorrow off. I can borrow my Uncle's car. I know the Island well, and, yes, I would be happy to take you around the Island."

Brian looked at her. She was beautiful. In the dim light of the bar, he could still see her dark eyes twinkle and her long black hair shine with an effervescent glow. He smiled and said, "I'll look forward to it."

Chapter 32

John Whalen woke up and looked at the young girl lying next to him. She was totally naked. Small in stature, she was very pretty. Her hair hung down to her waist and she had a perfect set of white teeth. Getting up, John lit a cigarette and looked outside. His room overlooked the pool. Sitting down at a small table, he thumbed through a book placed there on the sights of Bangkok. North of the city was where, during WW II, the Allied POWs had attempted to build a bridge over the River Kwai. Trips could be arranged to see that area as well as fishing trips and more. Looking over at the girl, she started to stir. Opening her eyes she looked at John. Stretching, she smiled, sat up and asked, “You want to boom-boom again?”

Smiling, John could feel himself being aroused by the simple sight of her body. Butting out his cigarette in the ashtray, he went over to the bed and wrapped his arms around her. “Okay,” he laughed, “let’s boom-boom.”

An hour later, both John and the girl were dressed. He found out that all the girls took on American names and hers was simply “Fun.” Although it was a strange name, he decided to use it as opposed to asking her what her Thai name was. They went down to the dining room and John was surprised that they had a Thai and an American menu. Seeing American style breakfasts, he ordered a cheese omelet, home fries, and toast, with fresh orange juice and coffee. Devouring every bit of food, Fun watched in awe.

“Americans eat too much, get too fat,” she said laughing. Just as they finished, Keith came down with a rather plump Thai girl. She was very pretty and spoke English well. Keith sat at the table next to him and ordered breakfast. The girls knew each other and started talking rapidly in Thai. “What are they saying Keith, do you know?”

Keith shook his head, “Fuck if I know.”

Finally, Keith’s girl, who they called Star, asked bluntly, “Would you like us for the week? It’s better that way. Fun really likes you,” she said nodding toward John “and I like Keith. We could have lots of fun this week together and you no have to worry about getting other girl. Many girls at bars not pretty like us."

John and Keith looked at each other. "What do you think?" Keith asked.

"Sure, why not. So what do we do?" Star got up and in minutes came back with the same Thai man that had come to John's room. He asked for $125, which they both paid. Smiling he said, "I arrange for driver for you today. His name is Town. He number one driver. He take you anywhere you want to go."

In minutes, a young man, not more than 18 or so, came to their table. "My name is Town. I will be your driver. I show you Bangkok today and tonight take you to number one bar. Thirty dollars for week. This OK?" Taking $30 from his pocket, John handed it to Town saying, "That's good; we'll see you later." Looking down at the money, Town smiled, folded the money and put it is his pocket before leaving.

Later, the four of them got in Town's car, which was driven from the opposite side, and had a tour of Bangkok. Both Keith and John were surprised at how modern the city was. Most men were dressed in Western style business suits, and the women dressed similar to what would be found in an American city. It seemed everyone was busy, the traffic brutal, and the weather hot. After some time, John suggested they go back to the hotel and use the pool.

That evening, they went to a local bar. Packed with American servicemen, they had an excellent band that played rock and roll music. Whalen shouted over to Keith. "It's great to hear the rock music. All they play where I'm at is country."

"Same with me," Keith shouted over the din of the music.

The next day they drove up to where the bridge over the River Kwai had been built. As they left the city, the countryside slowly changed to what looked like Vietnam. Once again, Water Buffalo and rice paddies dotted the scenery.

****

Brian had agreed to meet Amy at the restaurant where she worked at 8:00 AM. As he walked up to the hotel, he saw that she was already there seated in a Mustang convertible. Smiling at him as he walked up, she said, "You need a ride, soldier?"

"Nice car. Your Uncle has good taste."

"It has a V-8 engine in it too, with a four barrel carburetor. It's fast, and I love speed, so you better hang on."

Amy weaved through the busy streets of Honolulu and headed toward Diamond Head. Stopping, they got out of the car and looked out at the ocean. "This is a beautiful place," Brian commented. "You ever been stateside?" he asked.

"Yes I have, several times, but never out of California. When I was in high school, we took a trip to San Francisco, and I went a few times with my mother. It's expensive. I would like to see more of the United States and hopefully I will someday. I'm an engineering major. Are you surprised to hear that?"

"No, I'm not. There's talk that West Point and the other service academies will be allowing women soon. I think it's good."

"I may end up taking a job in the states next summer. This September I'll be a senior. There aren't a lot of jobs for engineers on the Island, but in California there are. Let's get back in the car. I'll show you some of the pineapple plantations."

Amy and Brian spent the day driving around the Island. On the mountainous roads leading away from Honolulu, Amy proved that she did like speed as they careened around sharp corner after sharp corner, prompting Brian to say, "Amy, your driving is more dangerous than the VC."

At the end of the day, they put the car away and stood quietly in front of her Uncle's house, which was only a few blocks from his restaurant. "I had a great day Amy. One of the best I ever had. You're amazing. Bending down, he put his arms around her and kissed her gently. I can't thank you enough. It meant a lot to me."

"I liked the day too Brian. You're amazing too. Not like any other soldier I have ever met."

"Most of the girls I knew back at West Point, I guess I don't know how to say it, just wanted to go out with a cadet from West Point. They hung around like leeches. It was easy to sleep with them. They didn't have any standards, that's for sure."

They walked for a while again, Brian holding her hand. Seeing a small park-like area with benches, Brian steered her to one of the benches where they sat down. He looked at her dressed in simple shorts and a silk top. He never saw anyone more beautiful or sincere. Taking her face in his hands, he kissed her passionately. I would love to sleep with you Amy more than anything. But if I did, I would regret it. I want to see you again, after my time is up in Vietnam. It's only a few more months, and I probably won't be in the field that much longer. I know you're thinking that I'm just lonely, but that's not it."

Reaching into his pocket, he felt for the small box with the bracelet. He handed it to her and said, "I bought this at a jewelry store here. When I bought it, I wasn't even sure why I did, but I want you to have it."

Removing the gift-wrap and opening the box, Amy held the bracelet in her hand. "It's beautiful. Do you know, with all the coral we have here on the Island, I don't have any at all." Amy put the bracelet on her wrist and looked at it. "I love it Brian, I really do. It means a lot to me. I would like nothing better than to see you when you get done with your tour. I do want to get to know you."

"I can get thirty days leave when my tour is done. I'll take some of it here. I want to write you when I get back to 'Nam. But I have a couple more days here. I know you are working, but maybe we can get together."

"We will," Amy said, holding Brian in a long embrace, "we will."

Chapter 33

It seemed that R&R had just started and was over in what seemed like two days instead of six. Keith and John stepped off the plane at Da Nang and were immediately greeted by the distant sound of artillery. "Welcome back to 'Nam," Keith said cheerfully.

"Why are you so happy?"

"Shit man, I'm getting short, so are you. Fuck, we'll be going back to The World soon."

"Hey Keith, our clerk back on the Hill said that he heard that the tours are going to be reduced to ten months starting in September. You hear any of that shit?"

"I heard the rumors John, but whether they are true or not, I don't know. I guess Nixon is under a lot of pressure to get this thing over with. They want to turn the fighting over to the ARVNs, but hell, you know those fuckers will get their asses kicked by the NVA in a year. If I had to bet, I would say it's true. Not as many troops coming over, that's for sure."

Stopping to light a cigarette, Keith said, "John, it was great seeing you. I've got to get back and I know you're supposed to meet your L. T. friend in the next hour. I had a ball this week. I think Fun and Star did too. Did you ever know any girls that balled like that? I don't think I could have taken another week."

"No, I never have either." Taking his hand and shaking it, John said, "I'm really glad we met up. When I get back to Sandusky, I'll give you a call. We'll go out."

Waving goodbye, Keith strode off to hitch a ride back to his unit. "You better make it back. Don't let Charlie get your ass," he yelled over his shoulder.

Sitting down, Whalen looked at his watch. He had about an hour to kill before Brian's plane was due in. Walking over to a lobby-like area, he saw Sergeant Peterson reading a magazine dressed in civilian clothes. "Hey Sergeant, heading to Honolulu, huh?" Seeing Whalen, he stood up and said, "Well, you made it back from Bangkok. No clap, I hope."

"Not yet. I had a great time. Met an old friend from Sandusky while there and we hung out. The women are fucking unbelievable. I'm waiting for Brian. He should be here in an hour or so."

"Yeah, I wanted his allocation, but he pulled rank on me, so I was lucky to get this week. Murphy wouldn't let us go at the same time."

"How's things back at the Hill? Weren't you due to go back on patrol?"

"All we've been doing is daily patrols. Out in the morning, back at night. Easy duty. I don't know what's going on. We took a couple of casualties though. Two wounded from the third platoon. Booby traps. Couple men ran into trip wires. Look Whalen, there is going to be some changes when we get back. Murphy is leaving. You'll get a chance to say goodbye, but he's gone by week's end. Hewitt gave the company to Hathaway and Bromley is XO. We'll be getting a couple of new platoon leaders. And I don't think Calhoun will be with us that much longer. The West Point guys, well, the Army has a lot invested in them and they're losing them to Charlie awfully fast. I think in another month or so, they'll put him in a rear area. Hewitt is fond of him. I guess he served with his father. I'm concerned about Hathaway. He's become aggressive." Shaking his head, Peterson added, "I hope he settles down. We'll see I guess."

Whalen had an uneasy feeling about Hathaway too. But it shouldn't affect him too much. Peterson and Calhoun were still in charge of the platoon.

"Oh, good news for Calhoun. You may as well tell him when he gets here. He's a First Lieutenant now. His promotion came through."

Smiling, Whalen said, "I will. He'll be happy about that."

Peterson got up, grabbed his bag and said goodbye to Whalen. John sat back down and thought more about what Peterson had said. Maybe he should think about doing what Scarcelli had done. Murphy liked him; maybe he could get a job in the rear before he left. Mulling it over, he decided if he did that, he would be putting Peterson and Brian in a tough situation. No, he couldn't do that, at least not now. Maybe when Brian was sent to the rear, he would try then.

Lost in thought, John was starting to doze off when he was awakened by a violent slap on his back. Standing up quickly with fists clenched, he saw Brian standing there laughing at him. "What happened, boy, all those Thai women wear you down?"

"Fuck yeah, they did."

Both laughing, they started telling each other about their adventures on R&R. Whalen smiled as Brian told him about Amy and how he planned to see her when his tour was finished. "I really like her. I hope it's not the Vietnam thing. She's beautiful and her personality, well, I have never seen anything like it. She's a little girl in a woman's body."

"Oh, I almost forgot." John stood crisply at attention and gave Brian a mock salute. "First Lieutenant Calhoun, Specialist Whalen reporting."

"No kidding, my promotion came through?"

"It did, congratulations."

Whalen finished by telling John what Peterson had told him about Murphy leaving and Hathaway getting command.

"The fucker is a loose cannon, but now that he's got the company, maybe he'll settle down. He doesn't have the time for captain, so he'll stay a first looey. Fuck, that's strange," Calhoun said.

Chapter 34

Sergeant Jack Peterson stepped off the plane and saw his wife Janet for the first time in months. Dropping his bag, he ran to her and hugged her with all his might. So happy to see her, he didn't even notice at first that she was pregnant.

"Don't you notice something different about me Jack?" she asked. Stepping back, Jack looked at her and smiled, "You're pregnant," holding her again, he quickly pushed her away, "How long?"

"I'm in my seventh month, so it must have happened just when you were leaving. I think it's a girl this time Jack. I really do."

Walking through the terminal, Janet filled Jack in on what was happening at Fort Jackson and with their two boys. "My Mom is staying with them, but they really wanted to come with me"

"I know, but I'll be home soon." Jack purposely didn't tell her about the rumor quickly spreading on the tours being reduced to ten months. He didn't want to give her any false hope. "I put in for DI school last week. We have a damn good company clerk and he's leaving soon. I wanted to put the papers in before he left. I'm sure I'll get it. The captain and my platoon leader wrote terrific letters. I think I'll like being a DI, you know, working with recruits. My time on the range was all right, but it was boring after a while. I know the days are long, but you get a week off after each week cycle and it doesn't count against your leave."

"I know you'll get it Jack, and you'll be a great DI."

Chapter 35

Whalen was surprised to see the stack of mail Simmons handed him. He had letters from home, a letter from Pauline and, much to his surprise, a letter from Natalie. Taking the letters to his hootch, he stared at it for the longest time before opening it. It was awkward for him, especially after the week he had with Fun. He hadn't thought as much about her lately and wasn't sure how compatible they would be when he returned. Finally opening the letter, John saw that it was fairly short.

John,

I am sorry I have not written you, but I just couldn't bring myself to do so. I know that you will be home in the next few months, and I'm not sure how you feel about me. I will always love you, but I fear that this past year has created too many obstacles for us to ever overcome. Love is complicated and has so many parts that must all fit together to work. I want to see you when you get back. Please call me and we will get together. I will be finished with grad school this fall and will student teach in the spring to complete my certification. I hope that you are well and return safely.
Natalie

John wasn't sure what to make of the letter. He had planned on calling her when he returned, but as time went on, he knew that chances were remote that they could pick up where they had left off. Folding the letter, he decided not to write her back. For some reason his thoughts turned to Debbie Fisher, and he took the picture of her legs from his wallet and stared at it. "Crazy girl," he thought. Putting the picture away, he walked over to the mess hall for lunch.

Sitting down, his squad members came over and started asking him about R&R. Most of the men were new. It was odd how fast time had gone by. It seemed like just yesterday he had, as Scarcelli pointed out, "359 and a wake-up."

"So Touchdown, did you score?" one of them said in a feeble attempt to be funny.

"Hell, if you don't score in Bangkok, you'd have to be a fag. It was great. Go there when your time comes. Don't even think of the other places. Why aren't you on patrol today?"

"They got us on stand down until Hathaway takes over. Murphy is leaving later this week. We'll be here for a few more days. It's been quiet. Not much artillery going out. Maybe Charlie is quitting."

"Don't count on it. That's the way Charlie is. He'll come back; and when he does, watch out," John warned.

Chapter 36

Sergeant Peterson woke up suddenly in the middle of the night. Sweating, he sat up, careful not to wake his wife. He had dreamed that an NVA battalion-size force wiped out his entire platoon. Surrounded, they had fought to the last man. It was a reoccurring dream and each time it became more realistic. The one common thread was a Vietnamese colonel who had an evil look about him as his forces swooped down. He was the constant in the dream. Always there, always laughing at the end.

Lying back down, Peterson tried to sleep. Even in Hawaii, with his wife beside him, he couldn't get Vietnam out of his system. "It was Hathaway," he thought. He didn't like him, nor did he trust him. Captain Murphy was fair, reasonable, and didn't take unnecessary chances. Maybe Colonel Hewitt thought he wasn't aggressive enough, but he got the job done. Peterson got out of bed, lit a cigarette and stared out the window. Looking out at Waikiki Beach, he thought of all the servicemen from WW II and now Vietnam who strolled through this beautiful city with war on their minds. Looking over at Janet, he knew she was worried. Two boys at home, a child on the way, hopefully a girl, and her husband in the field fighting an enemy that at times seemed invincible. With only two days left, he vowed to make them the best two days of their married life. Who knew what would happen. He had just a couple more months in Vietnam, but those were the ones you worried about most. Lying back down, he drifted off to a troubled sleep.

Chapter 37

It seemed funny to see the mess hall so crowded; yet no food was being served. Today was the official day that Lt. Hathaway would take command of B Company. Captain Murphy was there, as were the platoon leaders, platoon sergeants and all the men. Lt. Bromley sat quietly with the first sergeant and the company clerk, Simmons, who had just days left before he left for The World.

Captain Murphy spoke first, thanking everyone and giving a special thanks to the first sergeant. He told everyone that he would most likely leave the Army after returning to the United States but still was not 100% certain. He wished everyone good luck and a safe return to The World and then asked Lt. Hathaway to say a few words.

Standing up, Hathaway smiled and thanked Captain Murphy for his efficient job in leading B Company. He spoke of his excitement in having command and how since he was a young boy, he wanted to have a military career. "We'll be aggressive, but we'll be prudent too," Hathaway said at one point. Finally, he introduced the two new platoon leaders, 2Lt. Bill Benson and 2Lt. Peter O'Keefe. Both were from OCS courses in the states and had just arrived in country. Turning to Peterson, just back from R&R, Whalen whispered, "Shit Jack, I hope they give us some easy patrols until we get these guys some experience."

"It's the Army Whalen, didn't you ever hear the expression SNAFU?"

"No," Whalen asked curiously, "what does it mean?"

"Situation normal, all fucked up," grinned Peterson.

Chapter 38

Colonel Hewitt welcomed Lt. Hathaway, Lt. Calhoun, Sergeant Peterson and Specialist Whalen into his office. Sitting with him was Lt. Saban from Military Intelligence.

"Hathaway, first I want to congratulate you on your command. We were impressed with what you did as a platoon leader. You have expressed an interest in a military career and this will give you a good start toward that. We know you're short, but you'll be the company commander for at least another six weeks or so. I know you can extend your tour, but you need more time in grade for captain, and it would be hard for me to circumvent that with Division in Chu Lai. So for now, let's focus on what we can do on this next patrol."

"Sir, I want to thank you for the opportunity. I'm excited and I think we'll do well. We've got a damn good company sir."

Nodding to Saban, Hewitt asked him to go over the details of their next patrol. Rolling out his map and holding a report in his other hand, he showed Hathaway the area they were concerned with. "Over here is where at least a platoon or maybe even a larger force is holed up. They are all NVA regulars, part of the same force we tried to bust up some months ago in this valley. They have spread out and have been wrecking havoc with elements of our AO for months now. They have been setting mines, hit and run operations, and using mortar attacks to disturb our firebase and LZ operations. And as you saw, they have been surging in on night lagers and perimeters. We have good information that they will launch an attack on one of our LZs in the near future. Could be Mary Ann, Baldy, Siberia, we don't know. These LZs are very vulnerable and anything short of keeping the grunts back, they will remain vulnerable. The best shot we have is to wipe them out before they get a chance. To prevent this from happening, we want to send your company in a three-prong approach to where we believe they are. This jungle area here is adjacent to this village where we know from our Kit Carson Scout that a large horde of supplies and ammo is stored. We want you to take your most experienced platoon and make a demonstration here. Get in the village. The NVA will not want to lose those supplies, so we are certain they will come out of this jungle area and try to move you out. The other two platoons will be back in this area to the south. We're planning on moving all of you in at night to minimize Charlie knowing where you are. When the shit starts, your two reserve platoons can move in and cut off their retreat. It's going to be close quarters fighting, so chances are we won't be able to give you much artillery support, but we will have Cobras ready. Any questions?"

Lt. Calhoun asked, "What if Charlie has more than a platoon in there? We know that they had at least a company operating in this area that total maybe 150 men. We could go in there and really get the shit knocked out of us."

"Negative. Our reports are accurate and they state that there is no more than a platoon, maybe 30 men at most."

Hathaway, with the eagerness of a new command, asked, "When should we be ready to move out?"

Saban looked at Hewitt who answered, "Day after tomorrow. We'll send you out in the opposite direction and back door you into their AO."

Sensing the meeting was over, Lt. Saban started putting his maps away while saying, "We'll have a final briefing tomorrow afternoon, say 1600?" Everyone nodded in agreement.

As they left, Hathaway turned to Calhoun, "You have the most experienced platoon, so I want your men to go in and hit that ville. We'll talk more about it on patrol, but obviously we can't use one of the new platoon leaders."

Peterson, with a worried look, spoke up. "L. T., I hope to hell those two platoons support us. They have all new guys there, except for Sergeant Blakely. They may shit their pants when the rounds start popping, and we could get our shit blown away."

"I won't let that happen Jack. I'll stay back with them and make damn sure we get to you in time."

Hathaway walked back to the orderly room as Calhoun, Whalen, and the other two squad leaders stared after him. Peterson spoke first. "I hope we can count on him. We may be badly outnumbered at first."

The night before the patrol, Whalen wrote letters home. The hootch was loud that night with the men getting in the last bit of fun before leaving on patrol. The makeshift bar in the far corner was packed with men from the platoon. All were drinking heavily and the eight track continued with the drone of country western music. Occasionally a Johnny Rivers song, *Tracks of my Tears,* would break the monotony. Someone yelled to Whalen to join them for a beer, and John yelled back that he would when he finished the letters home.

John struggled with the letters. He finished one letter to his parents and one to Pauline. Both were short. He had decided to answer Natalie's letter, but didn't know what to say. Finally, he scribbled out a brief note, folded it and put it in the envelope.

Natalie,

I was very happy to hear from you. Letters are important here, and we can never get enough of them. I think of you all the time and especially remember the times we shared together. I have always planned on calling you when I get home, and I agree there are no guarantees. We have been apart for a long time now, but what we had was an important part of our lives, and I think we owe it to ourselves to see if we can pick up where we left off. I will see you soon.

John

Walking over to the mailroom, John dropped the envelopes in the slot in the door and hoped that Natalie would reply to his note. Maybe there was still a chance that everything would work out. He knew from making love to Fun on R&R in Bangkok that there was a big difference. What he felt with Natalie was far better than what he had with Fun. Entering the hootch, the men all yelled and tossed him a cold Hamm's beer. John opened the can, cheered his men, and drank the beer down in one large gulp.

The next morning John woke up at 0400 and started to organize his ruck. Some of the men were starting to stir around him but most were hung over and would be difficult to get up. They weren't leaving until 1000, so time was not an issue.

The final briefing the day before had brought out nothing new. Brigade was confident the mission would go off smoothly and another element of the NVA would be destroyed. John walked over to the officer's hootch and went down the stairs to their bunker. The new officers were nervously getting ready and asking questions to both Bromley and Calhoun. Seeing John come in, Bromley took his cigarette out of his mouth and snarled, "Whalen, would you get these new L. T.s calmed down; they're bothering us."

"Hey," Whalen said, "you got the easy job, we got the tough one. Just relax. Don't let your men see how nervous you are. You're officers, goddamn it. Look and act it."

"I'm going over for breakfast Brian, you coming."

"In a minute. I want to finish this letter to Amy and drop it off at the mailroom. We can walk over together if you want."

As they walked to the mailroom, John asked Brian, "You're really serious about Amy aren't you?"

"John, I've dated a lot of girls and I mean a lot, especially in high school and at the Point too. I have never felt like this before. Never. I don't know if I love her. I just know that I want to see her again. I want to spend time with her and get to know her. I realize this isn't the best situation, but if I don't try, I know I'll regret it."

After breakfast, the men of B Company started to form up near the main gate. They left at different intervals by platoon and headed in different directions. It was two days to their rendezvous, the last part of it at night. The route Brigade chose was considered a safe area and everything went well. After the first night, the nerves started to jangle, as everyone knew the mission they had planned would soon be upon them.

After setting their night perimeter and getting the ambush set, Whalen and Brian sat down together. Whalen tore off a piece of C-4 explosive and set a match to it. Burning at a much higher temperature than the heat tabs, it was a much-preferred method of heating C-rations. While John was doing this, Brian held a poncho liner over him so the flame from the C-4 could not be seen. Stirring a can of cheese into the can of beef was one way to make the rations more palatable. Everyone had their favorites.

"Okay, I'm done." Lowering the blanket, John served some of his concoction to Brian and both sat down and ate. Opening a can of peaches, John stirred in an envelope of powered cream used for coffee and gave half to Brian.

"Damn near as good as the food in Hawaii," mocked Brian.

"Hey, fuck you," John answered angrily.

"So, we're staying here tomorrow I guess."

"That's right John. We're gonna send out some patrols into those small villes over there. We know they're clean, but if Charlie is watching, and we know he is, he'll think that's all we're doing. Then we gotta move our asses out after dark and get a lot of ground covered. I'm worried about booby traps, but the rangers were supposed to move through the same area today and clear it for us; so if they did, we should be okay."

"Brian, I want to tell you, I really value your friendship. I know you won't be in the bush much longer. Peterson told me back in Da Nang that West Point officers are too valuable and that they'll probably move you to the rear soon. I hope that we can stay friends. After this, you'll probably go stateside. Maybe we can stay in touch."

"I hope so. I would have had a tough time doing this without you. I don't know when I'll get moved out. With the two new platoon leaders and Hathaway as CO, I don't know. I think I'll be around for another couple patrols. We'll see. All I want is to finish this and go see Amy for a couple of weeks. I never stop thinking of her John."

****

Amy looked at her watch and saw that it was almost 10:00 PM. It was a slow night and the kitchen was already closed. Turning to her uncle she asked if she could leave, and he nodded yes, but first he wanted to talk to her. She was worried that she may have done something wrong, but as they sat down, she quickly learned that she hadn't.

"Amy, since your father died some time back, I have tried to help you as much as I can. I have sensed a change since you met that young man on leave from Vietnam. I know he liked you and that you liked him. I also know that you are afraid to go too far with him because he is not Hawaiian. I suspect he will be back;

and when he does come back, you must follow your heart in much the same way as we all do when love finds us. The world is changing and so is Hawaii. Your father would be proud of you. He is a nice man. He loves you already. I could see it when you were together, and I feel that you must love him too. Don't be afraid of it Amy. You go now. Get some rest."

Amy walked out, her knees quivering. She had been afraid to tell anyone, yet her uncle knew all along. She felt relieved and worried. She hoped Brian was all right.

****

The daytime patrols returned with no casualties and nothing to report from the villages they checked. Going through the motions of setting up for the night, they followed the same rituals. As a bonus, a chopper came in from LZ Hawk Hill with mail and a hot meal.

Brian had just one letter and it was from Amy. Afraid to open it, he found a quiet spot away from everyone and slowly opened the envelope.

Brian,

I can't tell you in words how much I enjoyed being with you. I loved our time together. The bracelet you gave me reminds me of you each day. Many of my friends have commented on it, and they are all jealous. I can't wait to see you again and know the time will come soon enough. My uncle told me yesterday that he could tell we were in love. I don't know if that is true, but in time we will find out. I hope you are well and have time to write.
Love,
Amy

Brian read the letter over and over, surprised at the words. Looking up, he saw John looking down at him. "Better get some hot chow before it's gone. Beats the hell out of C rations."

"John, I got a letter from Amy. Go ahead, read it."

"Oh, I don't know Brian, it's personal."

"No, go ahead."

Taking the letter, John read it and handed it back. "Well boy, I guess you did it. You got the charm. I hope it works out for you, I really do." John felt a little down, thinking of Natalie and the uncertainty of their future.

Reading his mind, Brian said, "Maybe things will work out for you and Natalie. She did write. It's a start."

As night fell, the men of B Company's 2nd Platoon quietly moved out. Most of the men had not been on night patrol and were uneasy. Slowly they plodded along. Each snap of a dry branch caused the men to jump. Occasionally some animal would be disturbed and would send a chill down the spine of the men. Finally, after what seemed forever, they halted. Crouching down, the men were told to get as comfortable as possible and to rest. They were just a klick or so from the village they were to assault at sun up. As Whalen moved down the rank to check on his squad, one FNG asked nervously, "If the NVA are in there, why don't we just blast the hell out of them with artillery Whalen?"

"Doesn't work that way. Charlie is dug in or can move out quickly. And we never can tell if we got him. We need body count for that. Look, you'll be fine," he said, patting him on his shoulder.

****

Lt. Truong woke up as usual at 0400. He had planned a busy day for his men. He wanted to set new mines in an area he suspected cavalry may pass through. Their mines successfully destroyed two personnel carriers the week before. He also wanted to send several men into the village they were guarding to transport more supplies to another NVA platoon to the north and a unit of Viet Cong to the south. They had become much more cautious since an American patrol had discovered a large cache of their weapons some months before. These weapons would be needed for a planned assault on one of their firebases. Colonel Nhung had many plans laid out for them. He had heard that the American forces were being reduced soon. This information had come from several recent POWs who had, under much torture, told them of the rumors. Soon they would be marching on Saigon. It was only a matter of time. Truong's platoon was strong right now. Almost 40 very well equipped men. Many of their weapons were captured from Americans. Truong smiled. The war was going well.

****

The sun started to peek over the horizon when word came down for Calhoun's squad to lock and load. Four men were chosen to advance on the village and throw smoke grenades. Then the rest of the squad would move in. Two men would remain back for support if needed. Calhoun, observing radio silence, hoped the other platoons were in position to support him. On his signal, the four men ran toward the village. As they came within range, they each threw a smoke grenade and watched them pop off. As the smoke began billowing through and around the huts, they charged in yelling to the Vietnamese. *"Di Di Mau. Di Di Mau."*

****

Private Phan woke suddenly. He sensed something was wrong. Although it was still dark, the sun would be up soon. Sitting up, he listened carefully and thought he could detect the sounds of an army patrol unit. He rolled off the mat he had been sleeping on with a Vietnamese woman and quickly got dressed. Sliding his sandals on, he motioned to the Vietnamese girl lying on the mat to get dressed and wait for him. Phan moved slowly from hut to hut until he was at the edge of the village. Crawling on his stomach, he inched closer to an area of heavy grass that dropped off to a small valley. Straining, he could hear the muffled sounds of an American platoon. Retracing his steps, he returned to the hootch he had stayed in and told the girl to quietly wake the others in the village and move them to the nearby tree line. Crouching as low as possible while moving as quickly as he could, Phan reached the tree line and its protective cover. In just moments he saw Lt. Truong. Running up to him, he told him of the American patrol.

"Did you see how large a force the Americans had?" he was asked. "Yes Lt. Truong, it was no more than a platoon."

"They probably have another platoon backing them up, but we will move to cut them off." Truong told Phan to pass his orders on to his squad leaders. They would shift around and come to the Americans through the village. That way they would have the huts for protection. In just minutes his men were in position where they waited for the Americans to come into their village.

****

As soon as the four men reached the outskirts of the village, Calhoun gave word for the platoon to enter. Expecting the NVA to attack their flank, the platoon moved safely into the head of the village. "What the fuck?" Calhoun scowled, "Where the hell are they?"

Peterson motioned for his men to continue moving through the village. Just as several of his men got up to slide forward, the NVA positioned in the village let out a devastating hail of AK rounds and machine gun fire. In the first few seconds, three men of the second platoon were cut down; the others pinned down and froze in position. Calhoun, crawling forward, reached his RTO and grabbed the radio. "Romeo Tango 22, this is Romeo Tango 24." As soon as Hathaway's voice came over, Calhoun yelled, "The NVA are in a strong position in the village and have us pinned down by heavy fire. We already have casualties. Get your ass up here." Throwing the radio down, Calhoun leveled his M-16 at the hootchs and started returning fire.

Whalen yelled over to Peterson, "Jack, we're getting killed here; there's no cover. We gotta move the fuck back."

"I know, but we can't right now. Where the hell is our M-60?"

"I can't tell. I think he's been hit." Crawling to his left, Whalen found the M-60 gunner face down in a pool of blood. His loader was seriously wounded and was unable to help

Whalen. Setting the M-60 up, Whalen began firing short bursts as best he could into the village. Someone behind him with a LAWS rocket sent a round into the village destroying a hootch. The medic attached to the platoon who had been left back at the rear started popping 40 mm rounds into the village with his M-79 grenade launcher.

****

Lt. Truong looked on at the fight. Convinced that the Americans only had at most a platoon and his first contact had caused numerous casualties, he prepared to send his men forward. "We will deal them a fatal blow," he thought.

****

Lt. Hathaway, a klick or so back, threw his radio down in disgust. Quickly giving the word, he instructed the first platoon to move out. He ordered the third platoon to stay back and lend support as needed. Moving quickly he could hear the sound of the firefight ahead of him. In his ten months in the field he had never heard so much fire. "Goddamn it, move it," he yelled, "those guys are catching shit up there."

Whalen continued to fire the M-60 until he ran out of ammunition. Returning to his M-16, he watched as he saw the NVA moving closer from hootch to hootch. Jamming in another clip, he carefully fired shot after shot at the NVA troops who moved stealthily from hootch to hootch. He sensed that his squad was either running out of ammunition or had taken on more casualties as their rate of fire tapered off. He cursed as he wondered where the hell Hathaway's men were.

Seeing some NVA crouch down around a hootch that was no more than 30 yards from him, Whalen reached into his deep side pocket and took out a baseball grenade. Removing the pin, he waited, stood halfway up and threw it as hard as he could toward the village. Falling back down he rolled sideways in case they returned fire. Hearing the grenade go off, he looked up and with some satisfaction saw that the hootch was now on fire. Hearing a familiar voice to his left, he saw Calhoun half crawling over, "John I lost my RTO, he got hit and they took out the radio. I hope Hathaway got my message. If he did, we should see him any second."

Just then they saw Hathaway's men come crashing over the small crest to their east. No sooner had they hit the area directly behind them than their M-60 gunner started firing rounds into the now advancing NVA. Lt. Calhoun, getting caught up in the excitement of the advancing troops, stood up and joined Hathaway's men moving forward toward the line of NVA. Stunned at the new platoon arriving, the NVA at first started retreating; but at the encouragement of Lt. Truong, his men kneeled and began firing rounds into the men of B Company. Lt. Calhoun stopped to insert another clip into his M-16 and was just starting to move forward when an enemy soldier saw him. The NVA soldier moved his rifle up to his shoulder to aim, but thought better of it and instead fired a short round on automatic fire. He grunted in satisfaction as he saw Calhoun grab for his legs and fall forward. In horror, Whalen watched as Brian fell. He started to run toward him when all of a sudden the words of Sergeant Hess came back to him. "*I took that hippie shit out of you Whalen. You're a soldier now. I knew you would be a good leader. Don't disappoint your men.*"

Stopping, Whalen watched as the NVA soldier who had shot Calhoun, started running toward the protection of the hootchs and tree line. Feeling a rage he never felt before, he methodically put his M-16 up to his shoulder and aimed. He fired once, then twice. As he lowered his rifle, he watched as the NVA soldier turned and saw Whalen start to fire. The NVA soldier lifted up his rifle and began to return fire when Whalen's first round caught him in his right shoulder. Spinning through the air, he was about to fire his AK-47 when a second round caught him in his stomach doubling him over. Dropping his rifle he winced in pain as he crashed to the ground in a heap.

The men of Hathaway's platoon were moving forward driving the NVA back with M-16s, M-79s and LAWS rockets. Running back to Brian, John found him laying face down. "Aw hell Brian," he yelled. Rolling him over he saw that he had been shot in the legs and had taken a round in his helmet possibly knocking him out. Finding no other wounds, Whalen cut his pants legs off at the knees and found that an AK round had hit him square in the knee. The round then apparently traveled down his leg exiting the side of his boot. One of the medics came running up and shook his head. "He's lost a lot of blood, I don't know. We'll get a tourniquet on him. If that dustoff gets here quick, they might be able to save him. The tourniquet isn't a good answer though, gangrene can set in, but it's his only chance. Stay with him. If he wakes up, don't let him go back to sleep. Got that."

Lt. Hathaway came running up and knelt by Whalen. "How bad is it?"

"Not good."

"Stay with him, the dustoff will be here in less than five minutes. We're going in after these gooks. I want to make sure they don't get away with this shit." Hathaway ran off, getting his men organized for an assault in the tree line.

Whalen, cradling Brian's head, saw his eyes start to flutter and heard a groan. "Where am I?" he asked, his teeth chattering uncontrollably.

"It's okay Brian, you're going to be fine. You're going back to The World to see Amy. You'll be with her soon."

Brian smiled, "Amy, I love her. I'll see her soon." He started to close his eyes as John shook him, "No Brian, you have to stay awake. Think of Amy."

"I'm cold," Brian moaned. "My leg, it hurts so bad."

"I know Brian, but we're going to get it fixed." John heard two dustoffs come in and the medics running out with stretchers. "Okay," one of them said, "we'll take it from here."

Standing up on weak knees, John was shocked as he saw the number of wounded. Walking around in a daze at what had happened, John heard one of his men call his name. "John, what do you want us to do?"

Whalen turned and looked stupidly at him. "What do you mean?"

"Well, you're the highest rank here. We need to know what to do," he said waving to the men left from his platoon.

"Where's Peterson?" Whalen asked

Shaking his head, the man said, "He was hit John, probably as we started to advance on the village. He's KIA."

Whalen, doing his best to hold back the tears, looked down at the ground when the words of Sergeant Hess came back again. "*Don't disappoint your men.*"

"Let's get in that ville and get the ammo and supplies out. I want two men posted in front of the ville and two men in back. Go from hootch to hootch and get every bit of ammo and rice out of there."

An hour later, Whalen had the ville cleaned out. The amount of ammunition and other supplies was small in comparison to what they had expected. Joining him on the outskirts of the ville was Lt. Hathaway. "What happened L. T. after you went in?"

He shook his head and with shaking hands took out a cigarette and tried to light it. After several attempts he succeeded. "No good John. We went in the tree line, and I lost one man to a booby trap. Trip wire and grenade. Blew him up bad. Not two minutes later, my point man got stitched in half by machine gun fire. It's hell in there, hell. The body count we got wasn't worth it. All we could find were eight gooks. Eight, John. And what did we lose? We've nine KIA and six wounded. We lost your platoon leader and your platoon sergeant. For what? Some fucking rice and ammo?"

Turning their heads they watched as a LOACH came into view, slowly thumping its way into their AO. Setting down just 100 meters from where Hathaway and Whalen were standing, they watched as Colonel Hewitt and Lt. Saban climbed out.

Walking briskly toward them, Colonel Hewitt started shouting before he was halfway to them. "You boys did a terrific job. I understand you have some good body count, destroyed their ammo and pushed Charlie all the way back through that tree line. Lt. Hathaway, I want to congratulate you, and I want your company to go on stand down in Chu Lai. It's been a while and your men deserve it."

"We'll pass on the stand down sir. We didn't get in the tree line, at least not very far. As for the body count, they got the numbers on us. All we have is eight gooks down."

Hewitt, who obviously had been given bad information, glanced at Saban and grimaced. Turning back to Hathaway, he said, "Why didn't you follow up by chasing Charlie through the tree line? Hell, you had him cold. He was on the run. We talked about that."

Hathaway stared at Hewitt. His blue eyes turned to ice as he stared coldly at the colonel. Thrusting his M-16 at Hewitt, he snarled, "Sir, if you want them goddamn gooks so bad, go in there and get 'em yourself. And take your L. T. here with you. We came out here and got our asses kicked for a fuckin' few bags of rice and some ammunition that wouldn't provide enough pop for a decent 4th of July. I lost my 2nd platoon leader and his platoon sergeant and a bunch of others. I don't want stand down, and I'm sure as hell not chasing Charlie into those woods. What I want is some choppers out here to get these men back to the Hill. We have one platoon that wasn't engaged. I'll stay with them and we'll continue to patrol."

Hewitt looked startled but didn't say anything. Breathing deeply after giving Hathaway a moment to settle down, he asked. "Second platoon? Was that Calhoun and Peterson?"

"Yes sir, it was."

"Hathaway, get your RTO over here, I'll get some choppers in here to take your two platoons back to the hill. I need someone for debriefing."

Hathaway nodded toward Whalen, "John take care of that when we get back."

Hewitt stared at Whalen and said out loud, "He's only an E-4."

"That's all that's left sir," Hathaway answered sarcastically.

"Son," Hewitt said, "when you get back, come and see me. We'll sit down and go over what happened." Turning around, Hewitt and Saban walked back to their waiting chopper. Hathaway and Whalen watched as it took off.

Whalen, still somewhat in shock, let out a small grunt. "L. T., you got balls giving a colonel shit like that. Old Murphy would have been proud. You were pretty gung-ho a week ago, what happened?"

"It's different when these men are your responsibility. They set us up John. Those fuckers at Brigade didn't know what was in that fucking ville. They didn't know there was a platoon of heavily armed NVA in here. I'm sorry about Calhoun and Peterson. Is Calhoun gonna make it?"

" I don't know L. T., I don't know. He was shot up bad. Fuckin' AK round blew out his knee and exited his foot. He lost a lot of blood. Was in shock when they took him out. He'll lose the leg, that's for sure. He has other wounds too, but I'm not sure how bad they were. Everything happened so fast."

"When you get back, Whalen, check on all our wounded. Then get over to the TOC and get me a report."

It took the choppers over two hours to pick up the remnants of the 1st and 2nd platoons. When they arrived back at Hawk Hill, they exited the chopper and walked quietly back to their hootchs.

Whalen went to his hootch and pulled the poncho liner shut that separated his area from the rest of the men in his hootch. Lying down, he started shaking uncontrollably; finally he leaned over the cot and threw up. Hearing someone enter, he saw the burly form of the first sergeant standing in front of his cot.

"I heard what happened. Calhoun is down at the Evac Hospital in Chu Lai. You won't get to see him. He's gonna lose his leg and then they'll transport him to Japan. He took a round in the thigh of his other leg too, but he won't lose that leg. Has a concussion from a round in the helmet. Also had a round graze his forearm. Despite all that, they say he should live. I know you were close to both of them. Nothing I can say at a time like this, but I wanted you to know about Calhoun."

"Peterson had young kids at home and his wife is pregnant Top."

Top, almost losing his composure, moaned, "I…I didn't know about his wife. That's terrible. Staring at the floor, Top looked up and said, "I understand Hathaway stood up to the colonel?"

"It was a tough morning Top. Charlie had the hoochs for cover and we were caught flat in the open. They must have either been in the ville or saw us coming. They waited until we started in and let go with everything they had. We fired some smoke, but the wind caught it, didn't give us much protection. We didn't get much of a body count. Top, there wasn't much in that ville. No people, not much ammunition, hardly any rice."

Top looked down at the plywood floor of the hootch again and with a troubled look sat down on the corner of John's cot. Taking off his hat, he rubbed his eyes with the back of his hand. Looking up, he shook his head and said, "It's a tough war John, very tough. Did you know a man by the name of Sargo?"

John thought for a minute. "I think so. He wasn't in our platoon, but I know the guy. He's tall, thin, kind of lanky. New York City accent."

Top nodded his head. "He was KIA today, but that's not the only problem. We can't find his body. He's BNR, Body Not Recovered."

"I don't understand Top, we got everyone in body bags as far as I know. Are you sure he was hit?"

"He's missing John, and one of the guys that moved in on the ville when Hathaway came up said he saw him take a round in the stomach and one in the shoulder. You don't recover from that. The kid that saw him get hit thinks he may have crawled away looking for help. Could have crawled toward the deep grass. Anyway, he's missing. That means we have to report him as MIA."

John looked quizzically at Top, not fully understanding the implications of that. "Is that a problem Top? Hell, if he's missing, I guess that's all you can do."

"It's not that easy. If I report him missing, his family will think he may still be alive. It would be seven years before the Army would officially list him as KIA. That means his parents would be praying every day for a miracle that ain't gonna happen."

"So what do we do Top?" John asked.

"I'm gonna report him as KIA, that's all we can do.

John, you probably know they want you down at Brigade for de-briefing. Do you want me to go with you?"

"No Top, I'll go. The colonel didn't like the idea. Said I was only an E-4."

"You'll do fine Whalen, you'll do fine." As he started to leave, Top looked back, "Whalen, I don't know how to say this, but in all my years in this man's Army, I don't think I've ever met a soldier like you. When you came here, we were told to keep an eye on you, being a war protester and all, but you are a helluva leader. I wish the Army had more men like you. You'll be proud of this service some day. I know you don't think so now, but you will."

Arriving back at the Orderly Room, Top looked at the mail on his desk. A postcard from Army Headquarters in Washington acknowledged Sergeant Peterson's request for DI school. His request had been approved. Tossing the card down, Top leaned back in his chair and wondered if the war would ever be over.

****

Janet Peterson had just sent the boys off to school and was about to make up a shopping list when she heard a quiet knock on the door. Usually nervous that bad news may await her, this morning she was expecting her friend Peggy. She was going to go shopping with her and she was due over any minute. Yelling to Peggy, she said, "Peggy, the door is open, come on in for some coffee before we go." Again she heard the polite knock on the door, only this time a little louder. Slowly, and with a worried look on her face, she walked to the door and opened it. Catching her breath, she closed her eyes as she started to slump to the floor. Standing on the porch was Major Stokely and Captain Barlow, the Protestant Chaplain. Janet knew they only came to homes to inform the wives that their husbands had been killed or seriously wounded. Reaching to quickly catch her, Captain Barlow maneuvered her into the house and had her sit down. "I'm sorry to have to tell you this Mrs. Peterson, but your husband Jack was killed yesterday while on an early morning mission."

Unable to control herself, Janet started sobbing uncontrollably as she said over and over, "Oh Jack, what will we do now? What will we do? I loved him so much. I don't know if I can go on without him. How about my boys, how am I ever going to tell them? He'll never see his daughter, never. It's a girl. He...he wanted a girl so bad."

Trying to regain some composure, Janet asked, "Will his body be coming home?"

"Yes, it will. Mrs. Peterson, I have to leave, but the Chaplain is going to stay with you for a while. Anything you need, we'll be here for you."

****

Amy woke up from a sound sleep with a feeling something was wrong. She turned on the light and saw that it was 4:00 AM. Laying back down she started thinking of Brian. She had a strange feeling that he was in trouble. She felt for the bracelet he had given her. Touching it gave her a feeling of warmth. She wished she could call him. He would be here soon, just a couple of months, she said to herself. She turned off the light and attempted to go back to sleep.

****

After Top left, John tried to compose himself. He watched from his cot as a rat ran back and forth from one of the cots across from him to his hiding spot in the far corner of the hootch. He obviously had found some remnants of food to his liking. When John had first arrived in Vietnam, he was shocked to see so many rats. But now that he was well into his tour, he had become somewhat accustomed to them. The Vietnamese people would capture and eat them, considering them an excellent source of meat. One of the men in the hootch had gone into a nearby village and came back with a large cat, thinking it would reduce the population of rats. After a week or so, the cat was found dead outside their hootch. It was obvious he had been no match for the Vietnamese rat that was nearly as large.

Finally getting up, John went outside. Although monsoon season was just weeks away with its cool temperatures and constant rain, this day was hot and the sun almost unbearable. Stopping by a pistoon, John relieved himself and walked to brigade headquarters. He reported to the colonel's clerk, who looked surprised when he told him the colonel was expecting him.

"Go on in," the clerk told him, "the colonel is in his office with Lt. Saban."

Not certain what the protocol was, Whalen walked in the office and saluted Colonel Hewitt. Hewitt motioned to a chair and told John to sit down.

"I've asked Lt. Saban from S-2 to join us. Lt. Saban, this is Specialist Whalen. He was one of Lt. Calhoun's squad leaders and was involved in this morning's action."

Saban simply nodded his head saying, "I remember," as he started jotting in his notebook.

John looked at Saban closely. He looked more like a college professor than an army officer. He wondered if he had ever been in combat.

Smiling, Lt. Saban looked up from his notebook and began. "Specialist Whalen, first I want to tell you how sorry we all are. I know that you lost some fine men today, many of whom you probably knew and may have been friends with. From the information we gathered, we felt this was going to be easy. It isn't often that we find that many NVA at one time. It was important that we deal them a major blow. I have some questions for you and then you can go back to your unit. Do you believe there was any way the NVA could have been tipped off? We know they were heavily entrenched in the jungle area that bordered the village, but it appears they either reacted very quickly or had a large portion of their men in the village at the time you entered?"

"L. T., I can't answer that for certain. I do know that when we sent our guys in, it looked clear. We then sent in the rest of the platoon, and the NVA let us have it with everything they had. Machine gunfire, AK, 40 mm, you name it. They caught us flat, L. T., out in the open with no cover." Whalen stopped for a minute thinking of those nightmarish minutes. "My opinion, for what it's worth, I think they had a couple of soldiers sleeping in the ville, probably with a whore. They are well trained, sir, and probably heard us approach. They were able to get out and get some men to the back of the ville where it bordered the tree line."

"You did return concentrated fire?"

"We did, but until Lt. Hathaway arrived, we were stuck. Couldn't move forward, couldn't fall back."

"What happened after Lt. Hathaway arrived?"

His men added enough fire support that we were able to dislodge them. He had some LAWS rockets that wiped out some of their hootchs and moved them back to the tree line, sir. We should have gone in with more men."

Lt. Saban continued writing in his pad with Colonel Hewitt looking on. Closing his notebook, Lt. Saban finished by asking about Lt. Calhoun and Sergeant Peterson.

"I don't know about Peterson. I guess he got hit when we moved on the village after Hathaway's men moved up. I did see Lt. Calhoun get hit. An NVA soldier stood up just before he started retreating. He lifted his AK up to his shoulder and fired several shots at Brian, er, I mean Lt. Calhoun. One of the rounds caught him square in the knee, another bounced off his helmet, and I don't know, I guess he was hit in other places as well. Fortunately, he got hit as Hathaway moved in and he had already called the dustoffs in or Calhoun wouldn't have made it. He lost a lot of blood and was going into shock when they lifted him off. I understand he lost a leg and was medivaced to Japan, is that right?"

Colonel Hewitt, looking distraught, answered, "Yes, that's true. He should live, but he'll be in rehab a long time. I have already sent word to his father, who as you know is a brigadier general." Shaking his head, Colonel Hewitt sighed, as he said, "I don't understand, our boys are so brave, we should not have had this happen."

Whalen, glancing up at a row of history books on a small shelf hanging behind his desk, nodded toward them as he spoke, "Colonel, I don't know if bravery wins battles. It may earn you a few medals, but I don't know about the fight. You must read a lot of history, Colonel. I don't know if there was ever braver men that sat in that Alamo, knowing they had no chance, or what about Pickett and his men at Gettysburg. As far as bravery goes, those VC and NVA, well Colonel, they never run; they stick with us even though we have air support and artillery, yet they hang in there."

Lt. Saban glanced at Colonel Hewitt who gave him a quick nod. Saban stood up, shook John's hand, thanked and dismissed him. John saluted them both and quickly walked out.

"What the hell happened Saban? We lost a lot of men. We didn't have good intelligence, did we?"

"Sir, I think the NVA must have moved the bulk of supplies, or maybe we didn't find them."

"Well, goddamn it Saban, it's your job to make sure we have good intelligence. I want a full report and get another unit in there to look that ville over with a fine tooth comb."

Several days went by and at the end of the week, Lt. Hathaway returned with the men of the third platoon. They found nothing more while on patrol and saw little of the enemy. Hathaway, after meeting with Colonel Hewitt, was surprised he was still in command of B Company. Whalen brought him up to date on Lt. Calhoun, but there was little news to tell him. The Army was typically tight lipped when someone was injured and medivaced.

One evening, while Whalen was playing Spades, the new company clerk who took over for Simmons came into Whalen's hootch and told him Hathaway wanted to see him. The clerk, who had served in the first platoon for six months, had been wounded and was given the clerk's job after convalescing, took Whalen's place at the Spades table.

Whalen entered the officer's hootch thinking that the last time he had been there was to see Calhoun before the ill-fated mission. Walking down the stairs of the officer's hootch, Whalen could smell the distinct odor of pot wafting from the hootch. Hathaway and Bromley sat on one of the cots passing a joint back and forth. Sitting down, Bromley offered the joint to Whalen. He took it graciously and inhaled deeply before exhaling and handing it back to Bromley. Looking squarely at Whalen, Bromley said, "If I had my way and the authority, I would make you a platoon sergeant and have you take over for Peterson, but as you know, that isn't going to work. I don't know what's going to happen here. Murphy is gone. Top is leaving in a week or two. Hathaway and I will be gone soon too. This company is going to be run by FNGs and I think they are going to be in trouble. John, the rumors we heard a few weeks back, you know about the men rotating home early, were true. The tour is getting reduced to ten months starting in September. Guys that came in November will be leaving then. You came in February, so you'll be gone in December, hopefully by Christmas. Since you won't have much time left, they'll discharge you, rather than having you serve out your last six months. I talked to Hathaway, and we think you've done a helluva job. You remember Stinson don't you? He was in your platoon?"

Whalen laughed, "I sure do, eats candy like a little kid. He's all right."

"That's him," laughed Bromley. "He's been driving the deuce and a half to Chu Lai for supplies and so forth. He's short, real short, and now with this new ruling on ten months, we suspect he'll be going home to that big candy store they call The World any day. I talked it over with Hathaway and we want to know if you would like to take his job. It's a helluva lot safer than the bush."

Whalen hardly had to think for a second. "Hell yes, I'll take it, but what about my squad? Sir, we've lost Peterson and Calhoun, what the hell are you going to do to re-organize it?"

"We have a new platoon sergeant coming in tomorrow. He did a tour with the 82nd Airborne. He's a damn good man. You have some experienced men in your platoon. I suspect he'll get to know them and pick a new squad leader. John, if we don't move you out now, chances are we won't be able to." Rolling another joint, Bromley lit it and handed it to Whalen, "Here's to "B" Company and our new truck driver. Good luck John."

Chapter 39

Whalen walked back to his hootch, lay down and fell asleep almost immediately. Waking up in the morning, he got dressed, shaved, and went to find Stinson. His hootch was the farthest one away from Whalen's. Walking in, he saw Stinson sitting on the edge of his cot lacing up his boots.

Standing up, he greeted Whalen warmly. "Well son-of-a bitch, I thought I would see you today. They tell me I'm getting awfully short, so you may have to squint to see me. So, you're the one replacing me, huh?"

"I guess I am," Whalen answered smiling. "Is it a good job?"

"Fuck yeah, it is. I'm not running today, but I'll go over it with you. Tomorrow I'll take you with me. I understand you have a military driver's license?"

"Yeah, they made a bunch of us get 'em when I was at AIT at Fort Polk."

Stinson walked over to the wall and grabbed a couple of folding chairs. Opening one up for Whalen, John sat down and lit a cigarette. "Each morning, about 0600, you go to the motor pool across from Brigade Headquarters. You check out a truck and make certain everything is okay. The motor pool sergeant will have a driving order for you. You take it and pick up anything on the Hill here that is going to Chu Lai. There will be another order for shit to pick up at Chu Lai to bring back here. That's the easy part. The hard part is all the junk everyone asks you to get for them. Sometimes you may have time but most of the time you don't. Big thing is you have got to get your ass back here before dark. Before you leave in the morning, the engineers sweep Highway One to Chu Lai and make sure it's clear. You don't want to be on it after dark. The VC are out then and they'll pop your ass with an RPG round or AK fire. It's fine during the day, but if you' re in Chu Lai and you don't think you can make it back before dark, you stay there. You got that?"

Whalen nodded. After a bit, Stinson said he would see Whalen tomorrow and left to visit some friend from the motor pool. Whalen walked back to his hootch and found the men of his squad sitting on their cots all with gloomy expressions on their faces. “What the fuck is with you guys?” asked Whalen. “You all should be happy. They’re reducing the tour to ten months.”

One of the men, a red haired Texan they called Cowboy, shook his head, “That part of it is great John, but we just heard you’re leaving the platoon for a job in the rear. Who the fuck is gonna take over? We’re happy for you. You did your thing here, but we’re worried that’s all.”

Not sure what to say, John stalled for time, choosing his words carefully. “Cowboy, they made me a squad leader after one patrol. I didn’t know what the fuck I was doing. It was a week before anyone even said a word to me. You guys have a new platoon sergeant coming in. He did a tour with the 82nd Airborne and I’m told he’s a damn good man. Plus, you saw Hathaway on the last patrol. He’s not gonna go out there and shake up Charlie’s ass the way we thought. Things will be all right, you’ll see. I don’t have much time left anymore either. I’m gonna miss you fuckers, but I know you’ll be fine. Hell, I didn’t do much anyway.”

Cowboy stood up, a big old cowboy hat perched on his head that he had brought with him, “Touchdown, we want to thank you for what you did for us. We all liked you, and every goddamn week we want a case of good beer from Chu Lai, none of that Falstaff shit in the rusted cans. You got that boy?”

“I’ll have a case a week for you, guaranteed. Hell, before Simmons left, he gave me a dozen bootleg ration cards.”

****

The next few weeks flew by for John. Stinson had taught him what there was to know about driving the truck to Chu Lai. In some cases he went in convoy with other trucks and at other times he went alone. He made two long overnight trips to DaNang and was able to eat in the Air Force mess halls there; again surprised at the quantity of food and sheer luxury they had in comparison to life on Hawk Hill.

When monsoon season hit, the road to Chu Lai was wet and difficult to negotiate. Although the temperature was still in the

70s, everyone was cold and constantly wet. There were only occasional glimpses of the sun and the rain constantly misted down. Returning to the base in early December, John was surprised to see the company clerk waiting for him in his hootch. Smiling, he handed John his orders back to The World. "Your DEROS is 20 December John. With luck, you should make it home for Christmas. We'll assign a new truck driver for you tomorrow. You can kick around here for a couple of weeks. Are you gonna tell your folks?"

John thought about it for a minute. He hadn't told them about the early outs. They didn't expect him until February. "No, I think I'll wait and surprise them. They don't expect me until February. If I make it home for Christmas, it will be a helluva Christmas present for them."

The last two weeks in Vietnam went slowly. John packed his duffel bag and said good-bye to all the men he knew. The officers were all new and had not served with him in the field. Their goodbyes were cold and odd, as if he was deserting them. John remembered when the first sergeant had left. John hadn't realized how much he had respected him until he had said goodbye to him. Top had orders for an AIT unit at Fort Knox, Kentucky.

Now it was John's turn to leave. On his last night on the Hill, he walked from hootch to hootch to say goodbye. He wondered silently how many of these men he would see again. Although the field had been quiet in recent weeks, John knew it was just a matter of time before Charlie would set up an ambush or some of the men would trip a mine. Casualties had been light, but those things had a way of averaging out. Before he left, he went into the Orderly Room and looked at the chalkboard that had the names of the men killed in action scrawled on it. John counted 22 men that had served with him since his arrival. Only one had been killed since he left the field. Twenty-one of the men had been hit while he was on patrol with them. Thinking back, he estimated another 30 or so had been wounded seriously enough to be medivaced. John took out a small notebook and carefully wrote down their names. He got their addresses from the clerk.

He promised himself he would write each of their parents or wives a letter after he got home.

The next morning, Whalen went to the motor pool where his replacement was waiting. "You ready John? If you are, get your ass in and I'll give you first-class service to the next C-130 leaving for Cam Ranh Bay. Arriving at Chu Lai, John signed in and was told he had about an hour wait before a C-130 would be headed to Cam Ranh Bay. After boarding the plane, John sat down and started thinking about Natalie and what he would do when he got home. He decided he would just simply go to her apartment and walk in. There was no sense in preparing her for his visit. He suspected she had a boyfriend, maybe was even living with him, but he would find that out soon.

The big C-130 landed in Cam Ranh Bay where everyone climbed off. Those returning to The World were told to report to a large area for men returning home that was set up just off the field. A string of hootchs were there and John was told to secure one, lock his duffel bag to one of the bunk beds and report to an assembly area at 1400. Arriving there, John estimated there were several hundred men waiting, all returning to The World. At 1400 a sergeant stood on a large podium and spoke into a bullhorn. "Listen up men, I will say this only once. You all have a number. Keep that number with you. If you lose it, you are fucked. Every four hours, around the clock, we have a formation here and we will read numbers. They don't always go in order, so make goddamn sure your asses are here. When your number is read, you get your duffel bag and report to the fenced-in area to my right. An MP will be there to check your ID and your number. Once you are in that fenced in area, you will board trucks and be taken to your plane for transportation to the states. It's a 24-hour plane ride. You'll be going to Japan and then to Seattle, Washington, and Fort Lewis for processing to your next duty assignment or for some of you, discharged from the service. If you just arrived here, it may be two days before your number is called. Make sure you are here for each assembly. If you're sleeping in the hootchs, we will have someone waking everyone up every four hours. Now, I'll start reading the numbers for today."

Whalen walked back to his hootch and wondered what we would do for the next couple of days. He watched a group of men standing in the corner. One was continually flicking his lighter open and lighting and re-lighting it. Curious, Whalen walked over, "You guys getting close?"

One of them shook his head, "Just got here last night, maybe tomorrow sometime." Looking at John, he asked, "Hey, you don't have any drugs do you?" Shaking his head, John said, "No. Last pot I saw was back on Hawk Hill."

The man playing with the lighter laughed, "We're not talking pot, we're talking H man, you know heroin. We need drugs bad." John looked at them and could see the signs of withdrawal clearly etched on their faces.

"I can't help you there boys. Good luck though." With that he walked off shaking his head. "Fucking 'Nam," John thought, "If it ain't Charlie, it's something else."

It was 10:00 PM at night, two days after arriving at Cam Ranh Bay, when John's number was finally called. He was surprised how quickly everything went after that. He boarded the bus and they were taken to a jet from, of all things, Flying Tigers Airlines. Boarding the plane, John was able to get a window seat. As the jet started to move, John took one final look at Vietnam. There, not 50 yards away, was a giant rat meandering along the runway. "How fitting," John thought. The plane landed at Tokyo for re-fueling. Everyone had to disembark and run approximately 200 yards to the terminal in 28-degree weather with nothing more than their light jungle fatigues on.

With the next stop, Seattle, the men on the plane started to get excited. The plane's wheels barely touched down when a giant yell erupted from the plane. The pilot came on the intercom and welcomed everyone back to The World.

Before they could leave, an army sergeant came on board and used the plane's intercom. "Welcome back to America. On behalf of the President of the United States, I want to thank all of you for a job well done. We all appreciate your service to our country and the world in helping maintain freedom. When you leave the plane, you will be going through customs. I have men stationed in the terminal before you get to customs that will take any contraband you may have, no questions asked. If the customs' agents find anything, you will be held here and could possibly be imprisoned. After customs, you will change your MPCs over to U. S. currency. From there you will be fitted for dress green uniforms. While they are being tailored, you will get a first class steak dinner. After getting your uniforms, you will be processed out of the service or to your next assignment. We have transportation to SEATAC airport waiting for you. Good luck, and again, welcome home."

It was while John was getting his final papers typed up that he thought of Debbie Fisher. He hadn't heard from her in months and wondered if she remembered her promise. While waiting for his papers, he dug into his wallet and found the picture of her legs that she had sent. That picture had been so important to him at the time. Finally getting his papers, he thanked the clerk who typed them and asked, "Is that all?"

"It sure is. You're a civilian now, but you are expected to wear your uniform until you get home." John looked down at the uniform. He had been promoted to Sergeant E-5 about a month before leaving Vietnam. He had been awarded the usual service awards, the Combat Infantryman's Badge and an Army Commendation Medal for meritorious service while in Vietnam. He was directed to an area where an Army bus took them to SEATAC airport. The airport was packed with people trying to get home. It was now December 23rd and flights out were hard to come by. After waiting in line for what seemed like forever, John finally arrived at the counter. He watched as the ticket agent politely asked him his destination. "Sandusky, Ohio, but I'll be happy with Cleveland." After punching the information in, the agent looked at John. "I can get you to Chicago, but I can only do stand-by from there to Cleveland. Do you want it?"

John thought about it and on impulse asked the agent, "What about Philadelphia?"

"Philly? Well let's see." After a minute or two, he nodded, "Yeah, that we can do. You'll have a bit of a layover in Chicago, but we can get you to Philly." John handed him the money and went to the gate where the Chicago flight was to take off.

Whalen had remembered that before Top had left he said that John would be transferred from Japan to Valley Forge General Hospital, which was in Phoenixville, Pennsylvania, a suburb of Philadelphia. If he couldn't get home, he would see if he could find Brian.

Sitting down in the gate area for his flight to Chicago, John noticed a young man with long hair, faded jeans and a paisley shirt staring at him. He was obviously stoned. He and the young woman he was with were chuckling and obviously talking about John. Although John vividly remembered his college days when he too did the same thing, this time it was different. Standing up, he walked over to them and asked, "You have something you want to say to me?" A little shocked, the young man, not wanting to back down in front of his girl friend, stood up. A little taller than John and about the same weight, he said, "No man, we were just looking at your medals and we were just thinking, wow, man, we are safe here in America. With people like you out there defending us against women and children in places like Vietnam, what could be better?" John, starting to seethe, was about to grab the man when out of nowhere a swarthy Army major appeared and gently grabbed John's arm. John noticed that he had most likely also returned from Vietnam. The major looked sternly at him and said, "Son, there's a bar right across the gate, and we got about a half an hour before the flight leaves. How about I buy you a beer?" John let go of the man's paisley shirt and walked to the bar with the major. "Thanks sir, I guess I don't need to get in a fight after returning from 'Nam."

The major pulled out a ten-dollar bill and ordered two beers. "What unit were you in?"

"The 196th on Hawk Hill."

The Major laughed, "You didn't happen to run into Colonel Hewitt did you?"

"Yeah, I did, a number of times actually. He was our Brigade Commander. He had a habit of coming out to the field just after we finished a firefight. He put us in a real jam a couple months back. Where did you know him from?"

"I served with him during my first tour in 'Nam. He was a company commander and I was a platoon leader. I thought for certain he was going to get us all killed. He's all military, that's for sure. They'll be calling for us to board soon. Son, sometimes you have to turn the other cheek. Things are tense in the states right now. I'm sure you heard of the incident at Kent State." John had heard about the Army National Guard shooting and killing four Kent State University students during a protest. Hearing of the incident at Kent State, being an Ohio college, had upset John. He had a number of friends who had gone there, some of whom were still there.

Thanking him for the beer, John got up and started for the gate. Turning, he asked the major if he knew anything about the hospital at Valley Forge. He did know about the hospital and gave John some advice on how to get there and how to get in to see Brian.

"I have to warn you though, it's damn depressing. Most of the amputees are there, hundreds of them. And the place is rundown, WW II vintage. Mostly wood, long corridors leading to the wards. Not a good place to be."

John thanked the major and went to his seat.

Arriving at Philadelphia, John wandered around asking different military personnel if they were heading to Valley Forge Hospital. Spotting a young captain wearing the insignia of the medical corps, John got lucky. "Sir," he asked, "are you heading to Valley Forge?" Putting his bag down he looked quizzically at John, "Yes I am," he answered, "why do you ask?"

"I'm just returning from Vietnam and my platoon leader and good friend was wounded. He's an amputee patient there, and I want to see him if possible."

Picking up his bag, the captain told John to follow him out to his car. "I'm stationed there, so I can take you. As far as getting to see your friend, it's not like a public hospital, but I should be able to help you. Shouldn't you be going home for Christmas? I'm sure your family is anxious to see you."

"They don't expect me until February, and I want to surprise them. I booked a flight home for tomorrow. I'm hoping to see my friend in the morning and still get home for Christmas."

"Amputees have rehab in the morning, but are usually back in their rooms by 1100 or so. What time does your flight leave?"

"Not until 1600."

"That might work. There's a bus that leaves every hour or so from the hospital to the airport. Do you have a place to stay?"

"No, I thought once I got there, I could crash in a chair for a few hours."

"Naw, you won't have to do that. I'm staying in the officer's quarters. You can stay with me tonight, and I'll get you in the hospital in the morning."

"I can't thank you enough sir, it means a lot to me."

The young doctor looked at John, "He must be a helluva friend."

"He is sir, he is"

The next morning, John put his uniform back on. It was early and John would most likely have to wait for Brian to return from therapy, but he was sure he would get to see him. Arriving at the hospital, he was shocked at its sheer size. It seemed to be miles of corridors just as the major at the airport had said. Virtually everyone there had been wounded in Vietnam. Many of the patients nodded to John or asked how things were in the Americal Division. John carried the division patch on his shoulder, tipping the patients off to his unit. After what seemed to be a mile walk, the doctor and John stopped at a remote wing of the hospital. "This is where the officers are. Most are amputees. I'll talk to the duty nurse. You wait here." Several minutes later the Doctor walked out smiling. "It's your lucky day. I know the duty nurse. She said your friend, Lt. Calhoun, would be back from rehab in about an hour. I suggest you go down to the canteen in the next building, get a cup of coffee and come back then."

Thanking him, John walked to the canteen and ordered a coffee and toast. After the hour passed, he walked to the ward and spoke to the duty nurse.

"I'll take you back there, but his mom and dad are here today. His dad is a brigadier general, and I don't know what he will say about you seeing him."

Pushing through a double door that led to Brian's ward, John saw Brian's father sitting in a chair idly thumbing through a recent issue of *Army Times*. Off to his left was the doorway to the room Brian was in. Not sure what to do, John hesitated. General Calhoun, looking up, asked, "Can I help you Sergeant?"

"Yes sir, I would like to see Lt. Calhoun. I understand he's in one of these rooms."

"Lt. Calhoun is my son. Where do you know him from?"

"He was my platoon leader in Vietnam sir. I was hoping to see him."

Standing up, the general stared at John for a moment before answering coldly, "I am sure Lt. Calhoun will be happy to hear one of his men stopped by to see him. I will tell him you were here."

John, feeling the hair stand up on the back of his neck, was doing his best to keep his temper in check. He hadn't flown across the United States, gotten within a few yards of his friend, only to get turned away by his father. "Sir, we were friends, good friends. I was his squad leader and was with him when he got hit. We were tight sir. I would like to see him before I go home to Cleveland. I flew here from Seattle to see how he is..."

Interrupting him, the general said, "You're an enlisted man and you were friends?" John could hear the dismay in his voice. About to just walk into Brian's room, John saw a very stately and smartly dressed woman walk toward them asking, "Robert, who is this young man?"

"Marjorie, he knows Brian. Served with him in Vietnam. He wants to see him, but I told him Brian needs to rest, and I am sure the sergeant is about to leave."

Brian's mother looked at John. "Are you the young man that was with him when he was wounded?"

"I am."

"Well then, I am sure that Brian will want to see you. It's all right Robert, I will take him in." Grabbing John by his elbow she led him to the door. Gray colored curtains hung between the beds. Stopping short of the door, she pointed to the rear of the room. "Son, you will find Brian in the last bed on your right. You go surprise him. He needs something like this."

Walking into the room, he saw Brian staring out the window. Despite the months that had passed since leaving the field, he didn't look well. Much thinner, pale and gaunt, he was propped up in bed holding the sports section of the Philadelphia paper in one hand. "Well, if I had known you had a window view, I wouldn't have come all the way from Seattle to see you."

Brian saw John and almost tried to get out of bed to greet him. Walking quickly over, John put his arms around his friend. After embracing, John sat on the edge of the bed. "It's damn good to see you Brian; almost didn't get in with your guard posted at the door."

"Ah, he can be tough, but that's the way he is."

"He seemed upset when I told him we were friends, me being a hippie-enlisted man and all."

Brian laughed as he reached out and grabbed John's hand. "I have thought about you a million times since I left Vietnam. I wouldn't be here if it wasn't for you. I don't remember much about getting hit. I remember going down and the next thing I remember is waking up in Japan. Everything else is just not there. The round to the helmet gave me a concussion. But, despite that, I do remember you with me before the dustoff came."

"I didn't know if you were going to make it. You were shot up pretty bad. I guess you had more wounds than what I saw."

"I took a round in the left leg, one in the thigh, another grazed my left arm. Did you know the NVA put Water Buffalo shit on their bullets? As if I didn't have enough wrong with me, I developed an infection from Buffalo shit. Can you believe that? Then I got pneumonia to boot. It's been slow, but I'm making progress. I work every day with my artificial leg. Hey, why aren't you home for Christmas? I heard about the early outs, and I figured you would be coming home soon."

"I hit Fort Lewis yesterday. I'm officially a civilian. I couldn't get a flight to Cleveland, so I booked to Philly and hitched a ride here with an Army doctor I met at the airport. I wanted to see you Brian. I was worried. I didn't hear anything."

"A few weeks ago, Hathaway stopped to see me. He filled me in on what happened after I got hit. Sounds like things slowed down. He told me that he had you driving one of the Brigade trucks to Chu Lai. I was happy he did that. I guess he turned out okay."

"He did. He was all right. Is he staying in the Army?"

"I don't know John. He's stationed at Fort Ord, California. He thinks he'll be making captain, but who knows?" Brian looked uncomfortable for a moment, not sure how to say it. Taking a deep breath, he looked at John. "Hathaway told me you got the gook that hit me. I didn't know that. I wondered if that son-of-a-bitch got away."

"No, he didn't Brian. I got him. I don't know if I'm proud of it, but he's dead." Changing the subject, Brian started to laugh, "Funny thing is, despite all the shit, there were some real characters over there, weren't there? Remember Simmons and his ration cards and bringing that girl in during stand down. I wonder what illegal stuff he's up to. Guy was a real con artist, wasn't he?"

"He was, Brian, a lot of crazy fools over there."

Just then, a young Army Nurse walked in. "Well Lieutenant, who's the handsome visitor?"

"Cindy, this is John Whalen, he was my squad leader in 'Nam. He saved my life. He just got back."

Cindy took John's hand and shook it firmly. "Brian will be going home soon and all the nurses are planning a party. He's a pain to take care of. He's too nice. We do better with all the surly complainers. We don't know what to do with a patient who is actually pleasant. But Sergeant, you'll have to get going. We need Brian for a while and then he'll have to rest. You can come back tomorrow."

"That's fine Cindy, I have a flight to Cleveland later today. Can I have a moment with him before I go?"

"You sure can. I'll be back in five minutes."

John pulled a chair up to Brian's bed. "Brian, what about Amy. Did you get word to her?" Looking over, John could see a small-framed picture of her on his night table. It was the picture he had carried in his wallet.

"Not really John. I don't know what to do. When I was in Japan, I wrote her a short note, telling her that I was on a special assignment and that I would be detained for a while. I haven't been in touch with her since."

"You have to tell her something. I'm sure she is worried."

"She is very pretty and I am sure she has moved on. She wouldn't want me with one leg. What good would I do her?"

"What was the name of that restaurant she worked at? I'm going to call her tonight."

Shrugging his shoulders, Brian sighed and said, "*Hawaiian Palace*. What about Natalie? Have you made a decision?"

"I'm going to see her, other than that I don't know." Getting up, John looked at his watch. "I have to get going. I'm going to come back in a week or two. The duty nurse gave me her number. I can call her and see how you are doing. She said you would be going home in a few weeks. Any idea what you're going to do?"

"I don't know. The Army won't want me. I'll see, but right now, I don't know. What about you?"

Grasping Brian's hand and shaking it, John said, "I don't know. I've been thinking about law school."

"No shit, you're kidding?"

"No, I think I'll study for the boards and find some school for the fall. You got me thinking about it and hell, I can't do anything with a liberal arts degree."

Seeing the nurse peeking in the door, John smiled and said, "I'm really glad I came. I didn't know what to expect. But I can see that you'll be fine. I'll see you soon, okay?"

"Thanks for coming. I'll see you."

"Real soon, Brian, real soon."

Leaving the room, John walked over to Brian's parents. "I have to catch the bus to the airport. Thank you for letting me see him." Turning to Brian's father, John said, "General, you should be very proud of your son. He is an excellent officer. The men respected him and would have done anything for him. I don't know what his army future is now, but he would have made a fine career officer." John shook his hand and saw the general was touched by what he said.

The general apologized, "I'm sorry about earlier. My wife tells me you saved his life."

"No I didn't sir. Brian did that. I was just there, that's all."

Turning to leave, John opened up the double door and just before walking out, looked back at Brian's parents. "Oh General, by the way, Colonel Hewitt, he was a pain in the you know where. Ask Brian about him sometime."

Laughing, the general smiled, "He is, and if my wife wasn't standing here, I would spell it out for you too."

John had little trouble getting to the airport and despite huge crowds at the airport, was surprised the plane took off as scheduled. He had decided to go to Cleveland and take a bus to Sandusky. It would be awkward calling anyone for a ride.

While at the Cleveland airport, John took the time to place a call to the restaurant where Amy worked. He hated to call collect but didn't have the change to make the long distance call. Amy answered, and he quickly told the operator that the call concerned Brian. Almost in a panic, Amy asked, "Is Brian okay? I have been so worried. He said he is on a special assignment, but I have heard nothing."

"Amy, this is Brian's friend, John. I don't know if he told you about me, but we were friends in Vietnam. He was never on special assignment. He was badly wounded in Vietnam and lost a leg. He has been in hospitals since August and is at Valley Forge General Hospital near Philadelphia right now. I think he loves you; but he doesn't think you would want him missing a leg and all."

Amy stopped John as he tried to fill her in. "That is silly. I am going to fly to the states and see him."

"Amy, I believe he loves you; and if you don't feel the same way, I think he would be better off if you didn't go."

After a long pause, Amy answered, "You don't know me, and it's a good thing I am not there, because if I was, I would kick your ass. I'm going to see him. Don't tell him. I will fly out right after Christmas."

Hanging up, John chuckled to himself. "I guess Brian was right, she is special."

****

Amy hung the phone up and sat down on a chair. Her hands trembled and she seemed powerless to stop them. Not sure what to do, she watched as her Uncle came through the doors from the kitchen and saw her sitting down.

"Amy," he said, "we will be opening soon. We need to get the rest of the tables set." Looking at her more closely, he sensed something was wrong and sat down next to her. "What is wrong? You look very upset."

Her hands still shaking, she looked at her Uncle with tears beginning to form in her eyes. "You remember Brian, the young soldier I dated while he was on R&R from Vietnam?"

"Of course, I do, Amy. Is he all right?"

"No Uncle, he was wounded very badly. He lost a leg and is in a hospital in Pennsylvania. His friend called to tell me. He said that Brian loves me. I want to see him Uncle, but I don't know. What if I can't handle that kind of love and I hurt him more. He was so nice, and I think I loved him. He never tried to make love to me. He wanted to wait, to make the moment special. Do you know what that meant to me, especially here in Hawaii with so much military? The men here just want sex."

Her Uncle pulled his chair closer and grasped Amy's hands in his. "Amy, if you don't go, you will spend the rest of your life wondering about him, and he will do the same. Love is silent and if it flows between you, you will both feel it without saying a word. If your love isn't there, he will let you know. He is an honorable man. You should go."

"What about the restaurant?"

"We are not that busy over the holidays. I will handle it. You make the reservations and go see him. I will pay for the ticket."

"I don't know how to thank you," Amy said.

"You have many times over by simply being my niece. Now you go and finish setting the tables."

****

Landing in Cleveland, John was able to get a cab to the bus terminal and was happy to see he had just a few minutes wait to board. John sat next to an elderly couple traveling to Sandusky to visit their children for Christmas. John was surprised when they told him that there was talk about ending the draft soon. President Nixon had already resigned himself to removing all the troops from Vietnam and turning the responsibility of fighting over to the ARVN troops.

Arriving in Sandusky, John looked at his watch. It was almost 10:00 PM. He was almost out of money and was worried he may not have enough for cab fare. Counting the bills in his hand, a cabbie was watching him from his window. "Hey soldier, you need a lift?"

"Yeah, but I don't know how much it's going to be?"

"Where do you live?" John gave him the address and was told to get in the cab. "I'll charge you $5.00. I was in the Army during the Korean War. Where you coming from?"

"I just got back from 'Nam. They let me go early. My parents don't know I'm coming home, so it will be a surprise. I'm just hoping they aren't in bed yet."

John looked out the window and saw that very little had changed since he left. The air was cold and a light snow was falling. "It was good to be home," John thought. Pulling up in front of John's house, the cab driver reached back and shook John's hand. "There's no charge. I'm glad you're home safe. Have a very Merry Christmas." John offered him the $5.00 for a tip, but the driver refused to take it. Walking nervously up to the house, he suddenly realized he didn't have a key to get in. Sighing deeply, he stepped up to the porch and rang the doorbell. Moments later his father opened the door dressed in his pajamas and robe. Seeing John standing there, he was speechless at first. Walking in, John hugged his father, "Gee, Dad, I thought you would be happy to see me, but I guess you can't even say hello."

Recovering, his Dad yelled to his wife, "Elizabeth, come here, you won't believe who's here."

His mother, making cookies in the kitchen, came to the front door wiping her hands on her apron. Stopping in her tracks, she was barely able to compose herself. "John, is that really you?" Rushing forward, she joined her husband in a long embrace. His mother backed away and looked up at her son, "You weren't supposed to be home for two more months. You didn't get hurt did you?"

"No Mom," John chuckled. "They're starting to let everyone go early. I'm glad I made it home for Christmas."

Hearing all the commotion, John's brother, Mike, came running down the stairs. "John, I can't believe you're home for Christmas."

Seeing Mike, John gave him a giant hug lifting his brother off the ground. "Hey, I have something for you." Opening his duffel bag, John removed a stack of Superman comics and handed them to his brother. "Remember a few months ago you sent some comic books to me for one of the guys in my squad?"

Mike nodded his head as he thumbed through the back issues, none of which he had. "Well, the guy really appreciated it; and when he got home a few weeks ago, he sent me these issues and told me to give them to you."

"These are great John. I wish I could thank him."

"You already did Mike."

Walking into the living room, John sat down on the couch. He was tired, more tired than he had ever been. He hadn't slept much at the doctor's quarters. His mother sitting next to him asked, "Can I get you anything John?"

Looking at his mother he could see that a year of worry was slowly being erased from her face. "I haven't eaten much in the last couple days. Do we have anything for a sandwich Mom?"

Getting up, John's mother nodded, "Of course we do John. You talk to your father. I'll be back in a minute."

John looked at his father who seemed a bit troubled. He kept crossing and uncrossing his legs. Finally he spoke, "John, I know it was tough in Vietnam; and if you want to talk about anything, you certainly can talk to me. I know it's not easy coming home after a year away like that."

"I'll be fine Dad. I'm just tired right now."

"Do you have any plans son?"

"Not really. I want to chill out for a month or so. You remember in my letters I talked about Brian, my platoon leader?" His dad nodded, as John continued, "Well, he was wounded. Wounded pretty bad, lost a leg. I'm going to see him, maybe even in the next week or so. He's at a hospital near Philadelphia. It's not that far away." John didn't want to tell him that he had taken the time to stop and see him before coming home. It was something his father probably wouldn't understand.

His father, a smile returning to his face, said, "Your grandparents can't drive much anymore. Their night vision is poor and they have had a couple of minor accidents in the last few months. They want to give you their 1969 Chevy Nova. It only has 6,000 miles on it, and it has the V-8 engine. It will be a good car for you. A lot better than that Falcon you drove."

John laughed as he thought about that car. "Are they sure Dad? Maybe they should sell it. I'm sure they could use the money."

"No John, they want to do something for you. The car has been sitting for two months. We'll go over tomorrow and pick it up. We have to get them for Christmas dinner anyway." John's mother returned with a ham sandwich and a glass of root beer. Looking at the root beer, John smiled, "Mom, they had plenty of Coke and Pepsi in 'Nam, but I didn't see any root beer. I meant to get one as soon as I landed in The World, but I forgot all about it." John picked up the glass and drained it in just a few seconds.

"Have you talked to Natalie John?" his Mom asked.

"No, I haven't. She doesn't know I'm home. I'm going to see her, maybe later this week. I don't think anything will come of it. I received one letter from her; that was all. But that's what we agreed to, so I don't know. I thought about her every day, but I just think that it will be impossible to start over with her."

"Did your dad tell you about grandma's car?"

"Yeah, he did," John answered between mouthfuls of food. "I'm thrilled Mom. I still remember when grandma got the speeding ticket and told the cop she couldn't read the speedometer because her eyes were so bad." Her parents chuckled remembering the incident.

"Mom, Dad," John finally said, "I'm awfully tired. I'd like to go to bed. We'll have plenty of time to talk tomorrow. I'm really glad to be home. I'm sorry I didn't call you, but I wanted to surprise you, being Christmas and all."

“It was the best Christmas present ever John. We are so happy you’re home safe and healthy.”

John went up to his old room and removed some of the clothes he had brought back with him from Vietnam. In a small bag were a bottle of malaria pills. He was supposed to continue taking them for 30 days. He set the bottle on his dresser and lay down on his bed. “How quiet it was,” he thought. “No artillery, no flashes of night illumination, and no Tammy Wynette music echoing through his room.” He closed his eyes and fell into a peaceful sleep.

It was the best Christmas John ever had. Relatives were streaming in all through the holiday to see him and welcome him back. Even Pauline came over to see him. He told her how much her letters meant to him. He was happy to hear that she was engaged and would be married that summer.

Chapter 40

Amy walked into Brian's room and as the duty nurse had said, saw he was sleeping. Walking over to his bed she looked at him. Bending down she gently kissed him on the lips. Brian opened his eyes and was about to say something when Amy spoke first. "So, soldier boy, are you disappointed it wasn't one of the pretty nurses kissing you?"

Brian, speechless, reached out and hugged Amy with everything he had. "John called you, didn't he?"

"Yes, he did. Why didn't you tell me?"

"I couldn't Amy. We were together only a few days. I didn't know what to think."

Amy sat on the edge of the bed and shook her head. "I had to come. There wasn't a day after you left Hawaii that I didn't think of you. Staring out the window, Brian caught her gaze. "What are you looking at?"

"It's snowing. I never saw snow before."

"I'm going to be discharged in the next few weeks. I'm still planning on going to Hawaii. I thought it would be good for me to get away. I've been here for too long."

Smiling, Amy nodded her head, "I would like that Brian. I have to fly back the day after tomorrow. I'm really glad to be here."

"I'm glad you came Amy. I know we need to find out if there is a future for us. We have time for that. I know I'm not the same person I was in Hawaii."

Stopping him, Amy reached over and kissed him again, murmuring, "Yes, you are Brian, you are the same man you were, only now you are with me."

Chapter 41

Two days after Christmas John woke up and left for Columbus in his Nova. It was important for him to see Natalie. He decided to surprise her and see what her reaction would be.

John parked his car in the same spot he always had. He saw Natalie's car was parked in her usual spot. He walked up the two flights of stairs to her apartment and stopped as he got to her door. He wasn't sure what to do. He gently knocked, but there was no answer. Turning the knob, the door was unlocked. Opening it, he saw Natalie sleeping on a mattress in the far corner of the room. An empty bottle of wine stood next to their eight-track player as it quietly played Simon and Garfunkle's *Sounds of Silence.* The distinct odor of pot clung to his nostrils as he walked in. It was obvious Natalie was alone. Kneeling down next to Natalie, John could see that she had changed. She looked older, her hair was unkempt and the apartment much messier than she usually kept it. She had a blanket pulled tightly around her. John reached over and shook her shoulder gently, "Natalie, it's John."

Slowly she opened her eyes and at first thought she was dreaming "John, is that really you?" Sitting up, the blanket fell from her. She quickly grabbed it, but John pulled it away staring at her well-rounded stomach. "You're pregnant?" he gasped.

"I was going to tell you John," she said pulling the blanket back. "I was, but you're home early. Did they finally let you go?"

"They're letting everybody out early. Who's the father?"

"I, well, I, I'm not sure, John. The crowd I'm hanging out with John, you'd love them. We had a big orgy a few months ago. John, it was surreal. It was. The sounds of everyone making love, it was just something I can't explain. I was really spaced out at the time and I guess I missed taking my pill. Anyway, it's wonderful isn't it?" she said patting her stomach.

"You're smoking pot while you're pregnant?" John asked with a bewildered look on his face.

"Yes, it settles the baby down. He loves it and it won't hurt him."

John stood up shaking his head. "Natalie, I came over to see if there was any chance of continuing our relationship, but I can't do this Natalie. I can't."

"We should try John. We could open up the commune we talked about. There is so much we could do."

Shaking his head, John sat back down beside her. "Too much has changed Natalie. We're not the same people."

"You killed over there didn't you? Your Mom said you were in combat. I can't believe you killed. The war is so wrong. Did you see what happened at Kent State?"

"Natalie, I don't disagree that the war is wrong, but when you are over there fighting, it isn't about what's right or wrong, it's about survival. It's about working with the guys in your company. It's about not letting the other men down. Those Viet Cong, Natalie, they wanted to kill me. If I didn't fight, they would have killed me. War isn't that complicated. Not when you're in it. It's simple. You fight to stay alive."

Hearing someone enter, John turned and saw a longhaired man walk in the door. Seeing John, he set the bag down he was carrying and walked over to him. "Wow man, I bet you're John. My name is Paul. I'm happy to see you. Natalie and I were hoping you could stay with us. We would love to have you. We can help you with your hostility man. We'll bring the peace back in your life."

"You're right, I am John, but I don't have any hostility and I don't want to live here with you." John got up and walked to the door without looking back.

"Hey man," Paul said, "we're just trying to help with your guilt from Vietnam. You need to mellow out. You can take yoga with us and learn how to deal with your hostility."

John stopped, looked at Paul, and said curtly. "I'm telling you again, I don't have any hostilities, and I don't have any guilt. You better start taking care of Natalie. You both look like hell and this place is a mess. I'm sorry Natalie. I wish you the best."

John walked down the stairs and climbed into his car. Lighting a cigarette, he blew the smoke out of the window as he listened to the radio. "It's just as well," he thought.

Maybe Hess was right. Maybe he never was a hippie. That's what he had told him. Hess said that he drove the hippie from him. Maybe it was just a college thing, a fad. Starting the car, he left Columbus and headed back to Sandusky. About to get off I-71, he veered back into the main lane and continued north toward Cleveland. Not sure what he was doing, he drove steadily until he was downtown. Parking in a ramp, he walked across to the Federal Building and punched the elevator button for the third floor. When the doors opened, he followed the sign that said Armed Forces Examining and Entrance Station. Walking through the offices, John peered around the corner and peeked at Debbie Fisher's desk. He waited until she was finished with an applicant and strode up to her desk. Putting both hands on her desk he stared at her until she turned from her typing and asked with a smile, "Can I help you?"

John reached for his wallet and pulled out the picture of Debbie's legs. Tossing the picture on her desk, he said gruffly, "You never answered my question Fisher. I want to know who took the picture?"

Recognizing Whalen, Debbie blushed, "Well Whalen, I see you made it. I'm sorry I didn't recognize you, but you look so different, your hair is shorter, and…"

"Fisher, you're stalling. I want to ask you out to dinner tonight, but not before I find out who took the picture."

Opening her drawer, she removed an envelope and showed John several pictures that were unsuccessful attempts to capture just her legs. "I took them with a camera that had a delay on it. I set it on my desk and took them myself."

John picked up the picture of her legs and put it back in his wallet.

"I can't believe you kept it all this time," Debbie said with a laugh.

"So, continued John, "do you want to go to dinner with me tonight?"

A crazy feeling surged through Debbie's body. She wasn't sure what to say. "I, I don't know. I'm a mess. I should go home and change, and…"

"You look beautiful to me and I want to take you just the way you are. I'll pick you up outside at five o'clock, okay?"

Debbie smiled again, "You aren't going to take no for an answer, are you Whalen?"

"No, I'm not," answered John. "You got that? Five PM."

I'll be there," Debbie promised. John turned and walked away, waving to Debbie as he left the room. Debbie nervously picked up the phone and with trembling hands called home. "Mom, I won't be home tonight for dinner. I'm going to go out with some of the girls here, kind of a post Christmas thing. I don't know when I will be home." One of Debbie's co-workers walked by her desk as she hung up the phone. "Are you okay Debbie? You look kind of funny."

"I'm fine," she answered. "Just fine."

Chapter 42

July 1984

John and Debbie left the realty office where John, an attorney at law, helped his parents sign the papers for their new retirement home in Florida. The Florida sun beat down on them as they walked through the quiet town back to their motel. Running ahead of them was their six-year-old son, Brian. Always quizzical, he stopped and grabbed the wrought iron bar of an old cemetery. Peering between the bars, he yelled back to his parents, "Daddy, is this where dead people live?"

Debbie, looking strangely at her husband, said, "He's your son. You answer him."

"Yes Brian, I guess it is. It's where dead people live."

"Why are some of these stones bigger than others Daddy?"

Stopping beside him, John looked at the graves and their headstones. Some were small and unimpressive, others quite massive, towering over the smaller ones.

"Well son, I guess some of the people were more important, that's all." Running ahead again, Brian stopped at a grave that was only yards from the black wrought iron fence.

"Daddy, what about this dead person. His stone is huge. Was he a president?"

John stopped and looked at the epitaph on the large tomb. His name was Harold Miller, born in 1892 and died in 1918 from wounds received in battle during WW I.

"Well Daddy, was he a president? Or maybe a King?"

Debbie reached out and touched John's hand. He seemed lost in thought. The words of Sergeant Hess came back to him again. "You're a soldier now and part of you will always be a soldier." For a moment he could hear the artillery rounds leaving Hawk Hill. He could hear the pop of M-16s, the radio crackle, and the thump, thump, thump of the dustoff choppers coming in to a hot landing zone. For an instant he felt the fear, the pain of seeing friends die, and the loneliness and futility of war.

"Well Daddy?" Brian asked again, his small hand tugging on John's sport jacket. "Was he a president?"

Kneeling down, John took Brian's hand in his. Closing his eyes tightly he thought of the war. It had never left him, always there in the recess of his mind. The constant tug-of-war of what was right, who was wrong, and what, if anything was accomplished, and in the end, the empty feeling of so many left behind. Opening his eyes, he gripped his son's hand, hoping that the words of the philosopher Plato were not true when he said "that only t he dead have seen the end of war." Speaking slowly, with a tear welling up in his eye, he answered, "No son, he wasn't a president or a king. He was far more important than any king or president who ever lived. He was the most important person in the world."

Wide eyed, Brian looked at his father, "Well Daddy, what was he?"

"He was a soldier."

GLOSSERY OF TERMS

AK-47	The Soviet- or Chinese-made assault rifle used by the NVA and Vietcong; not as accurate as the M-16, but much more reliable. Also known as a Kalishnikov after its inventor.
Ambush	A small detachment of men who set up outside the company perimeter at night.
AO	Area of Operation. Could be term used in field or your bunk area.
APC	Armored Personnel Carrier. A tracked vehicle carried over from WWII and Korea. APC bodies were mounted on 5-ton truck beds in Vietnam to create convoy-protecting gun trucks.
Arty	Artillery.
ARVN	Army Republic of Vietnam (South Vietnamese Army)
Bic (biet)	Vietnamese term for "understand."
Boucoup	Many, a large amount. From the Vietnamese French.
C-4	A plastic explosive carried by designated members of a squad in an infantry platoon.
CIB	Combat Infantry Man's Badge. An award given to those who served in combat.
Claymore Mines.	Popular fan-shaped antipersonnel land mine filled with BBs and one pound of C-4 explosive; designed to produce a directionalized, fan-shaped pattern of fragments.
Cs, C-rations, C-rats, Charlie rats, combat rations	Canned meals used in military operations.
DEROS	Day of Estimated Return from OverSeas.
Deuce and a Half	2.5-ton truck.
Di Di Mau	Vietnamese for "Go Away Fast."
Donut Dolly	Female Red Cross volunteer who served in Vietnam to increase morale.
Dust Off	Medical evacuation helicopter or mission.
FNG	Fucking New Guy.
FO	Forward Observer. An artilleryman assigned to a unit in the field to call in artillery.

Frag	A fragmentation grenade.
Fragging	The murder of an officer or NCO by a man of lower rank, generally by a hand grenade.
FTA	Fuck The Army.
KIA	Killed In Action.
Kit Carson Scout	Former Viet Cong who serves as scout with army field units.
Klacker	The arming lever for a claymore mine.
Klick	Kilometer (.621 miles).
L. T.	Short for Lieutenant.
LAW	Light Antitank Weapon. Long-range rocket fired from a plastic cylinder by U. S. forces.
LOACH or LOH	Light Observation Helicopter, notably the OH-6A, small helicopter used for observation.
Lock and Load	To prepare oneself for imminent action or confrontation. In other words, "Get ready and make sure your weapon is ready to fire!" The reference is to the loading of ammunition in a gun. The version of the command to chamber a round that's most familiar to World War II veterans seems to be **load and lock**, that is, load the ammunition and lock the weapon in firing position. More recently, the more popular version—and the only one used in this metaphorical sense—Is reversed to **lock and load**, that is, lock the weapon in the safety position and then load the ammunition.
LRRP (Lurp)	Long-Range Reconnaissance Patrol.
LSA	Lubricant, Small Arms.
LURPS	Long-Range Reconnaissance Patrol Members. Also, an experimental lightweight food packet consisting of a dehydrated meal and named after the soldiers it was most often issued to.
LZ	Landing Zone. Small areas in the field surrounded by barbed wire.
M-16	Primary weapon of the U. S. Army in Vietnam; relied on firing a large number of small caliber bullets; early models not as reliable as the AK-47, as they had to be kept very clean.
M-60	A rapid-fire machine gun capable of great destruction.
M-79	A single-shot grenade launcher.

MARS Call	Phone call from Vietnam patched through a ham radio operator to the U. S.
MOS	Military Occupation Specialty. 11B was infantry. 11E was armor.
MPC	Military Payment Certificate. Paper money used by U. S. forces.
NVA	North Vietnamese Army; army regulars. Also known as PAVN—People's Army of Vietnam.
OCS	Officer Candidate School.
P-38	A small opener for C-rations.
Pistoon.	A piece of PVC pipe stuck in the ground with some screen over it for troops to urinate in.
PRC-25	Radio carried in field by the RTO.
R & R	Rest and Recreation. Vacation taken during a one-year duty tour in Vietnam. Out-of-country R&R could be taken at places like Bangkok, Hawaii, Tokyo, Australia, Hong Kong, Manila, Taipei, Kuala Lampur, or Singapore.
REMF	Rear Echelon Mother Fucker. Someone who worked in the rear area.
Round eye	Slang term used by American soldiers to describe another American or an individual of European descent.
RPG	Rocket-Propelled Grenade.
RTO	Radio Telephone Operator.
Ruck	An aluminum frame and canvas back pack.
S-2	Military intelligence.
Shake and Bake.	An enlisted man who completed a short course and was given the rank of E-5.
Sheridan	A small tank used in Vietnam with limited firepower and great vulnerability.
Short Timer	Someone who had a few weeks or days left in Vietnam.
SOP	Standard Operating Procedure.
Stand Down	A period of rest and refitting during which all operational activity, except security, is suspended. Usually a few days in a rear area for infantry units.
Star Light Scope	Telescopic device used at night to increase night vision.
Stract	In military order.

The World	The United States of America.
TOC	Tactical Operations Center for company.
Top	First Sergeant. Second highest non-commissioned rank.
Track	Armored personnel carrier.
VC	Viet Cong. South Vietnamese sympathetic to the NVA.